North, Pearl.

The Book of the Night.

DATE		

BAKER & TAYLOR

THE BOOK OF
THE NIGHT

TOR BOOKS BY PEARL NORTH

Libyrinth
The Boy from Ilysies
The Book of the Night

THE BOOK OF
THE NIGHT

PEARL NORTH

A TOM DOHERTY ASSOCIATES BOOK
NEW YORK

This is a work of fiction. All of the characters, organizations, and events portrayed in this novel are either products of the author's imagination or are used fictitiously.

THE BOOK OF THE NIGHT

Copyright © 2012 by Pearl North

Edited by James Frenkel

A Tor Teen Book
Published by Tom Doherty Associates, LLC
175 Fifth Avenue
New York, NY 10010

www.tor-forge.com

Tor® is a registered trademark of Tom Doherty Associates, LLC.

ISBN 978-0-7653-2098-8 (hardcover)
ISBN 978-1-4299-8598-7 (e-book)

First Edition: September 2012

Printed in the United States of America

0 9 8 7 6 5 4 3 2 1

For Richard

ACKNOWLEDGMENTS

My heartfelt thanks to everyone who offered help during the writing of this book. In particular, Steve Ainsworth, Paulette Petrimoulx, and Todd Harlan. Your support, guidance, and friendship mean so much. Thank you.

CONTENTS

THE BOOK OF
THE NIGHT

PROLOGUE

Clauda's Journey

Clauda paced her room in the Tower of the Fly all night, unable to sleep. Only a few days ago, a fire had devastated the Libyrinth's crops. Now, everyone was scrambling to do whatever they could to keep the community alive. In the morning she'd fly the wing out to search for food. But what kept her up was not their dire situation, or her mission.

The Chorus of the Word was leaving for the Corvariate Citadel at dawn, too, and Selene was going with them. In all the months since they'd been in Ilysies together, Clauda still had not gotten up the courage to talk to Selene. It wasn't like her to hold back when she had something on her mind, but this was different. And now, she was out of time.

"You'll never know unless you ask," she said under her

breath. "And if you don't ask now, who knows when you'll have another chance?" She glanced out the window. The night sky was turning blue. She had to hurry if she wanted to catch Selene before she left.

She hurried through the rest of her packing and cinched her knapsack closed as if she could keep her courage from deserting her with a good stout knot.

She found Selene in her chamber. The tall Ilysian had her back to the door and was putting clothing in a saddle-bag. The sight took Clauda back to that day in Ilysies when Clauda had come to warn Selene of the queen's treachery and had discovered the depth of her own feelings in the bargain. "Selene," said Clauda.

Selene turned. Her face, usually serious, softened with a smile at the sight of Clauda. That had to be a good sign, right? "Hey. Thanks for stopping by," said Selene. "I'm glad I get a chance to say goodbye before I leave. We don't get to see much of each other these days."

"And it'll be even less now."

Selene hesitated, then said, "Well, until we complete our missions, anyway."

Clauda nodded. They stared at each other in silence. Clauda couldn't read the expression on Selene's face. She stepped closer. "Selene?"

Selene fastened the clasp on one saddlebag and turned from the bed, taking a step toward Clauda. "Yes?"

They were close enough now that Selene's fragrance of ink and wool filled Clauda's nostrils, making her dizzy. "Do you . . ." She didn't know where to begin. The words she wanted to say tangled themselves up in a knot and lodged in her throat, making it hard for Clauda to breathe, let alone speak. Her mouth opened and closed like a beached fish gasping for air.

Selene frowned. "Are you all right?"

Clauda nodded.

"Are you having a seizure? You haven't had one since the Redemption, have you?"

Clauda shook her head. She was losing her nerve. If she didn't do what she came here for soon, it was never going to happen. And words were not helping her now.

Selene put a tentative hand on Clauda's shoulder and leaned down. "Do you need to sit down?"

Clauda put her hands on Selene's shoulders and arched upward. She closed her eyes and pressed her lips to Selene's.

The brief, soft crush of their lips was better than any flight she'd ever taken in the wing. Selene tasted like barley, and there was a fraction of a second when her lips parted, just slightly, and Clauda felt as if she drank Selene in. This elixir warmed her from head to toe.

And then Selene gripped her shoulders and pushed her back. "Clauda? What . . . ?" Selene's eyes were wide and her mouth hung open. "What . . . ?"

Clauda looked up into Selene's shocked face and shook her head. The warmth that had filled her a moment ago turned to red-hot humiliation. "I'm sorry. That was a mistake." She backed away, out of the clutch of Selene's hands. "I've got to go. Have a good trip." She turned and ran without a backward glance, unable to bear the sight of Selene's shock and dismay a moment more.

She stopped in her own room to pick up her knapsack. She splashed water on her flushed face and took a few deep breaths, forcing herself to regain her composure. She had a job to do and nothing was going to stop her from doing it. People were relying on her. There were more important things at stake now than her silly feelings.

In the stable yard Clauda found a small delegation had gathered to see her off. Haly, Gyneth, Burke, and Rossiter stood in the doorway to the stables. Already they looked a little thin and they were sweaty and dirt-streaked from planting the new crop. The sight of them helped her to set aside her hurt. She was grateful she had something useful to do.

Everyone else was out planting seed as fast as they could, but it wouldn't be fast enough. It would still take months for the grain to grow and ripen, and they had only scant weeks of food left. Which was why Clauda had packed for a long trip. While the Chorus of the Word traveled to the Corvariate Citadel on foot in quest of the bloom and to elicit aid from the villages of the plain on their way, Clauda would be scouring the outer reaches of the land in search of food.

She'd head north first, to Thesia. No one had heard anything from the mining and industrial center since the Singers had taken over more than six months ago. It seemed impossible that a whole nation could become destitute in that time, but if such was the case, then she'd fly to the four corners of the world in search of food. There had to be something out there somewhere.

Clauda embraced each of her friends in turn. When she came to Haly, she closed her eyes and held her tight. "I will find something," she said. "I will."

Haly nodded. "Just stay safe, and come back to us, whatever you find out there."

Clauda would secure food for them if she had to cross

the sea to find it, but she didn't tell Haly that. Reluctantly, she pulled away and turned to face the wing.

As always, her heart soared simply at the sight of it: a thing of living metal, shaped like a crescent with the wings curving backward. The Wing of Tarsus had a face on its underside, human and serene. It was powered by the same energy cells used in all the technology left behind by the Ancients, and that power was directed by a human mind: Clauda's mind.

Her thoughts calmed and things became simple again. She placed her hand on the smooth, golden metal surface of the wing and the hatchway opened for her.

The inside of the wing was an almost featureless chamber. When Clauda had first entered it in Ilysies a year ago, she had been surprised to find no seats or controls of any kind. Only a statue of a woman, made of the same gleaming gold substance as the rest of the wing.

The door to the cabin shut behind her before she had a chance to catch one last glimpse of her friends. Just as well, probably. Last looks were bad luck. Anyway, she'd be back within two weeks with a hold full of pickled trout and Thesian goat's milk.

How long would it be before Selene and the rest of the Chorus of the Word returned from their mission? And what would Clauda say to Selene when they did? Well, there was no point in thinking about all that now. What was done was done. Selene was a good person. She'd forgive Clauda in time. Maybe they'd still be able to be friends. And in the meantime, Clauda had the wing. Compared to the tangle of desire and embarrassment that thoughts of Selene spawned in Clauda's gut, her relationship with the wing was simple and certain.

Eagerness to be aloft pushed her worries aside. Clauda faced the statue and recited the words Adept Ykobos had taught her when she was a patient and a prisoner in the Ilysian palace. "Mighty queen, mother of Ilysies, blessed, brave Belrea, open for your daughter, bathe her in the light of your righteousness." Then she kissed the statue on the forehead, mouth, and belly.

A seam of light appeared, running vertically from the crown of the figure to the feet. The seam widened as the statue opened into two halves, and golden light poured out. Clauda turned and fell backward into the statue's interior.

The light caught her and cradled her, as if with countless gentle fingertips, supporting and soothing her, surrounding her in warmth and light. As many times as she had done this now, these first moments of interface with the wing still entranced her.

Soon, her consciousness merged with the wing. She was no longer simply Clauda, or even the Second Redeemer or the Hero of the Libyrinth or whatever other foolish titles people saw fit to assign her. She was Clauda-in-the-Wing, and she could fly.

She breathed in, and lifted off the floor of the stall in a delicate maneuver that she'd mastered over these several months. She eased out of the stall and out through the stable doors. Once in the yard, she rose up until she was above the level of the wall, and the great plain beyond called to her. With a single thought, she sped over the yard and into the sky.

The blue sky and the yellow land reached out to welcome her, and she flew into their arms. How she loved to fly. She loved the way the ground blurred beneath her, and how the blue of the sky deepened when she flew very, very high. Clauda-in-the-Wing felt every ripple of air that passed over her golden hide as she soared far above the Plain of Ayor. She banked and climbed. The land scudded past beneath her, rolling brown hills dotted with scrub bushes and rocks. She went as fast as her heart and her mind would allow, until the air stung against her skin and the human part of her gasped for breath. The sheer joy of flying filled her with the perfect contentment of a creature doing what it was meant to do.

She slowed again, now hovering. The sun warmed her back and created thermals—rising columns of warm air. She climbed them, entranced with the diminishing land wheeling slowly beneath her. And then, when she was so high up that she could see the horizon of her world curving, she flipped onto her back and gazed up. The sky, still blue at the edges, had turned black directly above her. She wondered what it would be like to go higher still. What was that blackness and what lay beyond it? Someday she would find out, but not now. Now she had a mission to accomplish.

She rolled back over and headed north, toward Thesia. Her path took her over the Tumbles. Somewhere near here was the underground vault where she and Haly had been held prisoner. Selene had taken drastic action to rescue them that night, throwing an Egg into a fire and causing a massive explosion. That had been Clauda's first inkling that Selene was not always the calm and rational being she pretended to be.

Thoughts of Selene's passionate nature jarred Clauda's focus. At the same moment, a gust of wind struck her, carrying with it fine grains of sand that stung her golden hide. She nearly lost control of the wing, and had to fight hard to right herself.

Once she'd stabilized again, Clauda-in-the-Wing scanned the horizon for the source of the wind. In the south and the east the skies were clear blue, but in the north and west, in the area where the vault had been, heavy gray clouds massed on the horizon. There, in the center of the storm system, was a cloud unlike any she had ever seen before. It was oval, like an eye, and it shaded from mauve at the edges to purple to a center as black as the night sky.

The odd oval cloud rotated, mauve and sickly green tendrils spinning off from its outer edges. Clauda-in-the-Wing stared at it, both human girl and Ancient machine struck dumb. The wind picked up and the cloud blossomed. In the span of one heartbeat it grew from the size of Clauda's fist to an oval, whirling mass as wide as the wing was. But the wind was coming from behind her, pushing her toward the cloud. No, that wasn't right, either. With a sickening twist her perception shifted and she realized that it wasn't a cloud.

It was a vortex, and it was sucking her in.

She flipped around and started flying in the opposite direction with all her might, but still the ground below slipped away in the wrong direction. She felt the grip of the vortex now, merciless on her metal skin. Though she struggled, the ground below continued to slip away, faster and faster. There was no escape.

Then she might as well face this thing that was her doom.

Clauda turned the wing around. By now the edges of the vortex were beyond her field of vision. The center,

which from a distance had been as black as the void between stars, was now shot through with twining arcs of
lightning. At the very center, argent and black mixed in
equal measure.

Did Selene push me away out of revulsion, or surprise?
What would have happened if I had stayed?

The force of the vortex, ever stronger, now unbalanced
her and she tumbled, end over end, purple and black and
white flashing past her field of vision. As she left all colors
behind and entered the light-shot dark, her nose started
moving at a faster rate than the backward-pointing tips of
her wings. She stretched.

The pull was going to tear her apart, and just as regret
for not explaining herself to Selene and demanding an
answer seared her heart, she saw something that drove
all other thoughts from her mind.

Letters. The light and dark were not streaks of lightning against a black sky. They were strings of glowing,
incandescent letters. An *N* the size of the wing sped past
her and as she looked into the distance ahead, she saw
the strings of letters formed words; the words, sentences.

" 'We are all going on an Expedition,' said Christopher
Robin, as he got up and brushed himself. 'Thank you,
Pooh.' "

Those words made no sense to Clauda, but others did:
"Tucker Mouse took himself very seriously now that he
was the manager of a famous concert artist." That came
from her favorite, *The Cricket in Times Square*.

Clauda-in-the-Wing's tail caught up with her nose, and
she now sped down what appeared to be a tunnel made of
words.

"Once the fire lizards settled to the business of eating, Piemur glanced at Menolly, wondering if she'd heard the drum message."

" 'When he broke that commitment to art, to making beauty, to recording, to bearing witness, to saying yessiree to the life spirit, whose only request sometimes is just that you acknowledge you truly see it, he broke something in Hal. . . .' "

"After that I was lost for a long time, doing dreamtime without end while my body paid the price."

Finally, the tunnel ended quite abruptly and Clauda found herself in emptiness.

She remembered the first time she'd gone into the stacks of the Libyrinth. She'd followed Haly and they'd gotten separated and Clauda wandered among endless shelves of books, all of them looking just like the others to her. She had still been too young to read, and she'd heard the stories about people being lost forever among the shelves, eventually dying of thirst or starvation. Clauda had never felt more small, insignificant, or fragile than she had then.

Until now.

Nothingness stretched out around her, limitless. It was a space that was not quite black. More of a dark reddish brown, the color you saw when you closed your eyes. That unnerved her almost as much as everything else put together. She wasn't in outer space. This was something different. For the first time Clauda wondered how she breathed while meshed with the wing, and what it would mean if there was no air around them.

She swung around to face the way they came, and inside the statue, within the web of light, the human girl gasped.

Before her hung an object made of words and light. Strings of letters traced arcs of light like orbits about an incandescent center where distance made words and sentences coalesce into a glowing orb.

She was drifting, and as the distance grew, even those outlying arcs of words lost resolution, and the whole of the thing took on a characteristic shape she'd seen before. A spherical core within a flattened disk of light and all of it whirling about its center.

She'd seen this before, in a picture from an astrophysics text of the late Earth period. The caption had said that it was what the scientists of that time believed the entire universe might look like.

Po Awakes

When Po first awoke, he didn't remember where he was. He stared about at the gauzy draperies and ran a hand over the soft, clean bed linens. Then he heard her voice, and he remembered it all. He was in Ilysies. He was the consort of a queen.

Queen Thela sat on a couch nearby, humming to herself as she flipped through the pages of a book. Po closed his eyes nearly all the way and feigned sleep. Through his lashes, he observed her. Her recent deeds did nothing to diminish her beauty. She had the classic tall, lean, Ilysian form. Her hair was long and dark, threaded through with silver, emphasizing her power and maturity and picking up the pale blue of her eyes. Her long, aquiline nose was as graceful as the shallow curve of her lips.

Thela raised one eyebrow and turned another page,

absorbed in what she read. Po searched for the pen but could not see it, either near her or on her person. He didn't know if that was good or bad.

Despite his circumstances, a delicious sensation of lassitude filled him. Po stretched out in the silken sheets. Surely it couldn't be wrong to enjoy this feeling, even if it might not really be his feeling, but one designed for him by Thela, using the pen. When he'd dared to defy her, she had used the pen to control him. Following her first, dreadful experiment, she'd adopted a more subtle method of securing obedience. She'd written that he would only do what made her happy. "Your Majesty," he murmured, blinking at her sleepily.

She looked up at him and smiled. "Ah, Po, you're awake. I will summon breakfast for you."

Po lay back in the silken sheets. He felt like he'd been asleep for a long time. What had happened again?

Oh yeah, everything.

It had started when he met Ithalia, though she was really Queen Thela in disguise. She'd made him her consort, and then she set the Libyrinth's crops on fire and framed him for the deed. After that, Haly had no choice but to send him away with the Chorus of the Word. They'd gone to the Corvariate Citadel in search of the pen, and they'd discovered the place ruled by a madman who called himself the Lit King. But once again, it was Thela who'd been running everything. She'd used the Lit King to discredit the Libyrarians. His mob raided the villages of the Plain of Ayor and stole their food, and he hoarded it all in the Temple of Yammon, where Po and the rest of the Chorus of the Word were held prisoner. He'd tortured

Siblea and used Po to revive him, and Thela had permitted all of it.

But Ayma, the tavern girl they'd befriended, had led the citizens of the citadel in revolt and released them. Everything had been okay then. They had the pen and they found the food and were returning it to the people. And then, Thela's spy, Mab, snatched the pen from Selene and ran away with it. And Po had chased her.

That's how he'd wound up in a chamber at the top of one of the temple towers with Mab and Queen Thela. He sat up at the memory of rolling on the floor, limbless, mouthless.

Thela watched him, smiling. Loathing seethed inside him, but outwardly, he smiled back, and held his hand out to her in supplication. "Will you bathe me?"

Her expressions could be so warm. Now, her face was bright with pleasure. "Of course."

Po felt like he'd been run over by a herd of cattle. His muscles were so sore he could barely move, and he was so tired. He'd been hit with a mind lancet more than once recently, and it couldn't have been more than a day between his last torture session with the Lit King and Siblea.

Then he'd followed Mab up to Thela's chamber at the top of the tower. And there, desperate to prevent Thela from using the pen to kill his friends and take over the world, he'd used his kinesthetic sense for a purpose he was certain it had never been intended. "How long have I been asleep?"

"Three days."

She escorted him to a bench beside the tub. He sat. She lifted his robe up over his head, and then unbuttoned his undershirt. "First a bath, and then"—she nodded to the low table by the chairs—"something to eat. And then—" she indicated her bower. "I've missed you, Po."

Sweet words. Inside, he was full of burning barley fields and missing limbs, but he leaned against her, and rubbed his head against her neck. He tried to stop. He couldn't. He blushed. He couldn't tell if it was with desire or humiliation. Exhaustion came to his rescue. He swayed. "Your Majesty," he murmured, "forgive me." The room faded and he fell into darkness.

When Po came back to himself he was sitting in the tub, wrapped in Thela's arms. The hot water felt wonderful. Thela washed him. The queen of Ilysies herself bathed him and treated his cuts and scrapes with extract of accar leaves. His opinion of his place in the world was perhaps too low.

He closed his eyes as she ran the cloth up his arm, remembering what had happened when she'd written "Po can do me no harm" with the pen. She'd corrected it, and now, his every outward action was gauged to please her. He reached for her even as he thought of what she had done and how he could keep her from doing worse. But his actions never matched what he was thinking.

Except for when he'd performed kinesiology on her. Nothing had prevented him then from altering her perception of and desire for the pen. He was still so tired from the energy he'd expended doing that, but he needed to treat her again as soon as possible, to make sure the pen remained an object of peril in her eyes.

Breakfast arrived and Thela finished bathing him, then wrapped a towel around him. She guided him back to the bed and dismissed the servant, carrying the tray to him herself. At the smell of fresh bread, flatfish baked in butter, and oranges, Po's hunger awakened. He'd forgotten how much he missed Ilysian food.

When he had devoured every last scrap, Thela took the tray and set it aside. Why was she serving him herself like this? Was it because he'd been hurt? Some women liked to take care of a male who'd been injured, though usually that was after he had fought another male for her attention.

She returned and sat on the bed beside him. "How do you feel now?"

"Much better, Your Majesty. Thank you."

"I'm glad to hear it. I need to talk to you but I know what an ordeal you've been through. I don't want to push you too soon, but this is important."

"Of course, Thela, anything you need." Could he lie, if the truth displeased her? He didn't know. He had to hope she asked him nothing that incriminated him or put the Libyrinth or the Chorus of the Word at jeopardy.

"You were in the tomb of Endymion."

"Yes."

"That's where you found the pen."

"Yes, my queen."

She nodded. "And did you see her?"

"The last Ancient?"

"Yes."

"We did. Ayma and I. We saw her. She was . . . Thela, she was still alive!"

Thela's eyes widened. "Still alive? But everyone said she was dead, and even if she wasn't dead when they sealed her in there, how could she still be alive after all this time?"

"She's not like us."

"Of course not; she's an Ancient."

"I know, but that's not what I mean. She's not even human. Maybe that's why she can still be alive. She was never really alive to begin with. And now she's disappeared, but I don't know what that means, exactly."

Thela smiled at him. Po realized how crazy he sounded. "I know it doesn't make sense."

"Why don't you tell me exactly what happened, from the beginning?"

And he did. He told her how he and Ayma had become separated from the rest of the chorus and how they'd found the ladder that led down through the tunnel of books. "It was so hard to pass through that little door on the other side. The feeling of dread was like a physical force, pushing us back."

"But you did enter," she said.

He nodded. "Inside it looked like an old Earth palace. There was a harpsichord. We found Endymion, but we thought she was dead, she wasn't moving. Then she started to talk."

Thela leaned closer. "What did she say?"

Po's heart beat faster, just remembering the last Ancient. "She wanted me to hand her her pen."

Thela smiled and sat back. "The pen."

"Yes. Only, we didn't know that's what it was. We thought . . . that is, the chorus . . ." He didn't want to bring up the chorus, or things that had happened at the Libyrinth. But he couldn't stop himself. "In the legends of the Ayorites it's known as the Lion's Bloom. The people of the Citadel refer to it as Endymion's Rose. We thought we were looking for a device shaped like a flower."

"But the pen is shaped like a flower, in a way," said Thela. "And when operated, the end opens up like a blossom. Isn't it interesting, how time reshapes things?"

"I'm sorry, Your Majesty, I don't understand."

"Well, I mean, these legends. They preserve an incidental fact about the device—that it resembles a flower—but hide the most essential aspect of its nature. It is a pen for rewriting reality, and yet the stories—I am familiar with the Ayorite version—focus instead on what is most familiar and desired to those who tell and retell the tale. The Ayorites are farmers, so they talk about a plant that can make the plain fertile again. I find that fascinating."

Po said nothing, hoping that her line of questioning was at an end. He was in luck. Thela brushed the hair back from his forehead. "I hope I'm not tiring you. How do you feel?"

"Better, Your Majesty."

She smiled. "How much better?"

He didn't have to pretend to smile back. That was the weirdest thing. He kept expecting to have to put on a show of how enamored he was of her, but he didn't. It felt completely natural to stroke her thigh with the backs of his fingers and say, "Let me show you."

They embraced. Could he perform kinesiology on her while they made love? He was desperate to find out if the work he'd done to prevent her using the pen had held. As she straddled him, he had an idea. "With your permission, I would try something, Your Majesty."

Thela raised an eyebrow.

"I think I can bring you even more pleasure if I am in kinesthetic trance when we make love."

The corners of her mouth curved up. "I have wondered about that myself."

"Shall we try?"

"Are you strong enough? You've been through quite an ordeal."

He didn't mention that she had put him through most of it. He flexed his hips upward. "As you can tell, I am completely recovered."

"You fainted, earlier."

"Yes, but . . . I was hungry. Please, Your Majesty. Let me try."

"All right," she allowed magnanimously.

Po never knew exactly how he'd perceptualize a person's energy patterns and bodily functions until he entered trance. Usually he seemed to gravitate toward organic metaphors—usually plants, sometimes animals. But he had never performed kinesiology under such circumstances before.

Meshing with Thela's inner world was the work of an instant. The geography of Ilysies itself was his map to her state of being, with the Ilysi River representing her energy flow, and various regions corresponding to different parts of her body and mind. To his relief he saw the tool that represented the pen still lay within the half-buried temple at the bottom of the chasm in her heart center.

While they moved together in the outer world, Po let his awareness flow with the waterfall, plunging down the cliff face and through the shattered roof of the temple. The place was flooded. The dolphins in the mosaic on the floor seemed to leap as the surface of the water undulated. And there was the tool, submerged amid fragments of the golden roof.

In the center of the room stood a round dais. In the middle of the dais a piece of fabric drifted about in the water's current: a white robe trimmed with gold.

Something about that empty robe drifting in the water made Po want to leave right away and never come back. Instead he picked up the tool and used it to hack at the pillars and walls of the temple. Stopping short of real structural damage, he set the tool atop the cornice of one of the pillars, where the wall nearby and the curve of the ceiling formed a little niche. It was a secure spot, and obscure—out of the way, and hopefully out of Thela's thoughts.

Po redirected his concentration to her navel center, where it was the work of a moment to bring her to satisfaction with a light gust of wind across the flowers growing on the island in the middle of the stream.

Po emerged from trance light-headed. Black spots danced before his eyes. To disguise his disorientation he buried his face in the crook of Thela's neck and kissed her.

"Mmm. That was lovely, Po."

Po was afraid that if he moved, the shaking of his exhausted limbs would betray him. But Thela shifted and he was obliged to move anyway. He was so tired.

Thela propped herself up on one hand and looked at him closely. "Are you all right?"

He nodded. "Yes, Your Majesty. It's just . . . the pleasure we share together is so overwhelming."

She raised one eyebrow. "Sweet words, but you look pale. I shouldn't have let you do that. You're still weak from your experiences with the Lit King. I'm going to have Ymin Ykobos examine you, to make sure nothing more serious is amiss."

Po opened his mouth to protest, but he couldn't. "You are most kind, Your Majesty."

Blame

Selene refilled her water bucket and set it down on the rim of the well. She wiped her brow and looked out across the settlement surrounding the Libyrinth known as Tent Town. It had been transformed into one gigantic infirmary tent since the Chorus of the Word had returned from the Corvariate Citadel. Now the community members, weakened by starvation, sat in their dwellings or beneath shade awnings.

These awnings had been stretched between the tents and stone huts by the remaining members of the Chorus of the Word and those villagers of the plain who had joined them on the trek back home. For three days Selene and the others passed out cups of thin gruel and water, carefully portioned in order to avoid overfeeding. But a few of the most resilient Libyrarians were beginning to recover, and the frantic pace slackened as they began to take over the care of the others.

Selene was so tired she could barely remain upright, but she forced herself across Tent Town to report to Haly, who sat with Gyneth, both of them with their backs propped up against a large boulder, shielded from the sun by a swath of rough spun cloth stretched between a corner tent pole of the infirmary proper and a cart in which adzes were stored.

They looked like they'd aged several years in the weeks that Selene had been gone. Dark circles shadowed their eyes and their robes hung off their bodies as if there was nothing beneath the fabric but a collection of sticks. They both smiled to see her but their emaciated faces made Selene flush with shame. Was there any end to the ways in which she could fail those who depended on her? The question made her think of Po and the pen.

And of course Clauda, whose hurt face had haunted Selene all the way to the Corvariate Citadel and back. Why in the name of Time and the Seven Tales hadn't Selene stopped Clauda from leaving that morning? She could have explained right then and there, but no, she had let her go. At least now, finally, she could seek her out and tell her the truth. It would be her next order of business, as soon as she gave Haly a full account of the mission.

"Selene," said Gyneth, bringing her back to the present. His voice was strong despite his weakened condition. "Sit down before you fall down. You look worse than I feel."

Selene sat down on the ground at their feet. She wanted to ask them where Clauda was. She hadn't seen her. Instead she said, "How are you doing? Do you need anything? More water?"

"We're fine for now," said Haly. Selene had difficulty looking at her. It hurt to see her cloud of dark hair with no luster and the bones protruding at her wrists and collarbone. Selene focused on her feet, poking up under a blanket of gray sheep's wool.

"Everyone's been so busy taking care of us, we haven't been able to find out how the rest of the mission went," said Haly. "Obviously you were successful in gaining the support of the villages of the plain, but what of the rest? What happened at the citadel? Did you find any sign of the Lion's Bloom?"

"Yes," said Gyneth, "and where are Po and Siblea?"

Selene realized that the frantic pace of the last few days had been a blessing in disguise. There'd been no time to explain much of anything. But now she had to face Haly, once her clerk, now her Redeemer. The words to tell them of Po and the pen were thick in her mouth, like cold, congealed porridge. Selene forced herself to take a deep breath and get her emotions under control.

Haly and Gyneth listened patiently as she told them of all that had transpired on the Chorus of the Word's first mission. Keeping to her most formal tone made it possible for Selene to relate to them how they had found the villagers bitter to them at first, because bands of people dressed like Libyrarians had been raiding and stealing their food. She told them of their arrival at the citadel and how they'd found it a ghost town. "There had been a prison revolt, and all the Singers were killed. A man, a former prisoner who called himself the Lit King, had taken over."

Haly put a hand to her face. "The prison! Seven Tales, of course! How could I have forgotten about the prison? We just left them there!"

Selene shook her head. "You had all you could handle here. You couldn't be expected to—"

"I was in that prison. I never should have forgotten it. We should have gone right away and let those people out. This is my fault—"

"They weren't all imprisoned unjustly, Haly. Some of them were criminals, by anyone's standards. No. What went wrong—when it went wrong—was my fault."

"If I have to sit here all day while you two argue over who's to blame for a bunch of stuff it's too late to do anything about, I'm leaving right now," said Gyneth. "Even if I have to crawl. What happened next, Selene?"

Selene nodded and told them about Ayma, and about Siblea's desire to fight the Lit King and how they were captured and put in prison. "But Po and Ayma got away, at first, anyway. They found the Bloom, only it's not a terraforming device. It's a pen."

Haly and Gyneth looked at each other. "A pen?"

"A pen for rewriting reality."

Haly's brow creased. "Where is it?"

Up until now, everything she'd had to tell them had been easy. "My mother has it," she blurted, afraid that if she hesitated, she'd never be able to get the words out.

"Queen Thela?"

"Does she know what it can do?" asked Gyneth.

"Yes. Mab took it from me—"

"Mab? My old cell-mate?" said Haly.

Selene nodded. "She is, and always has been, my mother's spy. I heard her mentioned back when Clauda and I were at the palace in Ilysies. It stands to reason that Mother would have spies in the citadel. But I'd forgotten about it and I didn't connect the name with the old woman who was one of the Lit King's helpers. I didn't know her name, until too late.

"Mab heard us talking about the pen and she saw me use it. I'm sure she told Thela everything as soon as she delivered it to her."

"But are you certain Mab took the pen to Thela?" said Gyneth. "Perhaps she kept it for herself."

"Not likely," said Haly. "If she was loyal enough to endure all those years of imprisonment for her queen, it's unlikely she'd turn against her now."

"Besides, I believe Thela was at the citadel," said Selene.

"What makes you say that?" said Haly.

"While we were prisoners of the Lit King, he tortured Siblea. . . ."

Haly leaned forward, her face tight. "Is Siblea dead?"

"No. He survived. He decided to remain at the citadel to help the residents rebuild. They're going to make the temple a place of scholarship. They want to exchange books with us."

Haly smiled. "Exchange?"

"The Lit King had some books. Not as many as we do, but . . ."

"What were you saying before, Selene?" asked Gyneth.

It had been a relief to speak of something positive to come out of all that had happened, but Gyneth was right. She needed to stick to the point. "There was no purpose to the torture; it was all for revenge, because—"

"Because when Siblea was a censor he had tortured him," said Haly.

"Yes. The Lit King just seemed to want to hurt Siblea as much as possible. He hardly bothered with the rest of us, didn't ask us why we were at the citadel or anything. But he used Po to . . ." She felt ill. "To revive Siblea. He made him heal him so that he could take more pain."

"And Po feels what his patients feel," said Haly. "Tales. He's only fifteen."

"But you said Po escaped," said Gyneth, and Selene understood why. He was trying to deny what had happened. People did that.

"At first he did escape, yes. When the Lit King's people apprehended us at the Old Theater he and Ayma got away, and while we were locked up, they discovered Endymion's Tomb. Ayma told us what happened there, and I can tell you more later, but the main thing is that's where they found the pen."

"Did they use the pen?" asked Haly.

"Po did. Ayma told us about it later. He wrote, 'The Plain of Ayor is a green and fertile land.' All we knew was that suddenly roots burst through the walls of our cell."

"The soil itself turned green, and silverleaf bushes, big ones, erupted from the ground everywhere, uprooting all the crops," said Haly, "but then a minute later, everything went back to the way it had been before."

"Ayma told us that when they saw what was happening, Po wrote, 'What Po just wrote about the Plain of Ayor being a green and fertile land never happened.'"

"So changes made by the pen can be unmade," said Gyneth. "That's something."

"Yes," Haly agreed. "But I'm sorry, Selene, you were telling us . . . What were you telling us?"

In spite of everything, Selene smiled. "After Po and

Ayma found the pen, the Lit King's mob found them. Po gave Ayma the pen, told her to run, and let himself be captured so she could get away. Sound familiar?"

Haly opened her eyes wide in false innocence. "I don't know what you're talking about."

Gyneth laughed.

"Anyway, you asked why I think my mother was at the citadel."

"Oh, right."

"The Lit King was torturing Siblea with no purpose other than to do it. Po . . . Po tried to distract him. He told the Lit King he'd been in Endymion's Tomb. Siblea told us the Lit King didn't seem to care, but the next time the guards came to our cell, they came for Po and Hilloa.

"Now, Hilloa told us she heard one of the guards say something about a 'foreign whore.' And that the Lit King, when he came in, said that 'she' wanted him to ask about Endymion's Rose."

"So you think Thela put him up to that line of questioning?" said Haly.

"I think she put him up to all of it. The revolt, the raiding of the villages. It was all to discredit us with the people of the plain."

Haly and Gyneth looked at each other. Gyneth raised one eyebrow. Haly nodded. They believed her. Selene was surprised to discover how much that comforted her.

"So how did Mab wind up with the pen?"

Selene's cheeks warmed with embarrassment over her carelessness. "Ayma led the citadel in a revolt against the Lit King. She released us from our cell. She still had the pen with her but she couldn't write. She gave it to Po and

Po gave it to me. While we were discussing what to do, Mab found us and offered to help us. I didn't trust her." Selene had to stop looking at them in order to get through the rest. She stared at Haly's feet again and her voice became mechanical. "But we kept her with us so we could keep an eye on her. I used the pen to reveal where the stolen food was stored. When we got to the storehouse, the citizens were about to torch the building. They didn't know the food was in there. In the confusion, Mab broke away from Hilloa and Jan and she snatched the pen out of my hands and pushed me down. Po ran after her. They went back inside the temple. By the time I got inside, I couldn't find any sign of them. We searched everywhere. They'd just vanished."

"You think the pen was used to spirit them all away? To Ilysies?"

Selene felt empty now. Further self-recrimination at this point was a wasteful indulgence. "That would be my guess."

"We don't know that's what happened at all," said Gyneth. "Maybe Po caught up with Mab, got the pen from her, and used it himself."

"Then why haven't we heard from him?" said Haly. "He wouldn't just take off."

"No," agreed Selene. "I don't think so."

"Then, if Thela has the pen, why hasn't she made us all loyal subjects of Ilysies by now?" said Gyneth.

They all looked about them, as if expecting just such a shift in reality.

"It's true," said Selene. "With the pen, she can do anything she wants to us at any time."

"But the pen is tricky, right? Presumably she knows that, too," said Haly.

Selene nodded. "She'll want to try it out on small things first."

They all looked at one another. No one wanted to say what they were all thinking: Po.

"We've got to get it away from her while we still can," said Selene.

"Yes," said Haly, "but we need a plan. First of all, Selene, you have to get some rest."

Selene nodded in reluctant agreement. "I will, as soon as I see Clauda. Where is she? I haven't seen her since I've been back."

The way Haly and Gyneth looked at each other made Selene's breath catch. Something was wrong. Haly reached out and took Selene's hand. "We don't know where Clauda is. She hasn't returned."

Numbness crept up her arms and legs, stealing in toward her heart. "Hasn't returned from . . . ?"

"From the mission she went on the day you left."

Selene understood now why people sometimes described grief as a hollow feeling. She felt like she had a hole inside her now. For Clauda to be gone so long . . . it likely meant . . .

It didn't seem possible. Even when she was so ill in Ilysies and Selene had to leave her there, Clauda had exuded life. Her grin hung in Selene's mind now, indelible, side by side with that awful look just after she'd kissed Selene. Why hadn't Selene just held her tight? Why had she pushed her back, sought answers, explanations? What explanation was needed?

"I'm so sorry," said Haly.

"You're sorry?" said Selene, gently wresting her hand from Haly's and hugging her ribs. "She was your best friend."

"Is," said Haly. "We don't know what's happened, Selene. She could be anywhere. Let's remember this is Clauda we're talking about, okay?"

That was true. A flicker of hope sparked to life in the void within Selene. Before the Redemption, Selene had been forced to leave Clauda behind in Ilysies. Clauda had been bedridden with the shaking sickness. Queen Thela suspected Clauda of being a spy and had her watched. The odds had been hopeless, but not only had Clauda survived, she'd won. It was worse than foolish for Selene to think her dead. It was disrespectful. She stood. "Has anyone gone out to search for her?"

"No," said Gyneth. "By the time we realized she should have been back, we were too weak to do anything about it."

Selene nodded. "Then . . . I'd like to go looking for her. You're going to need people to deal with the pen and you'd probably rather it not be someone who's already screwed it up once. I know it's a long shot. She could be anywhere, as you say, but let me go look for her, please."

S elene was as pale as an overcast sky. She swayed on her feet. As heavy as Haly's sorrow over Clauda's disappearance was, she'd had a little time to become acclimated to it. Poor Selene. "Yes, go look for her, but on one condition: first, you rest."

Selene nodded, her mouth a grim slash.

After Selene left, Gyneth asked, "How are you doing?"

"Physically, or . . ."

"Both."

"Wobbly," she admitted, "on all counts. You know I just decided when Clauda didn't return that she'd made some great discovery and one day she'd walk back into town and tell us all about the adventures she'd had. But Selene reacted as if . . . as if . . . I don't want to say it."

"Then don't. We don't know anything."

"And Po, what happened to him? What's happening to him right now? Now I know how Selene and Clauda felt when I was taken prisoner by Ithaster."

Gyneth expelled a long breath. "Yes, but you survived that, and Po is . . . he's strong."

Haly sighed. "I sent him away to protect him."

"I know."

There was nothing more to say about that at the moment. Haly scooted forward and lay down, and Gyneth stretched out beside her. From this angle, she could see the sky beyond the edge of their awning. "This pen business—I know Selene would never make up such a thing, but . . . I can't quite get my head around it. I know I should be terrified that Queen Thela has something that's so powerful. We all saw what the pen can do. It's just, I haven't got the first idea what to do about it. I think my brain is rebelling against problems with no solutions, you know? I keep coming back to how I thought we'd all be dead by now."

Gyneth lay on his side, his head propped on one hand. "But we're alive." The gleam in his eye was warm.

Haly rolled onto her side. Her head pillowed on one arm she met his gaze. She could not hold all of what Selene had told her in her mind. It kept slipping away, pushed out by her grief at Clauda and Po's disappearances and, perversely, her own overwhelming joy at still being alive.

Gyneth leaned forward, and she met him. Their lips, rough and dry from malnutrition, opened. Haly's heart quickened at the wet, warm glide of his tongue on hers. She reached up and ran her fingers through Gyneth's silken hair. He made that wonderful little whimper deep down in his throat, and pulled her closer.

Later, she rested her head on his shoulder and stared up at the sky. "The worst part about this pen business is that there's so little we can do about it. It doesn't feel real," she admitted. "I haven't seen the pen. I know it's all true. Selene would never make anything like this up, but—"

"It's hard to grasp."

"Yeah. And maybe . . . maybe I don't want to." She rolled onto her back, looking up at the blue, cloudless sky. "I think I'm doing a terrible job leading this community," she said.

"You always think that," he said.

"No, really. I don't take in the big picture. I miss things and they come back on us. Like the prison uprising. If we'd reached out to those people right after the Redemption, Thela never would have had a chance to exploit that situation."

"You don't know what else might have happened. Maybe something even worse. . . ."

She looked at him. "What could be worse than our worst enemy possessing an object of ultimate power? Argh. I shouldn't be thinking of Thela as an enemy. Already I've gone wrong there."

Gyneth propped his head on one hand. His eyebrows drew together. "Do you think she will ever understand how working together benefits everyone?"

Haly thought about how Thela had sent Selene, her own daughter, to die in a trap. "No. I really don't."

"Then it doesn't matter what you call her," he said.

"You're right, and there's no good in playing 'what if,' either. I just . . ." She sat up. "I don't want to make the same mistake again."

Gyneth propped himself up on his elbows. "I know that look. What are you thinking?"

"Thesia," she said.

He nodded. "No one has heard anything from them since they were conquered, before the Redemption."

"I think we'd better see how they're doing."

3

Kinesiology

Po sat up in his gauze-draped bower and regarded Ymin, who stood just inside the doorway, her arms folded, her posture stiff and formal. This was the first time Po had seen her since she had left the Libyrinth a year ago. She looked a lot older. Po noted the tension at the corners of her mouth and the worry line between her brows. Did she regret her decision?

Of all the people in the palace, Adept Ymin Ykobos was at once his most dangerous enemy and his greatest potential ally. What would she do if she knew what he was up to?

Ymin had been his teacher for a very long time, and there was something inherently comforting in her presence. Despite himself, he relaxed. "Thank you for coming to see me, Adept," he said. "Though I fear Queen Thela is wasting your time. I feel much better now."

Ymin shrugged and came forward, taking a chair and moving it beside his bower. "In any case, it is good to see you." She smiled, though the tension never really left her eyes. "And under such auspicious circumstances. Congratulations on becoming the queen's consort. You are moving up in the world, my student."

Po returned her smile. "Am I? Is it better to be the consort of a queen than an adept?"

She widened her eyes and her smile became playful. "For a male? Most assuredly. Even with my training behind you, not many would choose a male adept over a female one. But if you sire daughters, your future will be secure."

And that would be where the entire matter of Po ended, as far as Ymin or any other traditional Ilysian was concerned. Was he, perhaps, overreaching when he abandoned what once had been his most cherished dream?

Because of the pen, the answer didn't really matter. As long as Thela had it, he needed to do everything within his power to prevent her from using it. And right now that meant convincing Ymin that he was fit for duty as Thela's consort.

He lay back and tried to relax as Ymin rubbed her hands together to warm them, and then placed one palm on either of his inner elbows. Would she be able to detect what he'd been doing with Thela? Probably not. Not by treating him. Kinesiology was not mind reading. Still, he watched her face as her eyes closed and she matched her breathing to his.

This was, ironically, one of the very few times he had experienced kinesiology from the patient's perspective. He was relieved to find that he felt very little: a vague tingling along his meridian pathways and, when she turned him and massaged the muscles of his back and shoulders, warmth and relief as the tension there eased. But certainly nothing to indicate any specific activity in his energy centers. It was unlikely that Thela could detect anything to give away what he did when he treated her.

When Ymin had finished, he rolled over again and looked up at her, wondering what she had sensed.

"You have become a powerful adept in a short period of time," she said, as if in answer to his unspoken question.

"I noticed that," he said. "I had only just obtained my abilities before the chorus left the Libyrinth, and now . . ."

"Now you are as good or better than I am, with all my years of experience."

Would she hate him for that? Was she glad he was Thela's consort, and not in direct competition with her? How humiliating it would be for her to be found inferior to a male. Did she know he had treated an Ancient? Probably not. If she did, it would likely have been the first thing she mentioned. "It seemed to me that my abilities got stronger every time I experienced a mind-lancet attack," he said, hoping to divert her attention.

Ymin pursed her lips and nodded. "There could be a correlation there. I often wondered if Clauda of Ayor's facility with the . . ." She glanced at the door and lowered her voice. "With the wing was a result of the severity of the mind-lancet attack she endured. A mind lancet disrupts the body's energy flow. As such, it may facilitate the formation of new pathways and thus new abilities. Though it's not a method I'd recommend." She was silent a moment. "I'm sorry for what you've been through."

Po's heart pounded. "Thank you, but . . . I made my own choices." He was inordinately proud of that fact, though he tried to conceal it.

"There was a gap in your heart center," said Ymin.

Po swallowed.

"You have a secret that weights heavily on you."

Po took interest in a lizard that was sunning itself on the window ledge of his room. Ymin had gone against Queen Thela before, in smuggling Clauda into the wing in order to let the wing's interface heal her. But that defiance had come with a high price. Clauda had stolen the wing and altered all of Thela's plans.

That Ymin retained her position here meant that she must have made some sort of deal with Thela. For information, most likely. He had to be careful. Giving her nothing could be almost as dangerous as revealing his plan. "I met a woman at the Libyrinth," he said. Hilloa's memory stabbed him. He had not permitted himself to think of her, until now.

Ymin breathed in. "I see. Don't worry, I won't mention it."

Po looked at her. "I love Queen Thela," he said.

She nodded. "Of course you do."

The door to his chamber opened and Po put his book down. Thela entered. "How are you feeling?"

"Much better, thank you."

Thela sank onto the couch next to the reflecting pond.

"I'm glad to hear it. I've been all day with harbormother Parnan and my feet are killing me."

Po got up and knelt at her feet. "Let me rub them for you."

She smiled at him. "I didn't want to ask, since you're still recovering from your ordeal, but . . ."

"I'm fine, really."

She wiggled her toes. "In that case . . ." It was no effort to keep his self-satisfaction out of his smile as he took her feet in his hands. In many ways, what Thela had written about him helped him to deceive her. He was incapable of giving himself away with a frown or a cross word. Outwardly, his every action was designed to please her, and it required no effort on his part at all. Po breathed with her and closed his eyes.

"Oh." Her feet jerked in his grip. "You're going to use kinesiology? Is that—should you do that?"

He looked up at her. "I'm strong enough, and it will feel even better if I do. Just from touching you right now, I can feel how tense you are."

She bit her lower lip. "Well, all right, then."

He closed his eyes and breathed with her again. Instantly he dropped into trance. It shocked him, how easy it had become, and at the same time, it was hard to believe he'd once feared he'd never be able to do it.

Now he beheld Thela's inner world as if he were a hawk hovering high above Ilysies. He dived down to her heart center and found the tool that represented the pen still tucked away in its niche within the ruined temple. That was good.

Hoping to keep her focus on pleasant things, he turned

to her naval center and planted seeds for a berry bush that would yield sweet fruit.

It took an enormous amount of energy to manipulate a person in this way, and by the time he was done, he was dizzy with exhaustion. But he couldn't let her see that. He didn't need Ymin Ykobos examining him anymore, and he needed Thela to feel free to accept kinesiology from him at any time.

Po took a deep breath and willed himself not to sway.

"Ah, that was lovely. Thank you, Po." Thela stood and held her hand out to him. He stood before taking it, lest she feel him tremble. He thanked the Mother he was able to get to his feet without stumbling.

Thela drew him close and kissed him. She guided him toward the bed.

So when you were in Endymion's Tomb, and she asked for her pen, what did you do?" asked Thela, as they dozed in each other's arms.

He hesitated out of sheer embarrassment. "I handed it to her. Or I would have, except Ayma stopped me."

Thela shook her head. "Wait, you had it?"

"It was on the floor. We'd missed it before because it was in shadow."

"If it was right there, then why didn't Endymion get it herself?"

"Yeah. I know," said Po. "I don't think she could move. She was in a chair, and . . . well, her body wasn't really her body and I don't think her legs were working."

"Her body wasn't really her body?"

Po tried not to answer. It was hard to tell what information might be dangerous for her to have. Probably all of it. But Thela was waiting and it was impossible not to tell her. "When her arm came off, it was metal underneath her clothes. And later, when I treated her, I saw the true seat of her consciousness. The body, the clothes, her face, all of that was just like, I don't know, a puppet or something. Decoration. Like how you wrap up a gift with elaborate bows but the important part is what's inside."

"You treated her?"

He hadn't meant to mention that. "Yes."

Her eyes widened. "Really. Po, that's amazing. What . . . happened?"

"It's hard to explain. First, she showed me how Eggs were made."

Thela sat up. "Po, you should have told me that immediately. How could you keep something like that from me?" Anger and uncertainty sharpened her tone.

The question was not really directed at him. She was not asking why he would withhold such information, but rather how he'd been capable of it when he was only supposed to do what made her happy. The last thing he needed was for her to question the effectiveness of her control over him. "Only because it doesn't matter. The method is impossible for any mortal being to attempt."

She narrowed her eyes. "How can you be certain?"

He told her about being outside of time with Endymion, and how she took a universe that was just being born and stopped it from expanding, and made it into an Egg.

"Oh." Her voice was soft, her eyes full of wonder. "That is what they are? Universes? Oh, my."

"The Ancients are far beyond us, Your Majesty. They

are not— I don't believe they are beings of flesh and blood. I don't know what they are."

She nodded. It struck him that she did not question his deductions. She had more regard for his intelligence than he would have expected. "What happened next?"

"This is the strangest part of all. When I started treating her, the vision I had was of a desert, but the grains of sand were Eggs, and in the distance was a great metal sphere. Only the closer I came to it, the smaller it became, until I held it in my hand. Adept Ykobos taught me that in kinesthetic trance we can perceive things that are not apparent, either to the ordinary senses, or to reason. Thela, I knew that within that sphere was the real Endymion."

"Inside it?"

"Yes. Only, the sphere was cracked. It wasn't supposed to be that way. I tried to mend it but I couldn't. And then, my hands sprouted feathers, and became a bird. They left my body and flew away with the sphere, and when I came out of the trance, Endymion was gone."

In the silence, Po clearly heard the waves beating against the rocks at the bottom of the cliff outside. Thela stared at him, though he wondered if she really saw him at all. At length, she blinked and seemed to come back to herself. "That is the strangest thing I've ever heard."

He nodded.

"Did she . . . what happened to her?"

"I don't know. She said she wanted me to free her. I'm not sure what that means. She wanted to join her friends."

"The other Ancients?"

He nodded.

"They're all dead."

Po suddenly realized that one interpretation of this

story was that he had killed a woman. Would Thela kill him and have herself branded?

"Or so we thought," Thela said. "The Ayorites call the Ancients the People Who Walk Sideways in Time."

He didn't mention that he knew that.

"Maybe death to them isn't really death," Thela went on. "If she was stuck in that chair, then maybe she was stuck in other ways, too, and you simply helped her move to a higher dimension. In any case, you did as she wished. What is most remarkable is that you were able to interface with her at all. This goes far beyond anything that has been accomplished with kinesiology in the past. I wonder what Ymin would say, if she knew of it."

4

A New Voice

It had been a week since the return of the Chorus of the Word and people were starting to resume their regular routines. Haly sat on a stool at the console in the Great Hall, searching through books for anything regarding devices that could alter reality.

Hilloa marched up to Haly with a stack of books in her arms. "We need to do something about Po and the pen," she said.

She was right, but Haly didn't have the first idea what to do about it. She listened to Hilloa's books. She'd noticed that often the books told her things that pertained to the current situation.

"The study of the origins of words may be regarded as a sort of archeology of our thought process," said *Wholeness and the Implicate Order*.

"Exhausted from old age, Moses' last act was to write down on a scroll all the important events that had happened to the Hebrew people," added *The Alphabet Versus the Goddess*.

No help there. "What do you think we should do?"

Hilloa stared at her. "I don't know! I thought you would . . ."

Haly nodded. "Let's break the situation down. This all-powerful device exists; of that there is no doubt. Apart from one momentary catastrophe, we have not been affected by it. We could be affected by it at any time. No one really knows where the pen is now, or what happened to Po or where he is now. We don't know that Thela has the pen. She's ruthless in accomplishing her aims. If she really had the pen, do you think there is anything Po could do to prevent her from using it?"

"His kinesiology—"

"Is a healing power, not mind control."

"But he—"

"Isn't it more likely that something else happened to the pen? That Thela does not have it at all?"

"We searched the temple from top to bottom. We never found the pen, or Po."

"So we don't know anything. Which makes choosing a course of action rather difficult."

"So you're going to ignore it."

"We don't even know what 'it' is," said Haly. "And we have plenty of other problems that we have at least some idea of how to deal with, and not a lot of time for dealing with those, so . . ."

"So you're just going to ignore the most intractable one."

"Welcome to my life. Where do you think any of us would be now if I let fear force me into rash actions?"

Hilloa leaned back, her expression shifting from anger to surprise. "Oh. So . . ." She lowered her voice. "You do have a plan, then."

Song and Silence. "I can't discuss this right now, Hilloa. Please, the best thing for you to do is keep researching. The more we know, the better equipped we'll be to deal with whatever comes next."

Hilloa nodded, as if she was in on some secret now, and headed for the Alcove of the Fly. Haly watched her go with a sigh, and returned to her own studies.

Two days later Haly walked into her office to find Jan, Hilloa, and Baris waiting for her.

"We want to go rescue Po," Baris said before Haly even had a chance to ask them what was on their minds.

She raised her eyebrows and put a pot of water on the glow warmer to buy time. "We don't even know where he is," she said at length.

"I think we do," said Hilloa. "We've been talking it over and we realized a few things.

Haly sat down and regarded them. "Go on."

"Well," said Hilloa. "When we searched the temple for Po, we found that one tower was different from all the others. The rest all had a room at the top, but this one tower didn't. Or rather, there was no door to enter by. Just a blank wall."

"There's a room there," said Baris. "It belonged to Censor Orrin before. But now, the door is just gone."

"And it's not bricked in," said Hilloa.

"You'd be able to tell that," said Baris.

Jan nodded. "We think Queen Thela, or maybe Mab, used the pen to make the door go away."

"Do you think they're still in there?" asked Haly.

The three of them looked at one another. "We think Thela was there, and she used the pen to spirit Po, Mab, and herself back to Ilysies."

Haly nodded. "Selene said much the same thing. But why are you all so certain she'd go back to Ilysies? If she does have the pen, she can do anything."

"Po did kinesiology on Endymion," said Jan. "An *Ancient*."

"Ayma told us about it later," said Hilloa. "The point is, Po's kinesiology is . . ."

"Wildly powerful," finished Baris.

"The Lit King kept having him heal Siblea so he could torture him more. It was hard on both of them. Bad. But Po . . ." Hilloa trailed off.

Jan said, "He just kept going. We thought he'd collapse at some point. We were worried it might kill him. He *was* in rough shape, but . . ."

Hilloa shook her head. "When we were taken out of the cell, at the end, he still walked under his own power. He had the strength to kill the Lit King."

"So . . ." Haly waited.

"We think the reason Queen Thela hasn't taken over everyone and everything with the pen is because Po's preventing her with his kinesiology," said Hilloa.

The rest all nodded in agreement.

Haly took a deep breath. It was an interesting theory. It would explain why, if Thela did have the pen, she hadn't used it. But was it possible to do that with kinesiology, however powerful the adept might be? Besides, there were other considerations. "If you're right, then how do you plan to rescue him without disrupting what he's doing and putting him, and the rest of us, in even greater danger?"

Hilloa nodded. "I thought that myself, but we also don't know how long he can keep doing that. And if he's caught . . ."

"I understand your concern," said Haly. "But going to Ilysies at this time is reckless. We have no idea what is really going on. You're likely to do more harm than good. I know this is hard for you to understand but, sometimes, you just have to wait and see."

"You sent Po with the chorus to keep him safe," said Hilloa.

Haly swallowed against the lump that had suddenly formed in her throat. "Yes. I know."

"The other day when we talked, I thought you had a plan but you've done nothing. How can you abandon him?"

Haly closed her eyes. Hilloa was only a couple of years younger than she was. How could she make Haly feel so old? "I'm not. I simply have the experience to know that acting rashly can cause more harm than good. Sometimes, caring means waiting until you find the right course of action."

"What if Thela is using the pen on Po right now? The citadel people have all kinds of stories of the things the Ancients did to their slaves with it. We can't just sit here and do nothing!" said Hilloa.

"Yeah. Po could be in a lot of trouble right now," said Jan. "Bad."

They all stared at Haly as if she had sprouted a second

head. "You sent him with the chorus to keep him safe!" said Hilloa.

Haly couldn't look at them. She stared at her cooling tea. "I know. And I don't take this lightly. You know, after I was taken captive by the Singers, Clauda and Selene were in much the same situation as we are in now." She wished she could have Clauda talk to them about this, but Clauda was missing, too. *Tales.* "Clauda wanted to turn right around and go after them, but if they had, they'd have been taken captive as well. Selene wanted to get help, and they did, and though nothing went the way anyone planned, it did all work out, eventually." She had to believe this was for the best. "We are not forgetting or abandoning Po. We are doing the best for him by being smart about this."

They all nodded silently, but she had the distinct impression that her words were written in evaporating ink.

They'd only been gone a few moments when someone knocked on the door. With a sigh, Haly stood and answered it.

It was Burke. "Today is Palla's interment," she said.

Palla, Haly's old crèche mistress. She had died in the first Redemption, when the population of the Libyrinth had fought the Singers with rifles and fire irons. Many had died. Haly missed Palla the most.

Libyrinth children were raised communally, but most of them had parents here. Haly's parents had died when she was a very tiny baby, and Palla was the only mother she'd ever known. At the mention of her name, images flared to life in Haly's mind, some of her best and worst memories. Palla smiling indulgently at her as she proudly scrawled her first words upon the crèche floor in palm-glow. Palla reading to her from *Charlotte's Web*. Palla hugging her in congratulations when she received her first assignment as a clerk. And Palla dead on the floor of the Great Hall, her mouth full of blood and her empty eyes staring.

Burke held her gaze, nodding understanding. "No one is going to argue if you act as next of kin. And not just because you're the Redeemer."

Haly was about to agree when someone said, "They all thought I'd lost it . . ." The voice was so soft she could barely make out the words, but she definitely heard them. "What?" she asked, turning, but no one was there.

"Haly?" said Burke, giving her a concerned frown.

"Did you hear that?"

"Hear what?" said Burke.

"That's odd," said Haly. "If I didn't know better I'd swear I just heard a book voice."

"But they don't come to you anymore unless you concentrate on them."

"I know."

It started as a whispering, but when she focused on it, words emerged. "I'd always been taken with Bohm's concept of explicate and implicate orders."

Haly looked about the room, realizing for the first time that she had no idea *how* she could tell which voice came from which book. It was just a part of her overall ability.

And just as she'd always been able to pinpoint a book voice in the past, now she knew the words she heard came from no book in this room. "This is very strange. It's a book, I'm positive, but normally the nearest books are the loudest. How is this one breaking through the Song of all the others, seemingly from a distance?"

"It must be a very special book," said Burke.

Haly nodded. "I've noticed that the particular bits the books recite to me don't seem random."

Burke sat down and leaned toward her. "What do you mean?"

"Well, like for instance, when I was outside of the vault, I didn't hear just any book, I heard the instruction manual for the vault, and not just any part of the instruction manual, but the part that dealt with opening the hatch. The passages I hear from books often seem to be commenting on whatever is happening at the time."

"You think there's some connection between that and this particular book making itself heard over all the others?"

"I don't know."

Burke shrugged. "Maybe you really need to hear whatever it has to say."

"Is it going to tell me how to keep doing this every day?"

"Doing what?"

"Leading the community."

Burke chuckled. "You don't need a book for that, Haly. You do fine."

"Why does everyone think that but me? Well, and Hilloa."

"Well, competent people always underrate their performance. As for Hilloa, she doesn't know what it's like to be responsible for other people's lives."

But Burke did. She had been the Libyrinth's only physician for years. She had helpers now, but she was still the most experienced doctor they had. Haly let Burke's understanding smile warm her. She took a deep breath and nodded. "Yes. I would like to act as next of kin for Palla."

The Libyrarians believed that the world was comprised of seven Tales: Birth, Peril, Hunger, Balance, Love, Death, and Mystery. Each tale had a guardian spirit embodied by an animal. The seven towers of the Libyrinth were each assigned one of these animals, as were the seven alcoves in the Great Hall.

When Libyrarians reached puberty, rituals were performed to determine their tale and corresponding animal guardian. And when they died, their body was placed at the top of the appropriate tower, exposed to the elements until nothing was left but bones. Then the bones were placed in a box engraved with the person's name and placed in the stacks, behind their favorite book. It was up to their next of kin to place the box where it belonged.

As Haly wandered the closely spaced shelves beneath the Libyrinth, she clutched the box holding Palla's bones to her chest. This was where she had spent much of her childhood, but it was dangerous to be down here now that the Libyrinth had regained its full power and function. The shelves were no longer stationary. Like a Victorian-era clockwork device on a grand scale, they moved in response to a request made to the console in the center of the Great Hall, bringing the requested book to the scholar.

At one time, getting lost in here was the great peril, but now, one could get lost and squashed. So interaction with the console was suspended for the duration of the interment. This was one of her few opportunities for Haly to revisit her beloved shelves.

How strange it was to walk here in silence. At one time, the voices of the books would have clamored for her attention, but now all she heard was the gentle, persistent hum of the Song inside her—unless she focused her mind on a specific book or touched it.

There was very little light. A few stray traces of palmglow still lit the way to particularly useful areas, but for the most part, the phosphorescent gel had died and left the shelves in darkness. Haly put one hand out to the books on the shelves and felt her way along.

"Behind the child blared the noise of the TV set; the sound worked but not the picture."

"When finally he found the bottom of his sadness he looked up and wiped his eyes on his forearm."

"It's true that you could ask the same question a hundred different times and get a hundred seemingly different answers. But the S'kang concept of "truth" was indirect, malleable, subtle."

At least it still smelled the same down here. The dry peppery smell of old books filled her nose and brought with it wave after wave of memories. The time she met her first Nod, the time she had brought Clauda down here and confessed her ability to hear the books. And then, of course, the last time she'd been down here, with Gyneth, when they'd given the Libyrinth its heart back and found her parents.

They were properly interred now, too, behind *Rebecca* and *One Flew Over the Cuckoo's Nest*. Haly thought about visiting them, but decided against it. She'd never even known them.

But what was Palla's favorite book? Haly would have chosen *Charlotte's Web*, but that book had been burned over a year ago by the Singers when the Singers were still known by the Libyrarians as Eradicants.

But Palla had loved statecraft. It was she who had introduced Haly to the works of Mencius, Winston Churchill, and Mobeus. Their works had guided her in the past months. Yes, any of their books would be fitting resting places for Palla's bones.

Haly focused on Mencius. "But you don't think about tomorrow when people are feeding surplus grain to pigs and dogs. So when people are starving to death in the streets, you don't think about emptying storehouses to feed them. People die and you say *It's not my fault, it's the harvest.* How is this any different from stabbing someone to death and saying *It's not me, it's the sword?* Stop blaming harvests, and people everywhere under Heaven will come flocking to you."

Haly lifted the box holding Palla's bones over her head to slide it behind the books, where it could rest on the shelf space in the back. All of a sudden she stopped, as the full magnitude of it hit her all at once. She pulled the box back down, clutched it to her chest, and sank to the floor.

What was she doing? How could she be here and not be surrounded by the voices? How could she have let herself lose them? How could she have let them fall silent, and for what? For the Song. To be the Redeemer. The figurehead of an alien religion. And for this she had forsaken the books. How could she have made such a monumental mistake?

The Redemption, the Song—they were transient. Even when they were permanent they were transient. You couldn't hold on to them, and not only had she allowed herself to rely upon them wholeheartedly; she had founded an entire community upon them.

Up there in the Libyrinth, and outside in Tent Town and in the fields were people who were relying on her. Five hundred souls and more, and each and every one of them was counting on her to make the right decisions. What if she made a mistake? Or rather, another mistake.

No. Her vision wavered and her tears streamed down her face in hot rivulets. No. She didn't want this. Her breathing came in gusts and staggers and she wanted to throw up. She put Palla's bones on the floor and sank down on her knees, resting her face against the wood and the carving of her nurse's name. "Put it back," she begged, her voice soft.

So many had died. And now everything was different. How could that be? How could everything change so much in such a short period of time? How could she change so much? Who was she? And where was that world she used to know? "Put it back," she pleaded, with Palla, with the books, the Song, the Libyrinth, with who or whatever would listen. "Put it all back, please."

She wanted to be ignored. She wanted to be quiet and small. She wanted to stay in the background while other people made the important decisions. She wanted the books to talk to her of their own volition. She missed their interruptions so badly. How could she not have noticed that? It was as if she'd been walking around for the past year or more with a huge hole right through her chest and she'd never even noticed. How could she be so empty and still be alive? "I want to go home."

She wanted none of it to have happened: the quest, the

torture, the capture, the war, the fire. Everything was so different now. And they'd lost so many. It wasn't fair. She hadn't asked for this. She hadn't asked for any of it. She sat up suddenly, lifting her face to the word-filled darkness. "Put it all back!" she screamed.

The rage in her voice frightened her. She sank back against the shelves and buried her head in her arms and lost herself in the tide of her emotions.

It was some time before she noticed the tiny hands in her hair. A slight tugging and it may have been going on for some time, she wasn't sure, and then, a piping voice: "What does she say?"

Nod. That much, at least, was still the same. Nod wanted to hear a story. Haly sniffed and lifted her head and swallowed. The creature was about a foot tall, with red pebbly skin and exaggerated facial features. And bald. And without sexual characteristics of any kind. Why had she always thought of Nod as he? Haly wiped at her face and coughed, and gave a shaky laugh.

Nod had a book in its hand, which it pushed at Haly. "What does she say?"

Haly took the book from Nod, and at once her fingers knew it, even before it spoke to her. "On the contrary, I've found that there is always some beauty left—in nature, sunshine, freedom, in yourself; these can all help you. Look at these things, then you find yourself again, and God, and then you regain your balance." *Anne Frank: The Diary of a Young Girl.* Oh.

Nod and Anne had been her companions during her time of captivity among the Singers. And it was because of Anne, because of the words she'd written, that Haly had stood up to the Singers, had embraced the role of Redeemer, and through it changed a religion. However daunting circumstances might be now, it was nothing compared to what they'd been that day in Siblea's office in the Corvariate Citadel. The Redemption was widely considered a miracle, but the real miracle had been her finding the strength to challenge Siblea and the other censors. That was the first miracle. And every other miracle had stemmed from that one. Maybe that was enough reason to believe that this could all work out. Fresh tears came to her eyes but this time they were tears of gratitude. "Thank you," she whispered, though to Nod or to the book or to herself, she couldn't be certain.

"What does she say?" came another voice, and Haly saw another Nod emerge from the shelves across from her.

"What does she say?"

"What does she say?"

Two more Nods appeared and they all sat at her feet, their scrawny arms wrapped around their scrawny knees, waiting for her to read to them. Before long, a whole troupe of them had gathered. They sat down in front of her in a semicircle. More arrived by the second. In the space of two more breaths there were hundreds of them. They sat on each other, clustered together so closely it was impossible to tell where one ended and another began.

"What are you, anyway?" she asked them.

They didn't answer. All of them sat watching her expectantly. The one that had first approached her reached out and nudged at the book in her hand.

Well, all right.

Haly read to them for an hour or more. "And whoever is happy will make others happy, too. He who has courage and faith will never perish in misery!" It was the most relaxed she'd felt in over a year.

At last she stood and placed Palla's bones on the shelf behind Mencius. She paused, and put her hand on the spine of the book. "When there's more grain and fish than they can eat, and more timber than they can use, people nurture life and mourn death in contentment. People nurturing life and mourning death in contentment—that's where the way of emperors begins." Yes. Definitely. She slipped Anne's book into the pocket of her robes and when one of the Nods . . . was it the first one who had approached her? Did it matter? When it leaped upon her shoulder, she let it stay there.

"At its heart, my theory was a simple one. If matter is an illusion and process is the whole of existence, then everything is information."

Haly stopped in her tracks. There it was again, the same voice she'd heard earlier in her office. It was closer now, she felt certain. Intrigued by the tale, she crept down the aisle, quickening her pace as the voice grew louder.

"A fallen leaf, a shooting star, a fly on the windowsill, all arise from the same process, the rules of which lay implicate in their structure. The key is understanding how to look."

Haly turned down another aisle, then doubled back when the voice grew fainter.

"This was the foundation of my approach and since I saw the secret of the universe everywhere around me, teasing me with its shy implicate order, I thought it best to go after it from as many possible viewpoints as could be brought to bear on the topic."

It was louder than ever now. Haly zeroed in on a shelf
in a part of the Libyrinth she'd never been in before. She
pulled a jar of palm-glow from her pocket and smeared
some of the phosphorescent gel on one hand, which she
raised to the shelf. "First there was transcendence."

The voice came from a black book with an image of a
fly in white on the spine. The title read, *The Song That
Changed Us.*

Haly pulled the book from the shelf, and ran for the
Great Hall.

H aly found Gyneth and Burke at the main console.
"Listen to this," she said, showing them the cover
of *The Song That Changed Us.* "They all thought I'd lost
it when I delved into the work of Dr. Bohm, but at that
point, after fifty years, m-theory had yet to yield its promised results. We were as far from a Theory of Everything
as we'd ever been, and I was reminded of Einstein's famous quote: 'The definition of insanity is doing the same
thing over and over again and expecting a different result.'
While my colleagues took the approach that if strings and
membranes had not yet cracked open the universe like an
egg and spilled its secrets, then the answer was to do
strings and membranes even harder, I decided to try a different tack.

"I'd always been taken with Bohm's concept of explicate and implicate orders. In fact, his ink dot and fish tank
thought experiments were my first glimpse of the truths
behind the mystery of spooky action at a distance, and
largely responsible for my entry into the field of quantum
physics.

"Bohm's unwillingness to hide his interest in spiritual matters and his belief in a connection between the numinous and the scientific ruined his reputation and cast his work, unfairly, into disrepute. More shortsightedness from the same sorts of minds that denounced me when I began my interdisciplinary experiments.

"At its heart, my theory was a simple one. If matter is an illusion and process is the whole of existence, then everything is information. Not just information, but fundamentally, the same information. A falling leaf, a shooting star, a fly on the windowsill, all arise from the same process, the rules of which lay implicit in their structure. The key is understanding how to look.

"Consider those stop signs that are painted onto the surface of the road. When viewed directly from above the letters are elongated, but when seen from the perspective of a car approaching the intersection, they look perfectly proportional. A more extreme example is a digital video signal. Until translated by the receiver, it is a stream of ones and zeros totally without meaning to anyone but a specialist. But to say that it is only a stream of ones and zeros is grossly inaccurate. The video is implicit, or as Bohm would say, implicate, in the data stream, but it takes the right viewpoint (i.e., through the receiver) to make that hidden order available to the viewer.

"This was the foundation of my approach and since I saw the secret of the universe everywhere around me, teasing me with its shy implicate order, I thought it best to go after it from as many possible viewpoints as could be brought to bear on the topic.

"They threatened my tenure when I brought a biologist onto my team. When I hired a composer, they fired us all.

Fortunately, by then my project had caught the attention of Bella Gunderson and we were able to continue working on her payroll, which was even better.

"I remember clearly one evening in early summer when I stepped outside the facility in Des Moines and stood staring at the sunset. I thought then that I would die happy if I could just solve this problem. It makes me laugh now. Because of course in the end it was not the information itself that changed everything, but the process by which we discovered it. Even then I should have known that once you learn how to make the implicate order of a thing explicate, it is a small thing to alter that order. When you can do that, then you can do anything and death becomes a quaint artifact of the past.

"Still, there is much to be nostalgic for in that time. We were so innocent, and our quarrels and our loves, that seemed so important, were so small and insignificant.

"Every evening, Fisher played concertos on the baby grand in the great room. And Cow and Mouse would curl up on the couch in front of the fire. Everyone had a nickname, except for me. The animal motif started with Stephenson, my colleague in physics, whom we all noted worked like a dog. Nichols, the biologist, who would eventually earn the moniker the Lion, for his temper, started calling him Dog and it went from there.

"Privately, I was quite hurt at being the only one of the team without a nickname, though of course later, after the demonstration in which I turned a fly into a rosebush and back again, I became known as the Fly, not just by our little group, but by the whole world over.

"While Fisher composed the song which, when played at the correct frequency, caused the hidden dimensions to unfold and express the information embedded within them, it was Avendal, our linguist, and Masters, our visual artist, who designed the device that streamlined the process and expanded it to the ability to manipulate that information, and thus reality. It was her whim to design it as a pen, though it could have taken many forms.

"But I'm getting ahead of myself. The pens came later. First there was transcendence. Since information from dimensions five through eleven cannot be properly observed by mere three-and-a-half-dimensional beings, the observers, too, needed to change.

"That was Nichols and Foster's project, and it was the one that created the most furor in the general populace. While authors as far back as Egan and Vinge had speculated on the ability to upload human intelligence into immortal, synthetic processing systems that did everything the human brain could and more, people freaked out when the notion became a reality. Until they grasped that they were being offered immortality.

"Within a decade, everything changed. Scarcity became a thing of the past. The human race became immortal, and we seven who wielded the pens were gods. Time ceased to have meaning to us. We could create universes at will, or stop them from being born and use their energy to power our other creations."

Haly stopped reading.

"The animals," said Burke. "Is this the origin of the Seven Tales?"

"Are these the People Who Walk Sideways in Time?" said Gyneth.

"Where is Hilloa?" said Burke. "She'll want to hear this."

"I don't know," said Gyneth. "I haven't seen her this morning."

A little tendril of unease wound its way through Haly's stomach. As she and the others searched for Hilloa, then Baris and Jan, the feeling intensified. By that evening, it was clear that the three of them were gone.

They've gone to Ilysies," said Haly, certain of it. She was with Gyneth in the room they shared. It was late, but she couldn't sleep. She paced instead.

"In all likelihood," he admitted.

"They're going to get themselves killed."

"Maybe, but maybe Vorain will catch up with them in time." The former Ilysian soldier had volunteered to take a team and try to intercept them.

"They had a pretty solid head start. We may have just sent Vorain and the others into peril as well, for nothing. This is my fault. I should have paid more attention when Hilloa, Baris, and Jan came to talk to me."

"You can't blame yourself for everything, Haly," said Gyneth. He sounded tired.

Haly was tired, too, exhausted with responsibility. It was just earlier today that she'd lost it in the stacks while laying Palla's bones to rest. And now . . . another problem, and she was somehow supposed to think of a solution, but she was completely out of ideas, and worse, out of the capacity to withstand another crisis.

They all thought it was easy for her. That just because the Song was inside her meant accessing it wasn't a conscious act. In the first place, she had to remember it was there, and it was shockingly easy to forget when faced with catastrophe. And she had to focus on her breath and calm her mind. Otherwise, she could be just as panicky as anyone else. It was work and yes, there were times when she didn't feel like making that effort. Sometimes she wanted to be weak. But everyone was depending on her, so instead she breathed.

Gyneth stood, and came to her. She leaned against his chest and let him put his arms around her, tucking her nose in his armpit. She'd read somewhere that male body odor made heterosexual females feel better. It was true. She held on tight, and she breathed.

"You can keep a secret, right?"

He pulled back and gave her a puzzled look. "You know that."

"Yeah. Here's the thing." Haly leaned against him. Somehow, she felt like she'd be overheard. Maybe it was just that once she spoke these words aloud, they'd become real. She hesitated.

"What?" said Gyneth. "Whatever it is, just tell me."

The urge to tell was just too strong. "I don't think I can do this anymore."

Gyneth paled and he stepped back. "You mean . . . ?"

Oh, no. "No. Not that. Not us." She held up her hands. "I mean I don't think I can be the leader of the Libyrinth anymore. I'm terrible at it."

Gyneth seemed relieved. But then he shook his head. "You're mistaken. You're only seventeen but you're a wonderful leader. You're doing a great job! Why would you—"

"We almost starved to death, Gyneth."

"That wasn't your fault."

"Wasn't it? Isn't everything that happens here my responsibility?"

Gyneth narrowed his brows. "I think you're being too hard on yourself."

Haly was past listening. "I don't know what I'm doing and I don't think I can take it anymore. The pressure . . ."

"Yeah." Gyneth came and drew her into his arms. "Okay. It must be a lot, I know. For someone who says she doesn't know what she's doing you've accomplished amazing things, but I can understand why you feel this way."

T he next morning, Haly went to the infirmary to talk to Burke.

The Libyrinth's healer was at her worktable, grinding accar leaves.

"I think we need to revisit the question of who should lead the community," Haly said, sitting down beside her.

Burke raised her eyebrows. "But Haly, you're our Redeemer."

Haly shrugged. "So what? What does that even mean, day to day? So I had a big part to play in bringing about the Redemption. Just a part now, mind you. Other people were just as indispensable, which is something everyone seems to forget. Anyway. The Redemption happened, and now it's over. So what makes me qualified to lead this community? And should we even have one single leader, anyway? Shouldn't we have some sort of representational government? I just don't think we thought any of this through."

Burke waited until Haly was finished. "Okay, first of all, you are qualified, because you hear the Song inside you all the time. It does make a difference."

"Just think what a disaster I'd be without it," countered Haly.

Burke gave her a look. "Second, no one has a window into the future. You and all of us had our hands full getting the community organized and running. It is regrettable that we didn't reach out to the citadel sooner, but hardly surprising, or negligent, that we did not."

Haly opened her mouth to protest but Burke held out a hand. "And third, you are seventeen years old and I am sorry that I did not see what an unfair burden sole leadership of the community is to you. Of course you don't have to do this all by yourself."

Haly blinked at her. She had been braced for more argument and now, suddenly, she felt as if a great space had opened up before her, filled with possibilities.

5

The Confidence of the Queen

Apart from missing his friends, Po found that the worst part about being Queen Thela's consort was the boredom. Except for when he was entertaining Thela, he was alone. He had his own chamber, with couches, bathing pool, desk, and bower. A sumptuous room— though not overlarge—it had everything he needed. There was even an adjoining, private exercise yard.

His meals were brought to him. He had no reason to leave, and was, in fact, not permitted to, by custom. Other than Thela's visits, there was little to divert him from worrying about the Libyrinth, about getting caught, about what Thela might do with the pen if he failed.

At least now he was recovered enough to walk about. He pulled aside the sheer white curtain that veiled the archway and ventured out into his exercise yard. It was twenty feet square and open to the sun above. Lush grass cushioned his feet and tickled his nose with a rich, earthy smell. The whitewashed wall surrounding the tidy lawn was solid up to shoulder height, and above that, bricks with a latticework pattern in the shape of a four-petaled rose continued upward several feet. Through the spaces he could see the ocean, and on either side, other exercise yards nearly identical to his own.

He watched the waves rolling in from the vast blue sea that stretched out to the horizon. He remembered his first sight of the Corvariate Citadel, and how for a moment he'd mistaken its distant gray bulk for the ocean. How unhappy he'd thought he was at that time—framed by Thela for the fire that destroyed the Libyrinth's crops. Haly had sent him to the citadel with the Chorus of the Word in order to protect him, but it had felt like exile.

Those problems seemed small and manageable in comparison to what he faced now. That heartbreak, humiliation, and guilt seemed self-indulgent, a luxury. He envied his former self.

Scattered about in the grass were weighted spheres for exercise and balance. Just because he was confined did not mean he could let his body go to seed. He was expected to stay attractive for his queen. Po picked up one of the smaller spheres, made of polished granite, pink threaded through with green, and hefted it. At first his body protested, but soon disused muscles remembered the pleasure of work.

Po discovered that the physical exercise actually helped him feel better. Much of his exhaustion was due to the kinesiology he'd performed. Using his body seemed to counterbalance all the inner energy he'd expended. He did several sets of exercises, then lay in the grass in the sun and napped.

"Po, what are you doing out here?"

It was Queen Thela. Po opened his eyes to find himself still lying in the grass in the yard. The sun had gone down beyond the roof of the palace and he lay in shadow. The grass had collected the evening dew and become cool and damp, making his muscles stiff. "Your Majesty, I fell asleep."

"Tsk. Such a male. Come in now, you'll catch cold."

Po obeyed her.

Thela rang for a servant and ordered a hot bath drawn. "I need it as much as you do," she said. "The day I've had. I've never been able to understand how people expect to simultaneously pursue a policy of isolationism and maintain Ilysies's status as the most powerful nation on the continent. It makes no sense."

She disrobed and sank into the hot water with a sigh. Po sat on the edge of the tub and rubbed her shoulders.

"Mmm." She dropped her head back. "Plata thinks she can turn recent events to her advantage. She's courting Jolaz, who she perceives as less expansionist than myself. Carys whispers of a challenge, but I don't see it. There's a reason I didn't deflect criticism of the Redemption debacle onto my heir. I could have made it out to be her fault and replaced her, but Jolaz is loyal to a fault, steady, and sensible. She'd much rather wait for a natural succession than deal with the controversy of a challenge.

"It's more likely that Carys hopes to sow suspicion

between us and take Jolaz's place for herself. Then I'd be facing a challenge for certain. Carys fancies herself clever, but there's clever and then there's too clever. Perhaps I should find something urgent for her to attend to in eastern Shenash."

Challenge. Not every heir took the throne when the old queen died or retired. Some did not wish to wait that long. Though rare, it was accepted custom that an heir who felt that the current queen presented a danger to Ilysian sovereignty could challenge her mentor. By tradition they met in the ring with knives, but there were exceptions to that practice as well.

Po thought of the robe floating in the water in the partially submerged temple in Thela's heart center. Everyone had loved the old queen, Mata Tadamos. She'd been Ilysies's ruler for thirty years before she named her daughter heir, and she probably could have reigned for another thirty if not for the sudden illness that forced her into retirement. No one saw her after that, and months later she'd been reported dead. Had she lived out her reign, Thela would have been in her seventies before the crown became hers. There'd always been a lot of idle speculation about the old queen's demise. A popular palace rumor was that Thela had simply walled her mother up in her bedchamber and assumed the throne.

Po looked at Thela, who lay with her head tilted back, her eyes half-closed. He knew firsthand she was capable of terrible things. And yet she trusted Jolaz. What would happen if Thela's rule really were threatened?

She'd use the pen to defend herself. He had no doubt of that.

"They forget that a year ago the Singers were on the threshold of taking over everything. Now, our old rival, Thesia, is humbled and the Singers are no more."

"Mmm."

"All under your reign, Your Majesty."

Thela opened her eyes and looked up at him. Had he said too much? But he was incapable of any outward action that displeased her, wasn't he?

"You make an excellent point, Po. I will have to remind my critics of it. Come, leave off massaging me. Get in here, you're cold."

Po slid into the warm water and Thela's arms. His concerns about not having enough opportunities to reinforce his kinesthetic manipulations had been entirely unfounded.

"You are not like other males," said Thela.

Po returned her smile. "I hope that pleases you."

"It does," she said, surprise adding a lilt to her words. "I find I like having a consort I can talk with about other things besides pleasure. It's nice to be able to share with you what has transpired in my day. And I like hearing about your experiences with Endymion.

"I'm not used to a male having experiences beyond my own, but I find it doesn't bother me. It makes you more interesting. And you are helping me to understand the pen better."

He ran his hand up and down her arm. She liked that. She tilted her head back and closed her eyes. "The pen frightens me," he said, in all honesty.

"Mmm. Me too," she said. "And it should frighten us. Anything that powerful can't help but be dangerous. But don't worry. I won't use it until I understand it, and can control its effects."

"Is that possible?" Po cursed himself. He'd spoken the thought aloud, and he hadn't meant to.

"Of course it's possible. Don't be too overawed, Po. Just like all the other devices of the Ancients, the pen is a tool. It can be mastered."

That was what Po was afraid of. But all he could do was smile and say, "I know you'll do what's best."

The next morning when he ventured outside to work off the muzziness of sleep, there was someone in the yard next to his, a young man who looked a few years older than him. Hoping not to be noticed, Po observed him as he did push-ups. He wore the tight-fitting pants of a bull dancer, and his upper body was bare. He was slender and sinewy, with coal-black hair and a prominent, aquiline nose. He was a perfect specimen of manly Ilysian beauty. Po, with his brown hair and his snub nose, could never hope to compete with a male like that.

Why did Thela keep Po around? The only reasons he could think of were that she valued his kinesthetic abilities, thought he had useful information from his time with Endymion, or she genuinely liked him.

The other male noticed Po and shot him a fierce grin full of menace. He came to the dividing wall. "You may be her favorite now," he said, "but she'll soon tire of you."

Po didn't answer him. Everyone knew the queen had more than one consort, though such a thing was unheard of anyplace but in the palace. Ordinarily, rivals for a woman's attention would fight. Sometimes these battles were spontaneous and sometimes they were planned in advance and the woman, her friends, and family members attended as spectators. How were such rivalries handled here?

Since he didn't know, Po decided the best thing to do was nothing at all. Still, he didn't turn his back on the male as he bent and picked up a sphere and began his workout.

The other male put on a display of physical prowess. He did handstands and backflips, even did leg presses while balancing on his hands. Of course, he was a bull dancer. Traditionally, the queen selected her consorts from among the bull dancers.

Po was amused to realize he felt no need to compete with the other consort. He thought of his fights with Baris, and of this male's competitive show. Both seemed equally ridiculous to him now.

". . . And my hands became wings and flew away with the sphere. When I came out of my trance, Endymion was gone," said Po.

Thela leaned forward, her face eager. They'd just made love, and Po had taken the opportunity to reinforce his energy work, preventing her from using the pen. Now they reclined in bed, and the conversation had turned to Po's experiences with Endymion.

"But what about your hands?" said Thela.

Po lifted them and flexed his fingers. "As you can see, they were unharmed."

Thela narrowed her eyes in thought. "I must consult

with Ymin about that. It seems to me there should be some effect."

He had to agree, but he'd rather simply be grateful to have escaped unharmed.

"What happened to her?" asked Thela.

"I don't know," said Po. "Before the trance, she kept saying she wanted to go and be with her friends—the other Ancients."

"Who are all dead," said Thela.

Po shrugged. "What does that really mean for people like that? I mean they're—the Ayorites say they are descended from the People Who Walk Sideways in Time."

"That's their name for the people who created our world," she said.

He nodded.

"The People Who Walk Sideways in Time . . . that means they can travel in time, or that they transcend time? I suppose it amounts to the same thing. What do you think, Po? Do you think they created the world, or did it emerge from the ocean, as our tradition says?"

Po was nervous at first, until he realized that he was protected from displeasing her by what she had written of him with the pen. "Well, I think the world came out of the ocean, as is said, but . . . where did the ocean come from? When she showed me how an Egg is made, she said it was her and her friends' parents who did that. So, yes, I do believe that the People Who Walk Sideways in Time made our world."

Despite his earlier confidence, Po held his breath, waiting for her response. She rolled onto her back and stared up at the canopy of gauze above the bed. "So what do you think happens to us when we die?"

Po was so surprised that for a moment he couldn't speak. When he recovered, he didn't know what to say.

"Do we become like those people, living outside of time, or is it just . . . nothing? Or is it as some of the Old Earth books say, and we are punished for what we've done wrong, burning for all eternity?" She turned again and stared at him, waiting expectantly. There was an intensity in her gaze that he could not fathom. This was more than idle curiosity on her part.

His words were not his own. They came from someplace outside himself. "I think we drift off, as in a pleasant dream. We go on for all eternity, but it is for us but an hour—an hour of complete happiness. There is no suffering, and no punishment."

"Mmm," she said, and drew him closer. "I like that." She rested her head on his shoulder, and her breathing deepened. Po lay listening to her, and thinking of a robe floating in the water.

D id you have a happy childhood, Po?" asked Thela.
        Po blinked in surprise. He considered the question. "Yes, I guess I did. I had to put up with some teasing from my cousins, and they were girls so I couldn't do anything about it, but . . . other than that, it was nice. I was too young to realize there was anything different about my appearance and it was too soon for the rest of the family to be concerned about it. Life was quiet, uneventful. We had the land and the village. It was good." Something prompted him to ask, "What about you?"

"Yes. I was very happy." Thela smiled. "I grew up in

the palace. My mother, even though she was the queen, always had time for me. We played together every day. And when she made me her heir, I worked at her side. You know, she was every bit as wise and kind as everyone thinks."

All Po could think of was that gown floating in the water. "You can tell me anything, you know," he said, the words coming unbidden once again.

Thela stared at him a long time before saying, "I know. And I know that everyone thinks I killed her."

He waited.

"I did." She lay back and was silent. Her eyes were closed, but wetness glimmered in her lashes. When she spoke again, it was in a rough whisper. "She had the little lion inside. The cancer spread to her brain and the adepts could do nothing about it. Though she'd always been kind, she'd never been stupid; those who thought they could take advantage of her good nature never got very far. But she changed. Everything changed.

"It wouldn't have been so bad if she had understood what was happening to her. If she'd known, if she'd still been herself, she'd have stepped down immediately. But no matter how many times I explained it to her, she forgot. She would not relinquish the throne, and she became suspicious of me. Others took advantage of the situation. Ilysies was in jeopardy because of her impairment. When she signed a disadvantageous trade agreement with She-nash, and had it delivered in secret, I knew that was only the beginning. I had to act.

"In her condition, the public spectacle of a challenge was unthinkable." Thela rested her head on his shoulder.

She pulled him close and buried her face in the crook of his neck. He was shocked to feel her tremble. Tears dampened his skin. *Mother.*

Thela lifted her lips to his ear. Her voice was barely audible. "No one else knows this. I used Ease. She drifted off as if she were floating out to sea."

Outwardly, Po stroked her back, and said, "You did what you had to do." Inwardly, he felt frozen with fear. If she ever thought there was the slightest chance he might divulge this secret, he'd be dead. The control she'd exerted over him with the pen was both what enabled this disclosure and what protected him. But if she ever lost confidence in the words she'd written . . .

He continued to soothe her as his mind raced. Thela had killed her own mother, whom she appeared to have loved. And she'd nearly caused Selene's death as well. A mother, a daughter. What was a consort?

The next time Po went into the yard, the other consort was there again. "What's your name?" Po asked him, to preempt his threats and bragging.

"Myr." He stared at Po, apparently thrown.

"I'm Po."

Myr gripped the wall. "Sleep lightly, Po."

He sighed. "They want us to be rivals, you know."

"They? Who's they?"

Po had to think about that. "The women. They want men to fight each other because it makes it easier to control us."

Myr wrinkled his nose as if he smelled something funny. "You're even weirder than everyone says."

"Who says?"

"The other bull dancers. Everyone says you used to be an apprentice to Adept Ykobos. Is it true?"

"Yeah."

"That's why the queen favors you? You have special skills?"

"I guess so."

"But you're ugly."

Po couldn't help himself. "That's not what Thela thinks."

The other male did his best to hide his reaction but Po caught that first twitch of his mouth. It was true then; Thela's frequent visits were cutting into his competition's time with her.

"I should climb over this wall and kill you."

"What's stopping you?"

Now Myr looked sullen.

"Thela would be displeased if you did away with me, wouldn't she?"

He looked like he'd bitten into a rotten lemon. "I should have been given the opportunity to best you before all the court."

"It seems the queen is less than conventional."

Myr narrowed his eyes. "Others besides myself may not be pleased by that."

"What have you heard?" Unlike him, Myr got out every day for practice in the arena.

"Nothing. Not that I'd tell you, anyway."

"You'd do well to," said Po. "Both our fortunes rest with Thela."

"If I have something to tell her, I'll do it myself."

"But you have to see her first."

Myr pounded a fist against the wall. "Your cock will wither and snap off like a dry twig."

"I don't believe in curses from jealous males," said Po. "But if you change your mind and decide to cooperate with me, I may be able to help you."

"Go stab your mother while you're at it."

Po's gut churned. He took half a step forward before mastering himself. It made no difference. Myr had already gone inside.

6

Vanishing Point

The discovery of *The Song That Changed Us* created a great stir. The Great Hall, always a hub of activity, now bustled night and day as people ran to and fro with notes and books, showing one another passages and arguing points of interpretation.

Haly was in the midst of an argument with Peliac over the possibility of uploading human consciousness into a silicon-based computer processor when the hall suddenly fell silent.

"It would be worth it, just to never have to eat pickled turnips again," said Peliac, her voice ringing out clear and true. And then that, too, faded to silence and they all stared at the newcomer standing in the archway.

Haly remembered him. His green livery was faded now, but his regimental bearing remained the same. His standard hung limp with no wind to unfurl it but she knew it bore the boar of Thesia just the same.

Haly quickened her pace until she stood before the Thesian envoy. "Welcome to the Redeemed Community of the Libyrinth," she said.

He stared at her. Haly wondered if he recognized her as the shy young girl who had handed him a letter—how long ago?

It seemed ages, but it had only been a year or so.

"Greetings," he said. "I bear a message for the Redeemer, from the first administrator of the New Republic of Thesia."

"I am the Redeemer," said Haly. It surprised her how naturally those words came now.

The envoy produced a scroll, and presented it with a bow. "I have been instructed to await your response, Holy One."

Haly took the missive in her hand. The parchment was smooth. She refrained from listening to the letter. "Come to my office," she said.

Gyneth joined her and they all sat down in Haly's little office. She made tea. When they were all settled with a steaming cup, she broke the seal on the scroll and unrolled it.

The handwriting was neat and close-spaced.

Dear Holy One,

Felicitations on the Redemption. We regret our tardiness in offering our congratulations but the last eighteen months have been eventful ones for the New Republic, as we are confident they have been for you as well.

Recent events of an anomalous nature have caused

us to regret our unintended isolation from the communities of the Plain of Ayor, and in particular, from the Libyrinth. Thesia and the Libyrinth have a long-standing tradition of cooperation. Though both communities have recently undergone transformative changes, we see no reason that tradition cannot continue.

In fact, it is in hope of renewing our long-standing ties that we write to you now. A strange storm has appeared near our southern border, in the region commonly known as the Tumbles. The phenomenon is persistent and appears to be growing. We respectfully request, nay, implore, the Redeemer's presence at her earliest convenience.

In return for such consideration, the New Republic of Thesia is prepared to be generous with its mineral resources. Since time is short and the future ever more uncertain, we hope to make negotiations unnecessary with the following formal offer:

50 metric tons gold
200 metric tons iron
200 metric tons copper
200 metric tons nickel
1,000 metric tons aluminum
20,000 metric tons other assorted minerals of recipients' choosing, excepting gold

If this is not agreeable, pray bring your counteroffer with you. All reasonable requests will be entertained.

Yours Sincerely,
The First Administrator of
the New Republic of Thesia,
on behalf of all citizens of Thesia

Without a word, Haly handed the letter to Gyneth and watched as he read it. She knew exactly when he got to the part about payment. His eyebrows crept up his forehead, nearly disappearing beneath his bangs. But by the time he'd finished reading, he'd carefully schooled his features to neutrality again. "The letter does not state the cause of the storm," he told the envoy.

"That is because we do not know the cause. It is the first administrator's hope that the Redeemer, with her special relationship with the Song, may be able to provide us with a clearer understanding of the anomaly."

Haly and Gyneth exchanged a look. She remembered her conversation with Burke. The physician had more or less given her leave to take a break from the Libyrinth, and Haly had been wanting to visit Thesia since she'd recovered from the famine. "Will you excuse us, please?" she asked the envoy. "I need to discuss this with my advisor. You may wait in the Great Hall, or take some refreshment in the dining hall if you're hungry."

The envoy departed.

"Well," said Gyneth. "If you wanted to visit Thesia, here's your excuse."

"But things are so up-in-the-air here right now. Po and Clauda are missing, the pen . . . Not to mention Hilloa, Baris, and Jan taking off."

"You're not the only one who can handle those things, you know."

"Yeah, but . . ."

"But the first administrator seems to think you are the only one who can deal with this strange new storm. And besides . . ."

"That's a lot of metal," they both said in unison.

* * *

Haly thought carefully about which books to take with her on the journey to Thesia. *The Book of the Night*, most definitely, and the *Dhamapada*. *Quantum Theory* by David Bohm, *The Diary of Anne Frank*, and Shakespeare's sonnets.

She stacked them all neatly and tied them up with a thick silken sash that Palla had given her when she left the crèche.

There. She looked about her at the satchel that contained a few changes of clothes, for herself and Gyneth, their bedrolls, and her books. That was about it.

She turned at a footstep behind her to find Gyneth entering. "Ready?" he asked her.

As she nodded, excitement tingled in her stomach. She thought of the last time she had left the Libyrinth. In secrecy and urgency. That journey had changed everything. "What will Thesia be like now, do you think?" she wondered aloud.

Gyneth shook his head. "We won't know until we get there." He picked up the satchel and the books, and she took their bedrolls. They went downstairs. A lot of people were gathered in the Great Hall to see them off.

Haly hugged Burke, Ock, Peliac, and Rossiter. Despite the undercurrent of worry among them; despite the unsolved mysteries of Po, the pen, and this new storm, Haly could not shake a feeling of freedom. She felt as if she were embarking on a vacation. "I managed the last time," she told Peliac in answer to the habitually dour woman's intense frown.

Peliac drew a deep breath, and expelled it. "See that

you do the same. And try not to change everything this time. I'm just getting used to the way things are now."

The crowd followed them into the stable yard, and helped them load two large baskets full of provisions into their wagon. Then she climbed up into the seat and Gyneth climbed up beside her. She was just about to flick the reins when there came a screech from the far end of the stables, where they joined with the Libyrinth. People shuffled aside as a tiny red form came hurtling through the crowd and launched himself at the wagon.

"Where does she go? Where does she go?" shouted Nod, climbing up the side of the wagon and onto Haly's shoulder. The little creature clung to her neck.

"Nod. I think you should stay here, and take care of the Libyrinth. Don't worry, Peliac will read to you."

The dour Libyrarian frowned at her. Haly grinned, gently detached Nod from her neck, and handed him to her.

Gyneth flicked the reins and they were off.

The morning of their third day out, Haly awoke to find the envoy already packed and mounted. "I have other stops to make," he said. "Just keep traveling north until you reach the mountains. From there, the road heads straight to Thesia. You can't miss it."

"What? You're leaving us?" Haly took a good look at him. His clothes were dusty and worn, his face lined. He sat on his mount as if he grew out of it. "How long has it been since you've been home?"

His mouth twitched and he looked out to the horizon. "Not that long, but everything is different there now."

"You mean since the uprising?"

"No. Since about a month ago, only . . . it's been much longer than that, in a way."

"You're not making any sense."

He looked at her and she saw anguish in his eyes. "I suppose not. But I'm just supposed to deliver the messages, you see. Regardless of whether or not those who sent them are still—I have to go."

He didn't wait for her answer. He nudged his horse into a trot. Gyneth ran after him, but he couldn't catch up.

For over a week, Haly and Gyneth traveled the plain. They stopped in villages from time to time, where they were greeted warmly and offered embarrassingly generous hospitability. More often they camped out under the sky, sitting around a fire at night, and later making love underneath the stars. It was the first time they'd ever had more than a few hours alone together.

"Come with me, my love, come away. For the long wet months are past, the rains have fed the earth and left it bright with blossoms. Birds wing in the low sky, dove and songbird singing in the open air above. Each nourishing tree and vine, green fig and tender grape, green and tender fragrance. Come with me, my love, come away," Haly recited from *The Song of Solomon* one night when there was only the barest sliver of moons and the stars crowded in on them from above, the way the voices of the books used to do, before the Song came and encompassed them all.

Gyneth sighed and rested against her, then slid down further to lay his head in her lap and gaze up at her. The stars reflected in his eyes were a haze of distant brilliance.

"Remember that first day, when I tried to put the salve on your wound?" he said.

She nodded. "I've never been so violent in all my life."

He lifted his hand to trace her scar. "I don't blame you."

She shook her head. "But it was misdirected. You were trying to help me." She ran a hand through his hair and smiled as he leaned into her touch. "It's strange now, to think of how we were then, so divided."

"I was certain you were damned."

She grinned. "I'll never forget the look on your face when I asked you what the Song was."

Gyneth sat up, eyes sparkling. "Oh, I was appalled! Quite scandalized by you. But that was nothing compared to when you tricked me into looking at printed words."

"Tricked? I didn't . . ." She paused. "Okay, yeah, I definitely tricked you. But it all worked out, didn't it?"

Gyneth drew her to him and kissed her. "Yeah. It all worked out."

Neither of them spoke for a little while, but later, lying in each other's arms with the embers of the fire burning low, Haly said, "And now we've survived the famine."

Gyneth, his head resting on her chest, drew the blankets up over both of them and nodded. "Yeah."

"What do you think we'll find in Thesia?"

"I don't know."

"Me neither. And I don't know what's going to happen with this pen business, either, or with Thela in general."

"Nobody does. Not even Thela."

"Gyneth, if things ever . . . when all of this is over, when the fires are all put out and we're left to our own devices, what do you think we'll do?"

"Mmm." Gyneth lifted himself up on his elbows and peered down at her. "We'll be so very, deliciously bored," he said. "And then, we'll sing in the morning." He kissed her. "Read in the afternoon." He nibbled her ear. "And make love all night long." He let his weight settle on her and the solidness of him felt good. She wrapped her arms around him and buried her face in his neck. It might never happen, she realized. This might be as much of not-putting-out-fires as they'd ever have. She didn't want to waste it.

As they traveled northward the land became hilly and more and more trees began to appear—large silver-leaf, taller than any she had ever seen except for when Po had used the pen, and other species as well, poplars and birch.

Travel became more difficult as the land grew more mountainous and thickly forested. In fact, if it hadn't been for the road, they would have had to abandon the wagon entirely.

Running as straight as an arrow through hills and valleys, the road was crafted of massive blocks of stone—the same gray stone the Corvariate Citadel was built from. On either side of it was a steep bank, and Haly and Gyneth had to get out of the wagon and push in order to get it up the incline. But once they were on the road, it proved to be amazingly well preserved, smooth and even. Their pace picked up dramatically.

"This is the way we experience time," said Gyneth as they rode along.

"Hmm?" said Haly. She was watching the trees go by, wondering when or if they would see any people. It had been days since they had passed a village, and that had been still in the plain. They were in Thesia now, the road was proof of that. Where was everybody?

"I've been thinking about Hilloa's sticks in a bag, and about dimensions. We only experience three spatial dimensions, but that doesn't mean that's all there are. Some people describe time as the fourth dimension, but we don't experience it the way we do the other three. We can only move through time in one direction. At best, we only have partial access to the dimension of time. I think . . ."

She watched his eyes as they looked out at the vanishing point of the road.

"I think that what we experience as time is only a cross section of another whole dimension. It's like . . . Did you ever read *Flatland*?"

"That author hates women," said Haly.

"I know, but the way he describes a sphere as seen by a two-dimensional being is apt in this circumstance. The two-dimensional man—"

"Man, because the women are what, dots, isn't it? One-dimensional? He probably wished we were."

"Anyway, from the two-D point of view, a sphere appears as a sequence of circles that increase in size and then decrease as the sphere moves through the two-D man's field of perception."

"You can just ignore it, can't you? I suppose, coming from the citadel and all . . ."

"Consider how we experience time. As a succession of moments. It's not a full dimension we're experiencing. What we're seeing is the cross section of a dimension that extends beyond the limits of our own perception."

Gyneth's words finally overpowered Haly's annoyance with the author of *Flatland*, and she sat silent, looking at the world around her in a whole new way. "The People who Walk Sideways in Time," she said.

"What?"

"The Ayorites believe that the world was created by the People Who Walk Sideways in Time. Come on, you've heard the stories."

"Oh. Yeah, I just never . . . huh. Wow. And *The Song That Changed Us* talks about them becoming immortal, which would make sense if part of what they transcended was time. So do you think—" Gyneth stopped, because ahead of them in the distance was a large shape, fast approaching. It looked like nothing Haly had ever seen before—somewhat like a collection of wheels and gears, it made a clicking sound as it rolled along at a startlingly brisk pace. The sound got louder and louder until, with a clack and a screech of metal against metal, the thing came to a halt in front of them.

It was a flat platform mounted on four enormous wheels, each taller than Haly herself. In the center of the platform a large, tightly wound spiral strip of metal was connected to a shaft that drove a cluster of gleaming brass gears, which were in turn connected to the axles of the vehicle through holes in the platform.

Racks stood along the edges of the platform, with all manner of pots and pans, bells, pocket watches, compasses, and keys—anything that was made of, or had parts made of, metal. They rattled and clanged together in the wake of the contraption's sudden stop, nearly as noisy as it had been while still in motion.

A dark-skinned man with classic Thesian features leaped from the conveyance. He wore blue velvet trousers, a green waistcoat, and a jacket of red brocade, all tailored in the form-fitting Thesian style. His calfskin boots hugged his calves like a second skin, and the jacket accentuated his lean waist and broad shoulders. He wore a top hat.

He stood before his conveyance, hands on his hips, looking them up and down with an expression of detached curiosity. He was not a large person, but he exuded vitality. "What are you doing on the road?" he demanded.

Haly and Gyneth looked at each other. Ignoring his rudeness, Haly said, "We come from the Libyrinth. We were invited by the first administrator to come and investigate a strange storm. Besides, we haven't heard anything from Thesia since the Singers took over. We wanted to see how things were here now."

He raised his chin. "As you can see, the clockmaker continues to bring peace and prosperity to the people."

They'd seen nothing of the kind. In fact . . .

"Where are all the people, anyway?"

"They are either in the cities or underground. Where else should they be?"

"Underground?" said Gyneth.

"Of course. Now, see here . . . I am the tollkeeper for the Southern Road and I didn't stop you in order to present the population distribution in the Clockwork Kingdom of Thesia for your approval."

"Clockwork Kingdom?" said Gyneth.

The tollkeeper ignored him. "I stopped you because you have not paid your toll. You must do so now or be taken into custody and remanded to a compensation facility where you may work off your debt."

"We didn't know there was a charge for using the road," said Haly. "Besides, we were invited to come. I have the letter—"

"Ignorance of the law is no excuse for disobeying it."

"It's a very good reason," said Haly, "when the law is not one of obvious moral mandate. And besides, we've been invited to come, and promised generous payment for doing so." Haly fished the letter from the first administrator from her satchel and held it out to him. "I don't think your administrator would like it if—"

He waved the letter away. "I have a job to do and a duty to uphold. You are on the road, you must pay the toll."

"Fine, we'll sort it out when we get there. How can we pay you?"

The tollkeeper returned to his conveyance, where he fetched a large wooden case. He undid latches, unfolded panels, and the case transformed into a desk, complete with chair. From a drawer he withdrew a pen and a long sheet of paper with a great deal of small print on it. He sat down at the desk and began filling in some blanks that were left empty on the form.

"You're writing!" said Gyneth.

The tollkeeper looked up from his work. "Yes, yes. What do you expect?"

"But the Singers conquered you!" said Haly.

He raised one eyebrow. "I don't know what you're talking about. Fifty years ago the clockmaker led us in overthrowing a corrupt monarchy that was stifling our development as a nation. Of course some concessions must be—"

"Wait, fifty years ago? The revolt was about a year ago," said Haly.

He laughed. "You don't know your history. Now, as I was saying, some concessions must be made to the venerable oral tradition of our Singer brothers-in-arms. That is why, once I remand your paperwork to the Thesian Compensation Board, they will enter it into the nearest liberator and process you."

Haly and Gyneth exchanged worried glances. Whatever the tollkeeper was talking about, it didn't sound very encouraging.

"Now, let me see . . ." The tollkeeper frowned at the form and began to scribble, muttering as he went. "Fifteen miles, at four wheels and two horses a mile is . . ." He jotted something down, ending with an emphatic stab of his pen. He looked up at them. "Seventy-five pounds."

Haly raised her eyebrows. "Seventy-five pounds of what?" she asked.

The tollkeeper sat back, surprised. "Why, of metal, of course! All tolls on the road must be paid in metal."

Haly's stomach sank. "We have no metal, apart from the fittings on the wagon and a few studs and fasteners on the horses' tack. Certainly nothing approaching seventy-five pounds."

"You said fifteen miles," said Gyneth, standing up. "We haven't been on this road more than ten."

"Nonsense," said the tollkeeper. "I am being generous. Look behind you."

They looked. About fifty feet behind them stood a post driven into the gravel at the side of the road. The number "15" was carved into its side.

"But we didn't get on at the start," said Gyneth.

"How can I know that?"

"Because he's telling you," said Haly. Fear made her

tone sharp. She didn't know what a "compensation board" was but she didn't like the sound of it.

"Look, it's all spelled out here," said the tollkeeper, handing the form he'd filled out to them. "Now kindly vacate your vehicle so I can collect what metal you do possess."

Gyneth sat back down. "No."

Haly looked at him, a question in her eyes. He shook his head, then flicked the reins and drove the cart forward, veering to the right, around the tollkeeper's vehicle. Suddenly a loud crack pierced the air. Haly flinched. She looked down and saw a bullet embedded in the side of the wagon. The tollkeeper pointed a pistol at them. "That was a warning. According to section nine of the traveler's code, cited in paragraph twenty-seven of the trespassers advisory form I have just served you, I am authorized to use force in securing compliance to the Traveler's Aid Law. And I assure you, I am an excellent shot. Please get out of your conveyance."

7

The Nod of Nods

Clauda-in-the-Wing hovered in nothingness and watched her universe slowly whirl. What did this mean? How could she exist at all, outside of existence? And what was her world, anyway? A thing made of words?

Out of the corner of her eye she saw another light. She turned to look and saw another shape, just like the word-universe from which she'd come. She flew closer to it—deciding to leave aside for now the question of how she moved in such a space—and saw that it was not precisely the same as her word-universe. The argent arcs of this one were composed of numbers and symbols instead. Equations.

As Clauda flew back toward her own universe she saw, in the distance, yet another whirling disk, and then another. She was in a space between universes, and apparently there was no limit to their number.

With a will, she hastened back to the gleaming arcs of words, of stories, which made up her world. All of this had been very interesting, and Selene would surely die of envy when she told her of it, but Clauda didn't want to be here. She didn't want to know that Selene, Haly, the Libyrinth, and everything else she'd ever known only existed within a glittering toy amid other toys. She didn't want to know how small she was. She wanted to go home. Now.

And was that even possible? Clauda coasted near the outer fringes of the word-universe and realized at once how vast it was. How had she wound up out here anyway? Just traveling from one star to another could take several lifetimes. How had she gotten all the way out here so quickly? How could she move between universes in what seemed to her to be a matter of minutes?

The only explanation she could think of was that this was a place created by the People Who Walk Sideways in Time, and as a result, time flowed differently here, even for a tiny, three-dimensional being such as herself.

She was certain now that the vortex that had sucked her in was a rip in the fabric of reality. She had first spotted the cloud near where Selene had blown up that Egg when Clauda and Haly were being held captive and tortured in the vault. Could an explosion like that be powerful enough to tear the very fabric of existence? That all depended on what Eggs really were, and no one knew that.

But if she was right, then eventually the whole universe, including her world, would deflate like a punctured balloon.

All she wanted to do was go home, but even as she searched for the rupture that had landed her here, she realized that mending the tear, if such a thing was possible, was more important, even if it could only be done from the outside. Even if that meant she'd be stranded out here forever.

She spotted the tear. One argent arc of light was broken, the two ends whipping about, spilling letters into the space between universes. But how was she to capture them, to bring them together and mend them? The wing, apparently, had many capabilities, but could it mend a universe?

Suddenly a new object appeared. This was not another universe. It was red. And it was moving rapidly toward her.

As it came nearer Clauda distinguished arms and legs, a head, a body. And then, as it came even closer she made out the distinctive, wizened features. The largest Nod she'd ever seen hung there before her.

At this point Clauda thought she'd taken in all the strange things her mind could hold, but she was mistaken; for as she gazed upon the enormous red creature, she saw a pattern on the surface of its skin. At first it appeared to be one of those fractals Selene had shown her once—all curving tendrils—only it was moving. Then something gleamed in the light from her universe, and what she'd taken to be part of the pattern was in fact an eye—a tiny eye in a tiny Nod. And it was surrounded by other Nods of all sizes, all moving and crawling about on one another.

This was no abstract pattern. It was a conglomeration. The whole Nod that she saw was made up of other Nods— Nods as small as her thumb, Nods as large as half a universe.

She'd wondered how the creature moved through space and it now appeared it did so by virtue of the Nods that made up its back crawling to its front. The whole thing was constantly reforming itself.

Clauda wanted to scream, but instead she bent her attention to the questions teeming in her mind: Could what she saw before her be considered a single entity? What was the connection between this . . . this Nod of Nods, and the creatures as they appeared back home? Did it recognize her?

As if in answer to her last question, the great Nod smiled, and reached out with fingers composed of more Nods, and grasped the wing.

Clauda tried to think, *It's me, Clauda*, at it, but she didn't know if it did any good. Could she use the wing's light, somehow, to communicate with it?

She was distracted from this speculation by the sudden presence of scores of individual Nods seeping through the walls of the wing and occupying the cabin. "What does she say, what does she say?" they chanted.

She whimpered a bit at that.

Meanwhile, in the space outside the wing, the Nod of Nods reached out toward the twisting ends of the broken arc of the universe with its free arm. That arm detached from its body and became another, slightly smaller Nod of Nods, gripping the shattered strand of what had once been Clauda's whole reality in its hands.

The original Nod of Nods quickly grew a new arm, and then sent that one after the other end of the broken arc in similar fashion.

Clauda, used to focusing her awareness outside of the wing's cabin, ignored the little Nods chanting around her and watched, rapt, as the two sub Nods brought the ends of the broken arc together and swarmed over the seam, sealing it.

"Wait!" Clauda cried out. She'd never really vocalized before while in the wing. It came out as a pulse of light. It reflected off the Nods that composed the hand that held her. In the strong illumination, she saw that even those were made of smaller Nods, those Nods also made of smaller Nods, and on and on, apparently without end.

The Nod of Nods lifted her up and held her before its face. "This is not a place for beasties to be. Even beasties with Maker toys."

"No, you're right, Nod," she said, and the light once known as the Sword of the Mother pulsed her words. "I want to go home. Please."

The other two sub Nods paused in their work of sealing the broken arc together, and the Nod of Nods reached out and tucked her back inside the tunnel of words as if it was stuffing an olive and she was the anchovy. Clauda observed the tunnel of words closing around her and laughed that such strange surroundings could be a comfort. But compared to all of that out there . . .

As the Nod of Nods released her, the little Nods melted away through the walls of the wing until at last there was only one remaining. "It is all story," it said, and then it, too, was gone.

As before, an invisible force dragged Clauda through the tunnel of words at breakneck speed.

"Was this the best thing that had ever happened to him, or the worst?"

"The cloak-and-dagger protocols, the risk of capture, and the soaring view from the windows of Joe's home could not have been better designed to appeal to the mind of an eleven-year-old boy who spent large parts of every day pretending to pose as the secret identity of a super-powered humanoid insect."

"Eventually, something would have to be done about his hands."

Clauda began to wonder if she would ever return to what she still stubbornly thought of as the real world. She lost track of time. Overwhelmed by all she had witnessed, and exhausted by uncounted hours spent merged with the wing, she fell asleep.

And awoke within a maelstrom.

The ground beneath her was nothing more than a blur as turbulent winds tossed her about like a toy. She urged herself to go faster in the hope of outdistancing this—whatever it was—storm? She cast about, searching for some familiar landmark. She was in the desert. Distantly, in the east, she could hear the voices of the Libyrinth, just as she had when she stole the wing and flew out of Ilysies. She was home again.

A gale struck her crosswise, scouring her metal hide with sand. She was caught in a sandstorm, one possibly created by the sealing of the rift in the universe. It was all she could do just to stay in the air as the violent winds pushed her this way and that.

The world became nothing more than a confusion of sand and wind, and she lost all track of time as she strained every human nerve and machine sinew to ride with the storm, constantly altering her speed and direction in response to the turbulent winds. To go against them would be disastrous.

Clauda was glad of her nap. She wasn't accustomed to

feeling tired while inside the wing, but it crept in upon her now, threatening to slow her response time. She couldn't afford that. A gust of wind hit her from above, pushing her nose down. She canted sideways, giving the rogue wind less surface area to act upon. The maneuver allowed her to maintain altitude, but in the next instant the wind changed direction again, coming from the left. It struck her tail with a force like a hammer blow and made her spin end over end. She fought for control but she no longer knew up from down and the winds buffeted her in such rapid succession that she never had a chance to recover from one blow before another knocked her in a new direction. At any moment she expected to slam nose first into the ground.

The sand carried by the wind scraped her living metal skin and caked in every groove of her hull. If the wing had been made of flesh she would be raw and bleeding by now. As it was, she ached all over. Clauda-in-the-Wing took a deep breath and forced herself to focus. A gust from below hit her nose and tilted her upward. At least, she hoped it was upward, because she used the momentum of that sudden jolt to carry her into a steep climb, accelerating with all the power she had, going faster than she'd ever gone before. If she could get above or out or through this storm, she might have a chance.

She powered right through a couple of gusts that might have sent her spinning again, and a moment later, she actually felt the winds lessening. A little flicker of hope flared to life in her heart and she maintained her course. The winds lessened a bit more and she began to make out vague outlines in the cloud of sand and air around her. Encouraged, she pressed on and at last she broke through the storm system—to find herself twenty feet from a dense forest of pines.

Panic gripped her. The trees were spaced no more than a hand's breadth apart. If she crashed into them at her current speed, they'd tear her apart. But backing up would put her inside the maelstrom once more and then she'd have the storm and the trees both at the same time—even worse. So she pulled up sharply, hoping to clear the tops of the trees. The strain of it was overwhelming. She felt as if her heart would burst, like her joints were pulled apart, like every blood vessel in her body was burning.

But she did it. She cleared those trees. Relief made her weak. Continuing her climb, she drew a deep breath. Below her, the storm hit the trees. What she hadn't counted on was the damping effect of the trees on the winds. Or the way the storm would respond to such a barrier by surging up and over it.

This time, when the storm took her again, her resources were spent. The first wind that caught her sent her tumbling, her vision a jumble of sand and air and trees. She struck a tree and bounced off of it, her mind reeling. Pain and disorientation added to her exhaustion and she was powerless against the raging winds. The ground rose up to welcome her home at last, and then all was darkness.

8

Thesia

While the tollkeeper held the gun on Haly and Gyneth, they disembarked from their vehicle. He motioned for them to sit on the back of his cart. Still training the gun on them, he took two sets of manacles from the conveyance. "Hold out your hands," he told them.

"You don't need to do that," said Haly. Her heart pounded. She'd thought she was all done with those things when she left the Singers' dungeon.

"I have work to do and I can't guard you at the same time," he said. He aimed the gun at Gyneth's forehead. "You first, behind your back, please."

"Gyneth . . ." Haly began, but then she stopped. What could she tell him? Don't do it? She looked into the tollkeeper's dark eyes. They were implacable. He'd shoot if Gyneth didn't do as he was told.

Haly heard the click of the first manacle, and seconds later, the other.

"Now you." The tollkeeper aimed the gun at Haly.

What would happen if they both ran? Would he miss them? For a moment Haly stared at Gyneth as all of this passed through her mind. But she couldn't tell him. One warning and the tollkeeper would shoot. She was confident of that.

The cold embrace of the iron around her wrists was like the unwelcome return of a despised master. Her heart felt heavier than her hands.

The tollkeeper looped a third chain between both their wrists and locked it to a loop on the floor of the cart.

"Let's see, use of irons, two pounds per person per hour," muttered the tollkeeper, scribbling away at the form.

The manacles around her wrists and ankles were heavy, already chafing her skin. Beside her Gyneth stood taut as a wire, his cheeks flushed with barely suppressed outrage. The tollkeeper took a tally of all their possessions and declared them worth five pounds.

Then he returned to his conveyance and snatched up a crowbar. He twirled it, approaching their wagon.

He spent a moment or two looking over the box-frame structure, then fitted one end of the pry bar beneath a corner hasp. There was a ping, and the fitting sprang into the air as if it had the lead in *Swan Lake*. So quickly it was hard to follow, the tollkeeper pivoted the bar and pulled a second hasp free. He caught it in his hat and by the time Haly was done marveling at that, he had spun again, this time leaping to the bed of the wagon. He pulled five nails from the backboard in as many seconds.

Within fifteen minutes his hat was full and what had been their wagon lay on the ground—a stack of boards and four axle-less wheels. Haly had forgotten her shackles.

"Use of tools for reclaiming of toll due," muttered the tollkeeper, "five pounds per minute."

The wagon and the horses' tack yielded one-and-a-quarter pounds of metal.

Haly and Gyneth sat on the back of the tollkeeper's cart watching forests and mountains and sheer rock cliffs whizzed by on either side. The noise was deafening, not just because of the clicking of the gears but also because of the rattling of all the metal hanging from the frames.

Haly leaned against Gyneth, taking comfort from the warmth of him. "We'll get out of this," she said, shouting to be heard over all the noise.

He didn't answer her. He stared off into the distance, where the line of the road disappeared over the horizon.

Near dusk they came to a place where the road cut right through the middle of a mountain. Sheer cliffs towered above them on either side, banded with colors of different kinds of rock. The cliff walls were pitted with tiny square holes and lights could be seen inside.

"Do people live in there?" asked Haly.

"Live and work," said the tollkeeper. He pointed and Haly saw baskets rising and descending between the openings, suspended from pulley arrangements anchored to the rock, and she noticed smaller holes from which steam and sometimes smoke emanated.

As they crested a hill the tollkeeper pulled a lever and they coasted downhill. A distant clanging emanated from deep within the mountain, but another sound soon drowned it out.

Beyond the mountain, a city came into view. It looked like a toy, glittering gold and silver in the fading rays of the sun. Spires and rooftops caught the sun and made her blink. Haly heard a constant whirring hum, as of thousands upon thousands of machines, like the tollkeeper's conveyance, all spinning at the same time. "That's Thesia?" she said.

"Yes, the Clockwork City," said the tollkeeper.

She had never heard it called that before.

The road led down into the city. The twilight streets were lit with lanterns hanging from posts, and up and down the smooth, paved lanes whizzed and whirred a variety of bicycles and motorcars the likes of which Haly had never seen.

She glanced at Gyneth and saw him staring rapt at a giant wheel with a seat in its center, and a woman dressed in a form-fitting gown and an elaborate hat turning a crank with her hand, propelling herself down the avenue. She turned a corner and nearly collided with a low-slung steam-operated car with six wheels and three smokestacks, each one of them burping smoke in little puffs as it rolled along.

They passed factories and shops selling everything from buttons to grandfather clocks. Gyneth shouted and ducked. A bird made of brass barely missed him as it flew through the air with a message in its beak.

Most of the devices were operated by the same kind of spring as the tollkeeper's conveyance: a spring made of a flat strip of metal, wound into a coil and slowly allowed to unwind in stages, powering the motions of the gears and pinions. "It's all the clockwork," she said to Gyneth. "That's what's making that sound."

Beside her, Gyneth gasped. He tugged her sleeve and pointed.

Towering above all the other spires and rooftops was a gigantic clock. Toothed disks the size of the dome of the Great Hall at the Libyrinth turned in stately motion as the hands marked out the hours and minutes. There was something terrifying about it—as if it were built on a scale beyond the scope of the human mind. The tollkeeper saw them gawking. "The clockmaker's greatest work," he said. "Fortunately we are only going to the Department of Compensation."

He brought them to a halt in front of a large building that stood across the city's central square from the clock tower. The building was faced with toothed gears of all shapes and sizes, interconnected with one another, but to what purpose Haly could only guess. She glanced at Gyneth, and saw his eyes following each gear to the next, searching for the function of the whole. If anyone could figure it out, it would be Gyneth.

The tollkeeper removed their chains and walked them, at gunpoint, to the building. As they stepped on the first of the stairs leading to the door, it sank beneath their weight just a fraction of an inch. There was a distinct click, and then one of the largest gears, resting above the double doors of the entranceway, began to turn, driving all the other gears into motion with it. The doors opened and chimes rang, announcing their approach.

"So that's it," said Haly. "It's the world's most elaborate doorbell."

Gyneth tilted his head, his shrewd gaze following the action of the mechanism. "I wonder if that's all."

Once through the doors, they found themselves in a large circular hall with gleaming white walls. Accents of gilt graced the woodwork, and the floor was white and tan marble in a checkerboard pattern. Haly and Gyneth's chains chimed against the polished stone as they moved.

They crossed the echoing marble floor to one of the gilt-limned panels that lined it. At the pressure of the toll-keeper's hand the panel sank inward with a click and then rose up, disappearing into the wall above it.

The hallway behind it was decorated in a fashion similar to the grand hall they left behind, but the next door they came to opened with the simple latch mechanism to which Haly and Gyneth were accustomed.

Inside a row of chairs stood along one wall, facing a long desk and seven chairs that stood on a raised platform at the other end of the room.

In the middle of the desk sat a wooden box with a slot in the front and a metal cylinder mounted on top of it. A coiled funnel protruded from the back, widening into a flared cone that resembled a large lily.

"Sit down. The Compensation Council will arrive shortly to hear your case."

Haly and Gyneth took seats on the hard wooden chairs facing the desk and the tollkeeper stood at the door, his hands folded behind his back.

After a little while, a door on the side of the room opened and five people filed in, ascended the platform, and took seats behind the desk. Two of them were men in long black robes—Singers, presumably. They were a sharp contrast to the other three, all of whom were dressed in the epitome of Thesian fashion. That much, at least, had not changed.

Taking their cues from industrial-era Earth, the two women and the man wore fitted jackets and elaborate neck cloths. The women wore skirts with bustles in the back, and hats piled high with feathers and flowers. The man wore trousers and equestrian boots, and a top hat with a small clockwork train that ran around and around the brim.

Once they had seated themselves, the tollkeeper stepped before them, extended one leg forward with the toe pointed, and bowed. "Madam Chair, Your Excellencies, it is my honor to present to you our latest case."

Haly expected the tollkeeper to introduce them to the compensation board, but instead he took the form that he had filled out after stopping them on the road. He fed it into the slot in the front of the device that was sitting on the table. The paper disappeared inside and the cylinder on top of the box rotated. It was difficult to see from where they sat, but it appeared that needles jutted up from underneath and pierced the cylinder at various intervals. Then, there was a small *whoomf* and smoke issued forth from the tube next to the horn. It was a smokestack, she realized. Then the cylinder, now covered with small indentations, shifted positions and began to rotate again, this time over a series of thin metal spokes. A voice issued from the trumpet at the top of the box. In a brassy monotone, it said, "Let it be known to the authorities of the Compensation Board that on the fifty-ninth day of the second year, two persons identifying themselves as Haly and Gyneth of the Community at the Libyrinth were found traveling on the Southern Road in an unlawful manner, having failed to pay the toll and, upon apprehension by the tollkeeper, being without resources to pay their fine." The sound was remarkably clear. So this was how they compromised with the Singers. Haly was struck by the ingenuity of it.

The voice went on to enumerate the weight they owed in bronze, copper, iron, or silver, and the various fines they owed, in a complicated system made no easier to follow for being delivered orally. "Noncitizen Haly and Noncitizen Gyneth jointly owe the People's Republic of Thesia the grand total of seventy-five pounds of iron, or its equivalent in other metals or labor, such determination to be made by the Compensation Board," it finished at last.

The woman whom the tollkeeper had adressed as Madam Chair removed the cylinder from the device and placed it in a case. "We have heard the tollkeeper's report," she said. "I now call this meeting to order. Given that the perpetrators in question are noncitizens, it is customary to give them an opportunity to address the board."

Haly and Gyneth stood. "We were invited here by the first administrator," said Haly, holding out the letter the courier had given them. "We were promised much more than seventy-five pounds, as you'll see, to come and look into a storm of some kind."

The members of the board looked at one another. "There is no such thing as a first administrator," said the chair.

A chill went down Haly's spine. "No. Something's

wrong. You were a monarchy only two years ago, and there was a revolution, and now . . . now . . . I had the impression you'd become some sort of republic, with administrators and . . . no?"

"We are a republic, and have been for fifty years, ever since the clockmaker general came. It is clear you know nothing of our country. Unfortunately, that does not exempt you from obeying its laws while you are here."

Gyneth stood. "We are unfamiliar with the laws and customs of the New Republic of Thesia, but your ignorance is far more dire. Standing before you is the one foretold by Yammon's prophecy, the Redeemer of the Word," he said, gesturing to Haly. "The Redemption is accomplished. She has united Word and Song and the Libyrinth is liberated."

The members of the board whispered among themselves. Then the chair, who was the oldest of them, leaned forward. "So you are this Redeemer we have heard so much of. Is it true that you hear the voices of the books and that you brought about the Redemption?"

Before Haly could answer, Gyneth stepped forward. "Yes, it is true. I, Gyneth, subaltern of Censor Siblea himself, was privileged to be present at the blessed event."

"I asked her, not you. You will refrain from further speech unless asked a direct question."

Gyneth opened his mouth but Haly nudged him. "What he says is true," she said. "I can hear the voices of books."

"What other special abilities do you have?"

"Other special abilities? What makes you think I have other—"

"We have heard that you are one with the Song," said one of the men in robes.

"Oh. Yes. The Song is with me. I . . . hear it inside myself."

The two Singers bent their heads together and the woman in the middle craned her neck to listen. The two other members of the board, on the opposite end of the table, looked rather put out.

The whispering came to a stop and one of the Singers said, "Well, surely, that must give you other capacities beyond the mortal realm."

Oh. She'd never thought of that. "I . . . I don't know."

"You don't know? What have you done to explore your gift?"

The expressions on their faces sharpened Haly's embarrassment. "Um . . . the Song gives me strength. It . . . keeps me centered and helps me make wise decisions." *Sometimes.*

The Singer at the far end leaned over. He was a fair-haired man in his midthirties. "You mean to say you have not explored your gift?"

Haly shrugged. "I've been a bit busy."

The woman looked at her colleagues, then struck a wooden block with a little mallet. The sharp sound punctuated the buzzing of conversation. "We will discuss this matter further. Tollkeeper, take the prisoners to the waiting room while we reach a decision."

The waiting room was small and stuffy. The tollkeeper directed them to a bench and then took a seat in a chair facing them. A sudden wave of exhaustion swept over Haly. It had been a very long day already, and there was no end in sight. She leaned against Gyneth and closed her eyes.

"They are ready for you."

Haly struggled to awaken. She sat up and rubbed her eyes. She could have done with a longer nap. The room was dim. Outside the window, the sky was dark. "How long have we been in here?" she asked Gyneth.

"I'm not sure," he said. He tilted his head and raised one shoulder, to wipe the drool from the side of his mouth.

"Come along now, hurry. Don't keep them waiting," said the tollkeeper.

"Who's out protecting the road from unlawful use?" asked Gyneth.

The tollkeeper ignored him. He held the door open and gestured for them to go through.

Gyneth leaned close and whispered in her ear. "It's just him right now, and there are two of us . . ."

But they were in the depths of a strange building in a strange city. She shook her head.

They returned to the room they'd been in before. This time the compensation board was already seated. The chair stood.

"The traveler's code is clear on the matter of unlawful travel. Perpetrators are to work off the balance of their fee, plus penalties, in a compensation facility of the board's choosing. Given the extent of your crime, you owe the People's Republic of Thesia a debt that will take years to pay off in metal. However, in light of your unique nature, it may be that you can perform for us other services instead."

"What kind of services?"

"That will be determined by the clockmaker general.

You will be placed into her custody, to serve her as she sees fit, until such time as your debt is repaid."

"But wait," said Gyneth. "That could be anything, and any length of time. That's not fair! You can't ask her to agree to something so vague."

"No one is asking her or you," said the chair. "And if I recall, you were told not to speak unless asked a direct question."

"I don't care!" said Gyneth. "This whole thing is insane. All we did was drive on your road a few miles. We didn't do anything wrong!"

"Tollkeeper, take him to the compensation facility. His sentence is fifty pounds of iron."

"No! Wait!" cried Haly. "I'll do it. I'll work for the clockmaker general. Just don't take Gyneth."

The chair gave her a wistful smile. "Oh, you misunderstood. The arrangement with the clockmaker general is for you alone. Your companion must still pay us his portion."

The tollkeeper reached for Gyneth. Gyneth pulled back. Haly stepped between them. "You can't do this! If you take him, you have to take me, too. I won't work for the clockmaker if Gyneth is imprisoned."

"Not imprisoned," said the chair. "Working in a compensation facility."

"Don't argue semantics with me," said Haly. She glared at the two Singers on the board. "When I was a prisoner in the Corvariate Citadel, I worked on the horn. I know what 'compensation facility' means." She turned to the chair. "You can explain to your clockmaker why you can't deliver the Redeemer after she walked right into your hands."

The chair shook her head. "You underestimate the import of your last phrase." She nodded to the tollkeeper.

He shoved Haly to the ground and grabbed Gyneth by the wrist. In the blink of an eye he had Gyneth's arm twisted behind him and a pistol aimed at his head.

"You still can't make her work for the clockmaker. Don't do it, Haly. Something's wrong here."

"Stay down," the tollkeeper told her.

Haly sat where she was. "I'm not getting up, and Gyneth's not fighting you. You can put the gun away. And I'll work for the clockmaker, on one condition. You release Gyneth as soon as I've satisfied the clockmaker." It was a bad bargain. Gyneth would still go to the compensation facility, and there was no telling when the clockmaker would be done with her.

"Do you still think you're in a position to make demands?"

"Yes," she said. "If Gyneth is dead he can't work to pay his fine, and I won't do anything for you and you might as well shoot me, too, so that's two fines you'll be short. And a clockmaker who will be angry about not getting her pet Redeemer. But if you accept my bargain, you'll have Gyneth's labor, for a time, and my service to the clockmaker. Isn't that better?"

"All right," said the chair, too soon. Of course she agreed. Haly had no way of enforcing her demands. Unless . . .

"And if you think you can just agree, and then when the time comes, ignore our bargain, I will invoke the power of the Song and curse you and all of Thesia."

The board straightened. "You said you had not explored your powers," said one of the members.

"I wasn't going to tell you all my secrets. Besides, if I'm working with the clockmaker, who knows what else I will learn?"

They glanced at one another. The man in the top hat leaned and whispered in the chair's ear. Haly heard "told you we shouldn't . . ." They had been a long time deliberating. Were they afraid of this clockmaker, whoever she was?

"Very well," said the chair. "You will serve the clockmaker for a period of two weeks and no longer. When that time has passed, you and your companion will both be free to leave."

9

Lost and Found

Needing to start somewhere, Selene decided to go with the assumption that Clauda had headed first for Thesia. She rode in that direction for days and tried not to think of the chances of finding one small Ayorite in the whole vast plain.

And then one morning she saw a copse of trees in the distance. She was not far from the Tumbles now and it appeared that some of the trees had been knocked over, perhaps by a storm. She rode closer to investigate.

A gleam of metal made Selene's heart freeze. She leaped from her mount and ran into the woods, where she found the cause of the fallen trees. *Seven Tales*.

Half of the wing's right side was buried in the ground. The nose had uprooted several trees that now lay across it, pinning it to the ground. Selene gave one of them a shove. It didn't budge. The wing itself appeared undamaged, but what of the person inside it during such a collision? Trembling, she crawled through the space between the trees and the left side of the wing, feeling for the hatch. She found it, and it opened for her.

It was dark inside, dark and silent except for the harsh rasping of Selene's breath. She fumbled in her satchel for her jar of palm-glow and opened it. In the pale green light, she saw the cabin of the wing upside down, the statue, still rooted in place, hanging from above. But no body. She searched all the corners. No one. There was still hope.

She looked at the statue again. Could Clauda still be in there? What if she died while still in there? Selene fought to breathe despite the tightness in her chest. From here, she couldn't reach the statue. She'd have to climb up. She'd need rope.

She went back outside to her saddlebag, but on the way something caught her eye. There, in the soft soil near one of the uprooted trees—a footprint.

Selene whooped for joy. She fell to the ground and she kissed that footprint—a small footprint. And then she spotted another. Now she was able to follow Clauda's footsteps, even out into the dust of the desert, though that was more difficult. She walked, leading her horse Goliath, her head bent to make out the slight impression of a toe here, the streak of a heel there.

Clauda's path across the desert meandered. She sometimes went in circles and Selene would find herself back in the same spot she'd been in hours before. That was a bad sign. Selene quickened her pace.

*   *   *

Clauda walked under the blazing sun. There was no shelter in this section of the plain, no water, no trees, nothing but a few scrub bushes and a lot of rocks. Her thirst was an agony. Her only hope for finding water and surviving this ordeal was to keep walking.

The wing had crashed nose down in a stand of trees. Half of it was buried, and felled trees lay across the rest of it. Clauda, already exhausted and without any tools, decided her best bet was to start walking east, in the direction of the Libyrinth.

Now, she wasn't sure it had been the best decision. The wooded area she'd crashed in was small and isolated, giving way to desert less than a day into her trek. She'd miscalculated how far away the Libyrinth was . . . and how hot the sun would be in the desert . . . and how very little time it took to start suffering from dehydration.

The sun was ahead of her. Yes. That meant she was walking east. Unless it was afternoon already. If it was afternoon then she'd gotten turned around and was walking west. Had the sun been overhead yet? She remembered it, but that could have been from yesterday.

It was hard to concentrate. Her mind flitted from the Nod of Nods to the tunnel of words to that day in Ilysies when she'd walked into Selene's chambers and found her packing. Why, in the name of the Boy Who Outran the Wind, hadn't she told her how she really felt?

Selene thought the only important thing about herself was her knowledge and her mind. That just wasn't true. Selene was a child of the goat, just like Clauda. Selene was brave and true and there was a sense of humor lurking in there somewhere, she knew it. Someday she'd find it, if she survived.

Why hadn't she come across a settlement yet? Why was she in the most barren part of the plain? She should have stayed in the woods with the wing. She was going to die out here and never drink from the fountain of Selene's laughter.

The horizon wavered with heat mirages. She strained her vision, hoping that the shining, undulating air would resolve into a complex of sandstone domes, but it didn't. Instead there was just the stick—the black stick poking up like one of the trees of the woods. Only this one wavered. One tree was not a forest. But it was the wrong kind of tree to stand alone in this area. The few trees here were hard-bitten, small and spreading, not tall and straight. It was no tree, or tower. Clauda walked on, mesmerized by the sight of the black, narrow form.

It had four legs. No, six. Two higher than the four that reached the ground, dangling uselessly in midair. What the hell was this thing? Was she hallucinating? Had she hallucinated all of it?

The sound of a hoof striking a stone jolted Clauda into sudden realization. A rider! It was a rider dressed in black and mounted on a black horse. Clauda's parched lips curved into a smile, making the chapped skin crack, but she didn't care. "Hey!" she shouted, her voice little more than a wheezing croak. "Selene! I'm over here!" She forced herself into a trot and waved her arms.

Her foot struck a stone and she stumbled, her face scraping on rock. She struggled to stand but her limbs were

weak from exhaustion and dehydration. "I'm here, Selene,
I'm here!" If she could see Selene riding then surely Selene
had seen her? But Selene was dressed in black, on a black
horse, and Clauda was the color of the plain. She tried
again to force her arms and legs to support her and once
again found herself gasping on the ground and breathing
in dust. She coughed.

A shadow fell upon her. It was like cool water washing
over her. She blinked in the absence of sun. She heard the
jingle of the horse's tack and the crunch of its hooves on
the rocky ground. In the sudden relief and cool of the
shadow, her sense of smell returned and with it the musk
of the horse and the aroma of something else . . . wool and
ink. She rolled over and looked up into Selene's frowning
face. "It really is you."

P aradoxically, as time wore on Clauda's trail got easier to follow because she dragged her feet, and sometimes there were handprints as well. Selene mounted up
again, hurrying as fast as she dared without losing the
trail altogether.

At first she thought the tan lump in the distance was
just another of the many rocks that had made her heart
race in the past two days. But Clauda's trail led straight
toward this one, and as Selene neared, she caught a glimpse
of coppery hair. She urged Goliath into a trot.

Selene never took her eyes from Clauda. The young
Ayorite lay on her side, one arm flung over her face to
protect it from the sun. At first she didn't move, and Selene had to fight for breath again.

But then Clauda pushed herself up. She waved her arms

and ran toward Selene, stumbled and fell, and was unable to get to her feet again.

Selene dismounted, grabbed the waterskin, and knelt beside her. Clauda's skin was dry and peeling from sunburn. Her lips were cracked. With what must have been the very last of her strength, Clauda clutched at Selene's robes and said, "It really is you."

Relief that Clauda was alive and able to speak poured through Selene. She gathered Clauda into her arms and put her waterskin to her lips. Clauda's eyes closed, but she drank.

When Clauda had her fill she collapsed back into Selene's arms and seemed to fall into a stupor. Selene resisted the urge to clutch Clauda to her chest and rock her. And then she realized that holding such impulses at bay had very nearly resulted in Clauda dying without ever knowing the truth of how Selene felt about her. To hell with that.

She pulled Clauda close, and held her tight.

Clauda leaned back against Selene and closed her eyes, lulled by the steady cadences of Goliath's gait and Selene's heartbeat. This reminded her of that day, months ago in Ilysies, when they had ridden away from the palace in order to speak in private.

Clauda smiled and relished the solidity of Selene, the warmth and strength of her arms around her. She cracked one eye open and peered up at her. Selene looked back at her and a grin broke across her face like the sun rising. Clauda turned sideways in the saddle. Selene leaned down, and pressed her lips to Clauda's. The kiss was tentative at first, just a light brush, but the moment Clauda kissed back Selene pulled her tight and plundered her mouth, leaving them both breathless.

"Thank goddess you're alive," Selene said. "I'll never let you go off without knowing how I feel about you again."

Clauda rubbed her cheek against Selene's. "Which is . . . ?"

Selene pulled back, stared at Clauda, opened her mouth and closed it again, and then finally, blushing, said, "It's easier to just show you."

Clauda and Selene lay together by the campfire. Clauda rolled over, resting her head against Selene's stomach and gazing up at the stars. "Things aren't as they seem," she said.

"What?" Selene pushed herself up on her elbows and stared at Clauda, brows drawn together.

Clauda realized her poor choice of words. "No, not with us," she said, taking Selene's hand and kissing it. "Never between us. I mean . . . Well, how long have I been gone, anyway?"

They hadn't discussed Clauda's disappearance, its cause or duration. First, Selene had been preoccupied with getting enough water and food into Clauda. After that Clauda had slept for a day or more and when she awoke she was determined to make up for all the time she'd wasted not kissing Selene and telling her how wonderful she was. It had been a nice couple of days.

"About five weeks," Selene answered her.

"Well don't you wonder why I'm not dead?"

Selene stared at her, nostrils flaring. "I've been trying not to."

"It's because," Clauda paused and pointed up at the sky. "Because beyond all of that, beyond outer space and the stars and the galaxies, there's more."

"More?" Curiosity sharpened Selene's voice.

"Yeah. Hilloa and Gyneth were right about there being higher dimensions and multiple universes. And that the sticks in the bag can be made of anything. Selene, I saw . . . Wait. Let me start from the beginning."

Selene was silent as Clauda told her all about her strange adventure. Clauda told her everything, the universe of stories, the math universe, the Nod of Nods, all of it. When she finished at last she turned, bracing herself for Selene's disbelief.

Clauda was certain Selene would dismiss it all as a hallucination brought on by a bump on the head. In fact, she herself had begun to wonder if maybe that was all it was, and part of her wanted to take refuge in that idea.

But Selene just stared at her with her dark brows drawn together. At last she said, "This vortex you encountered in the Tumbles. Was it near the vault?"

That was not what Clauda had expected her to ask. "Yes. Not just near. Right above it."

Selene stood and paced. Clauda could tell from the tension in her movements that she was upset. "What?"

"Don't you see?" said Selene. "I blew up that Egg. I think it tore a hole in the fabric of our universe, and that's how you wound up out there."

Clauda stared at her. "You mean you believe me?"

Selene sat down again and took her hand. "Why would you make all that up?"

Clauda shrugged. "Maybe I crashed and hallucinated it all."

Selene smiled. "Would you rather believe that? In a way, I would. What you're saying means I tore a hole in the world."

"It wasn't your fault. You did it to rescue us."

"And I could think of nothing else to do? Surely there must have been something else."

"I don't think so, to be honest. I was there, remember? Besides, maybe the explosion didn't tear a hole in the world. Maybe I hallucinated my whole trip beyond."

Selene gave her that wistful smile again. She reached out and brushed a strand of hair from Clauda's forehead. "You were gone for five weeks, with no food or water, and you're still alive."

There was that. "Oh." Clauda paused. "But I don't want you blaming yourself for this, Selene. Besides, the . . . the Nod of Nods mended the tear. And you're back from the Corvariate Citadel and you wouldn't be out here looking for me if the famine were still going on, so everything's okay now. We can go home and we don't have to worry about all of this worlds-within-worlds stuff. This world is enough for us, isn't it?" Clauda stopped because Selene had turned away from her and was hiding her face in her hands. Her shoulders shook. "Selene?"

Clauda took her by the shoulders and pulled her into her arms. She was shocked to find Selene's face wet as she rested it in the crook of her neck, and then a sob escaped Selene's lips.

Selene didn't cry. Why was Selene crying? Seven Tales, something was very, very wrong. Clauda held Selene tight, running a hand up and down her back and murmuring soothing words in her ear.

When Selene quieted, Clauda asked her, certain she didn't want the answer, "What's happened?"

When Clauda told her where the vortex was located, Selene confronted the full extent of her recklessness. She should have known there would be dire repercussions to burning an Egg. But at the time, she'd have torn a hole in the world with her bare hands if she could, to get Clauda and Haly out of that vault. At least the rift was mended, for now.

Something told her that getting the pen away from her mother and rescuing Po would be much more difficult. Clauda's optimism only intensified Selene's fear and guilt. Clauda assumed that they were on the threshold of a long and carefree life together. Nothing could be further from the truth, and it was up to Selene to tell her so.

It was too much. Selene opened her mouth to speak but the sound that came out of her was a hoarse croak. She bent her head as she felt the first scalding tears stream down her face. All she wanted to do was hide from Clauda's kind, questioning eyes, but most of all, from herself.

Clauda wrapped her freckled arms around her and held her tight to her chest and started to rock her. For a few moments, Selene's emotions got the better of her and she permitted herself to be comforted. It felt good. Clauda was so warm. Even dehydrated and half starved, there was such vitality in her. It always made Selene wonder if maybe the world was a more generous place than she gave it credit for, if Clauda could be so liberally supplied with energy. Since Clauda herself seemed to take it for granted, Selene also wondered at such times if it was her own suspicious nature that barred her from the secret wellspring.

Likely, she should not have kissed Clauda in the first place. As delightful as it had been, this past day had, in a sense, taken place under false pretenses. Once she knew that Selene's blundering had lost both Po and the pen and doomed them all, would Clauda want anything to do with her anymore?

More distractions. Clauda had told her the entire, wild story about her adventure between worlds. The very least Selene could do was give her an honest accounting of her own activities during their separation.

She gently extricated herself from Clauda's arms, dried her eyes, and proceeded to tell Clauda everything—the trip to the Corvariate Citadel, the pen, Mab, and how both Po and the pen were lost in an eyeblink. "I should have recognized Mab for who she was," she concluded.

Clauda sighed. "Stop it. Please. I can't stand to hear you torture yourself anymore. Come here." Clauda held her arms out.

Selene blinked. "I don't deserve your com—"

Clauda pulled Selene to her and kissed her on the lips. For a moment, Selene's whole world was a swirl of lush softness. And then the kiss broke. "Ah, wha—?"

"Well, that shut you up, anyway."

This close, Selene could see the flecks of gold in Clauda's eyes.

"You don't know yourself, Selene. You fault your virtues and exalt your flaws. Look how long it took you to kiss me. I suppose you felt you were exercising proper self-control all the time, too."

"Yes. And you're right. That was stupid of me, too."

"I'm not trying to give you more ammunition against yourself. I'm asking you to accept that you're not the best judge of your own behavior. I think you should let me take over that job for you."

Selene sighed and relaxed a little more, leaning into Clauda. "Okay. I'll try, but don't be surprised if I . . ."

Listening to Selene recount her tale in a flat voice, with her face forced into expressionlessness, was excruciatingly painful. Of course Selene would take all the blame on herself, despite the fact that she'd counseled the others not to trust Mab. Finally she fell asleep in mid-self-recrimination. "Don't be surprised if I . . ."

Selene's words trailed off as her head drooped and she began to list sideways. Clauda grabbed her around the shoulders and pulled her close, then eased her down onto the bedroll.

Selene murmured something at the shift in position, and then sank deeper into sleep. Clauda pulled the blanket up over her and brushed a few stray hairs from her face. She trailed one finger down the side of Selene's face, from her prominent cheekbone down the long, sloping curve of her jaw. She caught herself and pulled her hand away.

Poor Selene. Always blaming herself for everything. Even in sleep, she had a vertical crease between her brows.

Clauda wondered what it would take to make that worry line go away. Too tired to search for answers, she settled for lying down beside Selene and drifting off to sleep.

Selene awoke with Clauda fast asleep beside her, her head pillowed in the crook of Selene's arm. Clauda's coppery brown hair tickled Selene's nose, and for a moment Selene forgot about the pen and her mother and Po, and simply relished the moment. She was supremely uncomfortable, which somehow made it easier to allow herself to enjoy Clauda's warm proximity. Her arm was numb from the weight of Clauda's head resting on it; she had a full bladder; and any moment now, the stray, curly hairs brushing against her nose would make her sneeze. But Clauda was warm, and alive, and she must have pulled this blanket up over Selene when she . . . when *had* she fallen asleep, anyway?

Clauda opened her eyes, smiled, pulled Selene down for a kiss, and said, "Let's go see about the wing."

Half of the wing's right wing was buried in the ground. The nose had uprooted several sizeable trees, which now lay across it, pinning it to the ground. But the vessel itself appeared undamaged. "We'll need block and tackle to get it free, I'm afraid. We need to go back to the Libyrinth and get help."

Clauda nodded. She patted the gold flank of the wing. Selene saw tears in her eyes and turned away, but not before she heard Clauda murmur, "I won't forget you. I promise."

Later that day as she and Clauda sat astride Goliath, making their way toward home, Selene asked, "Is the wing alive?"

"Well, it's not just a machine. There's a . . . mind of sorts. It has memories and feelings."

"How is that possible?"

"I don't know. It's a creation of the Ancients. Anything's possible, with them."

For several miles they were silent, and then Clauda said, "So what happened to Po?"

"No one really knows," said Selene. "Most of us think Thela used the pen to whisk him back to Ilysies with her."

"But if she has the pen and it can do all you say it does, wouldn't she be doing a lot more with it? Things we'd, you know, notice?"

"I know. Hilloa thinks Po is using his kinesiology to prevent her from using it."

"Can he do that?"

"I don't know," said Selene. "He'd been through some pretty intense stuff. Mind-lancet attacks."

Clauda inhaled sharply.

"Right. Do you ever wonder if what you endured made it possible for you to bond with the wing the way you have?"

Clauda frowned. "I never really thought about it."

"That was Po's theory."

"Oh."

"Anyway, Hilloa thinks Po is with Thela and she, Baris, and Jan have taken off, without permission, to rescue him."

"They could get into trouble."

"Yes."

"Maybe we should go after them."

"Vorain already has. Besides, I want to get you back to the Libyrinth, safe and sound, before anything else happens."

"No."

"What?"

"You're not taking me back to the Libyrinth. I'm coming with you to Ilysies." Clauda grinned. "It'll be just like old times."

10

The Clockmaker General

They wanted to separate them right there at the Department of Compensation, but Haly refused. "No, I will go with him to the facility. I want to see for myself what this place is like."

The chair readily agreed. "Fine. You will perform your duties with a settled mind if you see for yourself." She turned to the man with a train on his hat. "Summon another tollkeeper to escort them." She hesitated. "No, make that two."

Two more tollkeepers, both attired similarly to their tollkeeper, but taller, arrived in short order and took Haly and Gyneth out of the Department of Compensation and loaded them onto the tollkeeper's conveyance. They rattled through the city until they reached the outskirts. There a complex of low, single-story buildings sprawled in the middle of an open square bordered by an iron fence. The buildings were red brick, with small windows.

Two women dressed in black skirts and waistcoats stood at the gate bearing rifles. "State your business," the one on the left said.

"Citizen guardians, we bring a new inmate, and an . . . observer."

"An observer?"

The tollkeeper explained the situation.

"Well, this is highly irregular," said one of the guards when he'd finished. "We don't normally admit anyone who isn't here to work."

"Here is the order from the Board of Compensation," said the tollkeeper.

She looked the written order over and showed it to her compatriot, who also read it. "Very well," said the latter, folding it and putting it in her pocket.

They opened the gate and admitted them. "We will show you your sleeping quarters first," said the tollkeeper.

They drove to one of the buildings; it was impossible to tell how it was distinguished from any of the others. Inside, rows of beds filled a long room and at each end were bathrooms. The beds were tidy, the mattresses a bit thin but actually quite a bit better than most of those at the Libyrinth.

Next they visited the dining hall. It was similar to the one at the Libyrinth: rows of long tables and benches stretched from one end of the room to the other. "How has your food supply been?" Haly asked the chair.

"Fine. The clockmaker provides us with all we need." The guard looked less than thrilled about that.

What was going on? Thesia had been in straits just as

dire as the rest of them. But now everyone acted as if they'd never been out of food. And while it was true that the Thesians had always had a mechanical turn of mind, they'd never amassed this concentration of gizmos in one place before. It was as if this were a Thesia with a different past than the one Haly knew to have existed.

At last they went to the work buildings.

"These are the forges," said the chair, pointing to a row of square structures with steel doors. Even from where they stood they could feel the heat. When one of the workers opened one of the doors, Haly took a step back.

"Don't worry," said the chair. "He won't be working the forges. Smelting is only for the experienced."

Lucky them, Haly thought.

The workroom was filled with the clang of metal on metal, the hiss of steam as red-hot brass was plunged into water to cool. "What are they making?" asked Haly as she observed a woman hammering a glowing strip of metal until it seemed as thin as a page of a book. The worker curled each end over to produce a loop, and then slid the strip into a long trough of water to cool.

"Springs," said the chair.

They moved past the metalworkers to another area. Here people trod a large treadmill, turning a winch connected to a metal rod with a slot in it. Workers took the cooled strips of metal and threaded them onto the rod. The loops held them in place. The strips were also slotted into another rod on a frame that ran in tracks on the floor. As the winch turned the one rod, it coiled the strips of metal upon themselves in tight spirals, pulling the rolling rack ever closer. Once the springs were wound, they were secured with a cable threaded through the loop and wound around the spring, attached to the loop again. After that, workers pulled them off the winding rod and sealed them in flat metal canisters.

Just as one of the workers was taking a wound spring from the end of the winding rod, the center anchor loop snagged and the whole spring came undone, uncoiling with such force that it struck the man and threw him across the room where he lay, limp and motionless. Another worker who'd been standing nearby was hit by the other end of the uncoiling spring. She held her hands to her face. Blood dripped from between her fingers.

"This is the most hazardous part of the process," said the chair, with calm understatement. "Apart, of course, from delivering the wound springs and mounting them in their stations."

"Gyneth can smelt," Haly said.

S he said goodbye to him at the gate. "Be careful," she told him.

"You too. At least in my case, we know what the hazards are."

"I'll be back for you soon," she said, and left before she gave in to the urge to cling to him.

She climbed onto the tollkeeper's conveyance and sat down beside the chair. They clattered down the street and across the square. They came to a halt outside the clock tower.

Haly couldn't say why, but just looking at the building made her hands sweat. She stared, trying to figure out what it was about the place that troubled her so.

The other occupants of the conveyance sat staring at her. "Well," said the chair. "This is it."

"But aren't you going to take me inside and present me?"

"No."

The chair and the tollkeeper both looked tense. The tollkeeper tapped his fingers against the wheel, as if barely containing the impulse to drive away.

"Go on," said the chair.

Thinking of Gyneth in the compensation facility, Haly disembarked from the conveyance and advanced toward the building. The closer she got to it, the deeper her fear became. It was an effort just to climb the steps. Haly couldn't explain it, but she felt as if she approached something so awful it would drive her mad just to lay eyes upon it. Whatever lay beyond that door, she did not want anything to do with it.

But Gyneth toiled in the spring factory and if she did not do as she was told she'd never get him out of there. She forced herself across the portico and she opened the door.

Inside the building it was musty and dim. The only light was what filtered down from the skylights in the dome above. She heard a ticking sound and looked up. The center of the dome opened up into the spire that reached for the sky. Gears the size of small houses rotated in stately progression, interlocking with pinions and driveshafts. A pendulum that appeared to be made of solid gold swung back and forth.

Just as the dome of the Great Hall back home at the Libyrinth had images of the Seven Tales spaced about it, so, too, did this dome, only here a clock hand, curved to skim the dome, pointed at the hour of the Fly.

In the middle of the rotunda sat a figure in a chair, and a small table with some books on it. A few paces away stood a harpsichord. Haly's footsteps echoed in counterpoint to the ticking of the clock as she approached.

The figure didn't move. Haly stared at it. She had never seen, nor read or heard, of anything like this. The . . . person, she supposed it must be, was humanoid, but so ancient it didn't seem possible that she—or he—could still be alive. And yet the eyes that stared back at her from their deeply recessed sockets gleamed with life. They reminded her of Prime Censor Orrin's eyes, only if the late leader of the Singer priesthood had been old, this person was . . . ancient.

A nose like a beak stuck out over lips withered to a flat, blue-black line. Cheekbones, brow, and chin stood out in sharp relief from the sunken cheeks and eye sockets. The skin was a rich golden brown, deeply lined. It made Haly think of a wood carving.

And that was only the face. There was so much more: the elaborate headdress like a pointed arch, the bits of foil and colored paper and plastic wound into the long, white dreadlocks. The clothing, a hodgepodge of every style Haly had ever seen, either here or from Old Earth books, all jumbled together layer upon layer as if she—he—never took anything off, but just kept adding. It made Haly wonder if there was a body at all, under all those vests and coats and frocks.

One hand, skeletal and lined, rested on the chair. The other arm ended above the elbow, where a jagged metal strut stuck out from the combined sleeves of an opera gown, a frock coat, a T-shirt, and a flannel suit.

So maybe this wasn't a human being after all. Was it a device of the Ancients? Whatever the being was, it was obviously intelligent and Haly was being incredibly rude, standing here gawking. She bowed and said, "Good morning, Clockmaker. I'm Halcyon. You wanted to see me."

The lips parted and a female voice at once faint and hoarse said, "Well, look at you." Her teeth were encrusted with wires and gems. "You're not like the others, are you?"

Haly shook her head. She thought she'd come to terms with being different, thought she'd accepted her odd origins and her unique abilities, but now she felt like a specimen under a microscope, horribly exposed, and afraid of something she could not even name.

"There's something funny about you," the clockmaker went on. "A little bit of you curls around and extends beyond cube space." She sniffed. "Are you an imp?"

Haly sat up. "Imp? You mean, like the Nods?" Her heart pounded. Dread overcame her at what she might be about to discover.

The clockmaker sniffed again and shook her head. "No, not an infrastructure maintenance pod, though there's a little bit of imp in you, isn't there? Hmm. I bet that gives you some unusual abilities."

"For as long as I can remember, I've heard the voices of the books. Only since the Redemption, it's only when I concentrate on a book. Now, I hear the Song."

"Yes, that makes sense. Your imp bits make you more aware of *The Song That Changed Us* than your meat puppet peers. Maybe you can help me." A long sigh escaped her. "I'm stuck. And that boy took my pen."

"Stuck? You mean in that chair? Can you walk?"

The clockmaker shook her head. "Didn't bother having legs made. What was the point?"

"Made? Then . . . this isn't your real body? Your original body?"

The truncated arm jerked up and a whirring sound came from somewhere under the sleeve. "What do you think, you stupid meat puppet?"

Haly was taken aback, at both the words and their vicious tone. Suddenly several aspects of the situation combined and . . . rotated, giving her a whole new view: the clockmaker's age, her statement about being "stuck," her reference to a pen, and Gyneth's observations about Time and the people who walk "sideways" in it. "You're the last Ancient," she said.

"What, do you want a prize for figuring that out?"

Haly realized that what she saw told her next to nothing about this being. She existed mostly outside of the spaces Haly could see, smell, hear . . . and yet . . . "You're not just stuck in that chair. You're trapped here," she said. "When Po used kinesiology to try to free you, it didn't work."

"Not all the way," said Endymion. "I thought I could get out through the hole in this world, but I wound up here instead, fifty years in the past. And now the hole is closed again. Damn imp." She looked about her. "Do you like what I've done with the place? I was in the mood for some steampunk." She grinned. It was a ghastly sight. "I am so bored. I want to die, like my friends all did. I was afraid, but Jane was right. I wish I could have gone with them."

"The others . . . your friends . . . the other Ancients?"

"That's right. Let me show you." On a table at her right, the side her good arm was on, sat a stack of books.

She picked up the book on the top of the stack. It was not like most books Haly was used to seeing. It was wider than it was high, and the covers were thick. She focused on it, and was surprised to hear nothing at all.

Endymion settled the book in her lap and opened it. The moment she turned the cover over, a picture sprang up out of the book and hovered in midair.

Seven kids about eight years of age, wearing party hats and waving noisemakers, cheered and laughed. They appeared to be in some kind of conveyance. The seats looked like the ones Haly had seen illustrated in *Buses, Trains, and Space Shuttles: A History of Post-Terrestrial Transit Design*. The windows behind them were reddish black, like the color you see when you close your eyes.

"The seven of us came for my birthday party," said Endymion. "This was me." She pointed at a girl with shoulder-length ash-blond hair, brown eyes, and a sprinkle of freckles across the bridge of her pert nose. "You see, even then we wore skins. The fashion was for hyper-realism at that time. I was supposed to get an upgrade the following week, but of course that never happened. Once we realized we were never going home, we made our own modifications. When you're on your own, you lose track. Forget to look in a mirror, even. I suppose I look very different now."

Haly did not answer.

"This was Grant." With her remaining hand she pointed at a boy with dark hair and a solid jaw. "No matter how many upgrades he got, he was never as smart as the rest of us. He was the first to go." She sighed. "It was so soon, we didn't even know how lucky he was.

"Now *this* was Pierce." She pointed to another dark-haired boy, this one with angular features and brilliant blue eyes. "All the girls loved him. He was so beautiful . . ." Her finger moved to a girl with curly red hair. "Rebecca. I used to hate her. But she was right, in the end. And Nancy . . ." Her finger moved to a blond girl who had her head turned away, looking out the window. "Always thinking of something else."

"Dylan thought he was better than everyone else, because his mother was the granddaughter of the first Transcendent. And she was an engineer. He wore the emblem of the Fly, so no one could ever forget the fact. We used to laugh at him, but he was the one who brought the pen along. He stole it from his mother and smuggled it along in his backpack. We weren't supposed to have such a thing, of course.

"And Lysander." Her finger moved to a girl with blond hair who looked right at the viewer with a frank, confident expression on her face. "We used to call her the Lion, because she was so brave. She was my best friend. We did everything together. The Ilysians were our idea," she said, great pride in her voice.

"The Ilysians?"

"Yes. We added them. With the pen. After we killed Dylan for it. But you see, we weren't supposed to be able to die. But I'm the only one who didn't."

"Do you miss your friends?" Haly could not imagine what it must be like, to be trapped in here for centuries, all alone.

"I don't know if they're really dead," she said. "Or if

something else happened to them. There's a ring of life around the edge of time, you see? And they jumped off it, into the abyss." She made a strange grating sound that might have been weeping. "Nobody who hasn't leaped knows what's there. Imagine, all those people, just . . . jumping. It was my idea, you see, to come here in the first place, and it was my idea to send them away.

"I miss them. I wouldn't even care about the player or the pen anymore if I could just . . . leave. Maybe you can help me."

"Because . . . some of me is outside of . . . um . . . cube space? Because of what the Nods did when I was born?"

"That's right, little meat puppet. You're special: part song and part book. Made of equal parts this world and mine. If anyone can carry me out of this prison, it's you.

"Now you're going to see something, hear something, that will frighten you. Just take the ball. That's all you need to do, for now."

Endymion opened her mouth, and kept opening it, wider and wider, and just as Haly thought it could open no farther, her jaw unhinged, and the upper half of her head fell back to reveal a little platform where her throat would have been had she been human. Resting in the center of that platform was a silver sphere about the size of Haly's thumb. She'd never seen anything so horrible and so strange.

The sphere began to move. It rolled around the edge of the platform in a lazy circle, then picked up its pace. The faster it went, the tighter the circle became until the sphere vibrated in place in the center of the platform where it had started.

A sound emanated from it, complex and multitonal.

At first Haly thought it might be the Song, but it wasn't. For one thing, the Song did not hurt.

At first her hands and feet tingled, as they had when the Horn of Yammon sounded, but then the tingling became burning and it spread to the rest of her body. Haly jumped up, expecting to see flames, but there was nothing. She clapped her hands over her ears, but it did not block out the sound.

This was the opposite of the Redemption. Haly's thoughts fragmented as the sound pulled her apart into tinier and tinier components, each one awash on the surface of a vast dark sea, cast about with the movements of forces beyond her understanding.

It was a moment and an eternity, and when it was over Haly found herself lying on her side on the cold marble floor. She sat up and wiped drool from the side of her chin. She felt as if she'd awakened from a dream in which impossible things had seemed perfectly normal and rational.

Haly stood and found Endymion, or at least her carapace, still sitting in her chair, the top half of her head hanging from its hinges.

The metal ball rested on its platform, unmoving. The sense that it was dormant now came to her, from the same place that book voices and the Song came. Did that mean Endymion was dead? She wasn't sure. Haly picked up the ball.

It was heavy in her hand. The smooth polished metal was pitted in places. Something leaked out from the tiny fissures, something oily. Haly wrapped the orb in a handkerchief and put it in her satchel. What on earth was she going to tell the Compensation Board? Their clockmaker was gone. Would they ever let her and Gyneth go now?

Maybe. Something told her the Thesians might not be entirely upset about the loss of their leader.

On the table beside Endymion's husk, where the picture album had been, sat another book. It was small. Haly recognized it as a paperback novel of the Old Earth late period, when paper and gasoline were still readily available and books were produced by the millions.

On the cover, a golden flying machine sailed over a desert plain. In the foreground, a girl and a boy held hands as they ran from three enormous beetle-shaped creatures. The girl led a goat by a tether, and the boy, a tall youth with sandy-brown hair, held a mind lancet in his hand.

Haly couldn't breathe. She looked more closely. The beetle-shaped creatures had silver faces, and what had appeared to be tentacles were in fact tongues, bifurcated many times over. The golden flying machine also had a face on its underside. It was the wing.

The top portion of the cover, where the title would have been, was torn away. Haly opened the book to the title page. "The Book of the Night, a novel by Roger Theselaides" it read.

11

The Queen's Consort

Every night after they made love, Thela talked to Po. She spoke of her mother, of Selene, and of her frustration with the more traditional elements of the Ilysian nobility.

"If we could recruit men for the army, we could rebuild our forces in months," she complained.

Admit men to the army? Was she insane? Po's thinking on a great many things had changed since he'd first left Ilysies, but giving men weapons seemed foolish and extreme. Of course he couldn't say that, and probably wouldn't even if Thela wasn't controlling him with the pen. He leaned back and looked at her.

The set of her mouth was rigid. A muscle jumped in her jaw. She was really upset. "I can tell you anything," she said.

"Of course."

"Things aren't going well. I may be facing a challenge."

The thought of being the consort of a failed queen, with all the uncertainty that entailed, soon gave way to a deeper dread. He wasn't thinking right. Thela would do anything to maintain her position. She'd use the pen. That was what he needed to worry about.

"What if you did?" he said, the words seeming to come from outside himself. "What if you were challenged, and lost the throne? What if you conceded without fighting? You've done so much for Ilysies already. Would it be so bad to retire to a quiet life in the country with a male who adores you?"

She stroked the side of his face, her eyes glittering. "Wouldn't that be lovely?" she surprised him by saying. "I get so tired sometimes." She closed her eyes and tears dampened her lashes. "Tired and lonely."

He rested his hands on her arms, caressing her inner elbows with his thumbs. He let part of his mind slip into kinesthetic trance and he said, "Well, why can't you?"

She looked at him with such yearning it burned a hole in his heart, and through it flowed the waters from the sunken temple of her guilt. The empty gown floated up in his mind's eye and wrapped around him. He couldn't breathe. "It can't be for nothing," she said.

Po released her arms and broke the trance. He gathered Thela close and held her. "She forgives you," he said. "She knows why you did it and she's grateful to you. Ilysies is grateful to you. You've done so much. It's enough, Thela." He didn't care anymore if the words were true.

She was quiet a long time and then she said, "And Selene? I sent her to her death. I thought I had to."

"It's not too late. She could forgive you, too, if you gave her the chance."

"Do you say these things because of what I wrote with the pen, or because you were redeemed and this is your wisdom?"

He couldn't answer that. "Would you like to be redeemed?"

"I saw it, but I was too far away. I couldn't feel it."

"I can help you. The ultimate goal of kinesiology is integration, and integration and Redemption are the same thing. But you have to know, it's not something you're ever finished with. You have to recreate it every day."

She sighed. "Can I be redeemed and do what I must as a queen?"

"Haly is redeemed."

She said no more, but held him close until she slept.

The next time Po treated her, he focused on the submerged temple. The first thing he did was pull the gown out of the water and take it outside. He spread it on top of the reeds to dry.

I think I've made Myr very unhappy," said Thela the next day. "I don't want you to be jealous and I don't want either of you to harm each other, but I think he's lonely. Will it bother you greatly if I visit him tonight?"

Po looked up from the book he was reading. "I'll miss

you, of course. But no. It's only fair. He's secluded for you; you shouldn't neglect him."

She smiled and turned to go.

"Just don't stay away too long, please."

Po hung the gown, now dry and restored to its former glory, from the branch of a tree on the island that represented the energy center corresponding to Thela's willpower. Then he turned his focus to doing something about the temple itself. He debated the relative merits of raising the temple above the water level, or simply draining the swamp. Ultimately, he chose the latter.

He became an alligator the size of an elephant and he swam up and down the river, using his snout to deepen the channel.

Come with me." Thela stood in the doorway of his room.

"With you?"

"Yes. I have a full day of meetings. I want you to experience this part of my life."

"You're going to bring a male into your conferences?"

"Why shouldn't I?"

He could say nothing more. Po dressed and accompanied her.

He served drinks while she met with the trade minister about the new treaty with Shenash. The woman, in her eighties, kept glancing at Po and then back at Thela with a bemused expression.

"The Shenashian ambassador of trade will be less than pleased," she said.

"Yes, but there's nothing she can do about it. They need our barley and we know it."

"Just so, Your Majesty." Her gaze drifted to Po once more. "If Your Majesty will permit me to comment . . ."

"Speak freely, Uphine."

She looked even more nervous now. "I don't like to question you, but . . . Is it wise to include your consort in conferences of state?"

Thela raised her eyebrows. "Include? He is serving us."

"Yes, but males talk. Everyone knows that."

"Well, yes, but he's not like other males. He will do nothing to displease me, I assure you."

Uphine sighed. "I tell you this as an old friend and your most steadfast supporter, Your Majesty. There's talk. Some say you are besotted with your new consort and your lust has clouded your judgment. Others . . . well, it gets worse."

Thela sat back, her eyes gleaming beneath lowered lids. "Tell me, Uphine. Tell me all."

"Well, some say that it's a fetish. Your fixation on a male so far below our standards. Others call you . . . dick whipped."

Thela laughed. "Dick whipped. Really? Oh, that's good! Who's saying these things?"

"Do you need me to tell you?"

"Plata."

"You made an implacable enemy the day you assassinated her mother."

"There's no proof I did that."

"But it would not have been effective unless the hand behind it was obvious."

Thela shrugged. "Well. So she slanders me. Losers lie, everyone knows that."

"If that is all it comes to, then you have no worries," said Uphine.

What had once been a stagnant swamp was now a thriving river, studded with islands. Fish leaped and birds flitted from tree to tree. Po was a breeze that swept the last of the swamp debris from the temple. It was just an ordinary structure now, not gold, not perfect. Its twin in the mountains, in Thela's perception center, was no longer perfect, either. It still gleamed, but it was bronze, not gold, and it wore a patina of age.

"Remember when you thought I was just a farmer?" Thela asked him one afternoon when they lay side by side in bed, resting as the day melted into evening around them.

"Yes," said Po.

"It was nice, wasn't it?"

"Yes."

She paused. "I'm sorry for what I did to you."

"I understand," said Po.

"That's the pen talking," she said.

"No," he said, but it was.

She sighed. "The only person I can be honest with can't be honest with me. But if I removed the control I put on you with the pen, you'd turn against me. I'd lose you, too."

"I forgive you."

"How can you, really?" she said. "I was wrong. I see that now. I could have offered the Libyrinth true friendship, not aid in exchange for control. I couldn't see it as anything but a rival. It seems strange to me now. We could have worked together."

"You still can."

Thela shook her head. "Selene has Haly's ear. She won't trust me, she can't. And Haly has every reason to listen to her, to hate me herself."

"Haly's not like that."

"All the same. Selene—"

"Then make amends with Selene first."

She started. "How?"

"First, you could say you're sorry. Then . . . I don't know. What could you do that would most help the Libyrinth now?"

"There's nothing I can do to help them. They've won."

"What does that mean?"

"They have everything they need. They've got plenty of food now, so long as I don't take it away with the pen. I suppose they're worried about that—the pen. And I'm sure they'd like to know what's become of you."

A sudden jolt of raw emotion made Po jerk. "Me?"

"Of course. I know Selene, and I can guess at Haly. They'll feel terrible about you disappearing. But I don't want to send you back." She paused. "I suppose we could visit. It might not be a bad time to leave Jolaz in charge of things here again. We could go there and they could see for themselves that you're all right. And you could do a lot to get them to trust me."

Something squirmed in the pit of Po's stomach. The way she said that . . . How complete was her integration? But she had no need to dissemble with him, to pretend.

He could not act against her. He could not even refuse to help. The thought made him shiver.

"Are you cold?"

"No."

Thela regarded him. "You're afraid. You think I mean to trick them again."

Po could not answer.

She sighed. "It is in the back of my mind, it's true. I can't help it. I can't stop seeing all the angles. But I don't intend it. I really do want to mend fences."

But would she still want to, if the opportunity to take advantage presented itself? Po lay awake, listening to Thela's breath slow and deepen. When she was asleep, he eased himself out of bed and sat on the couch, watching her. She showed no sign of waking.

How horrible it must have been for her, to stand out there in the desert, seeing the Redemption happening but not taking part in it. To be so close to what you needed, and to be denied it. Well, he knew what that was like.

The next time Thela came to him, she brought the pen with her.

Po fought for calm, but he felt like his heart was at war with his lungs. They battered against one another and he could barely breathe, let alone speak.

It must have shown in his face.

"Don't worry," said Thela. "I'm not going to use it. But I want you to try something. Since you are an adept and you were able to use kinesiology on an Ancient, and since everyone knows that the devices of the Ancients are alive,

I thought it would be interesting if you performed kinesi-ology on the pen as a way of learning more about it. You'll report everything you experience to me, of course. That will make me happy."

He could not refuse her, not when she used those last five words. "I don't know if it will work," he said.

"I know," she said. "Just try."

She handed him the pen.

Po's fingers closed over it. All he had to do was write "the pen does not exist," and the world would be safe. But he could just as easily walk across the sky. It would make Thela unhappy.

There were no pulse points or energy meridians for him to tap into, but then, that had been the case with Endymion, too. He grasped the pen lightly in both hands and closed his eyes. He focused on his breath and on the warmth of the living metal in his hands.

He plummeted through darkness toward a vast net-work of argent light far below. It took him a moment to realize he was not free-falling in his own body. He clung to a feather that twirled and whirled as it fell. The net-work below them spun like the images in the kaleido-scope his cousin had received for her eighth birthday.

They neared the network and Po realized the lights were not random. They were words.

"We must find a way to break into that tower and de-stroy the orb," said Yammon. Soon, Po and the feather were among the words. The feather sliced through the words with its gleaming sharp edge, and caught up the loose ends with its tip, reforming them in new configurations. "Bel-rea was a mighty queen, the first ruler of Ilysies."

But the rewritten letters did not shine as brightly as

those that had been severed. They were thinner, too. They looked fragile; a careless move might break them.

Po opened his eyes to find Thela watching him expectantly. "Well, what did you see?"

He told her.

"No real information about the pen itself then," she said. "Assuming, of course, that the feather was your kinesthetic vision of the pen."

"Simply a reiteration of its function, though it's worth noting that the pen erases as much as it writes. But what's really interesting is the network of words."

"What do you make of that?"

"That must be what the world looks like to the pen," said Po.

She nodded. "Or perhaps it is a quality of the world that permits the pen to function as it does."

They made love, and slept, and the pen sat on the table beside the bed and Po could not reach for it.

But he awoke in the middle of the night with an idea about how to help Thela and the world at the same time. He looked at Thela sleeping. She was proud. She would not admit a mistake even if she knew of it. And she certainly would not take advice from him. But she wanted the land to be fruitful. He knew that.

Po pressed against her side. She didn't stir. She was very deep in sleep. He sat up and took the pen in hand.

He thought long and hard about what to write. Whatever it was, it had to make Thela happy. That limited him quite a bit. In the end, he wrote two things: "Queen Thela will know Redemption," and "The story Kip told Po in the vegetable garden at Minerva's house in the town of Nikos is true."

He watched his words fade with satisfaction. His grand-sire Kip's tale was about how men used to be flowers that gave off a special pollen that fertilized the land, until the flowers fell in love with the women and became men. According to the story men's tears and blood caused plants to grow. Now, no matter what else happened, the land would be fertile.

Suddenly he realized he had not set a time limit on Thela's Redemption. He raised the pen to amend that when she murmured and rolled over. He barely had time to put the pen back on the nightstand before she opened her eyes and drew him to her.

12

Haly-in-the-Silence

Haly dropped the book as if it had grown teeth and bitten her. This was an Old Earth book, but with the same title as Iscarion's book. What did it mean? Theselaides had been born here and died here, so the Theselaides who wrote this book couldn't be the Libyrarian Theselaides. And why were there pictures of things from this world on the cover of an Old Earth book anyway?

She snatched the book back up again, collected the holograph album from the table and, with Endymion's consciousness rolling around in her pocket, she left the tower.

She strode down the steps and across town to the Department of Compensation. The board was in session. As she entered the room they fell silent and stared at her.

"I have done all that the clockmaker asked me, and she is satisfied with what I have done. I've completed the terms of my agreement," said Haly. This next part was a bit of a risk. "Furthermore, you may now enter the clock tower without fear." She noted the way the chair's pupils widened and the other members of the board glanced at one another. She sensed she was on the right track. "The clockmaker is so pleased with what I did for her that she has elected to leave this place in peace, and accompany me back to the Libyrinth."

The board bent their heads together and whispered. Seconds later, the chair said, "Tollkeeper, please go and verify what Halcyon the Redeemer has told us."

The tollkeeper stared at her a moment, betrayal in his eyes, then turned crisply and left the room.

They sat in silence, the board staring at Haly, Haly staring back at them. She wasn't about to tell them about the book.

When the tollkeeper returned, he appeared much more relaxed. He stared at Haly in wonder a moment, and then seemed to recover himself. He turned to face the board. "It is as she says. The atmosphere of dread is gone, entirely. I went all the way inside, and I found that the clockmaker . . . her essence has left us."

The board stood. "Gone? Entirely?"

The tollkeeper broke into a grin. "See for yourselves."

"I've fulfilled my end of the bargain," said Haly. "Release Gyneth now, before you do anything else."

The tollkeeper bowed to her. "Of course, Redeemer. I will escort you there now and release him personally. We all owe you a great debt."

"Then perhaps you can convey us to the border of

Thesia, so there are no further misunderstandings," said Haly.

He looked chastened. "Yes. Of course."

It was a beautiful, fresh morning, the air cool, and the land spread out before Haly and Gyneth, broad and flat now that they had descended from the mountains. "Well," said Gyneth. "Now it's just us."

The tollkeeper had dropped them off at the end of the road the previous night, making sure that they were amply provisioned for the rest of their trek, including providing them with a brand-new wagon, courtesy of the Board of Compensation.

He had offered to accompany them farther, but they declined. Now Haly took Gyneth's hand and stared at the distant horizon. "Yes."

She had not mentioned the book in her satchel. She did not want the Thesians to know about it, because there was no telling how they'd react. The most important thing was just getting Gyneth freed and getting out of there. Then, last night, when they'd been alone, she hadn't wanted to. They'd both been in a celebratory mood and she didn't want to think about that book and its implications.

But she had to show it to him sometime. As she reached into her satchel, her hands shook and she hesitated. As long as she didn't show the book to another person, she didn't have to think about it, either. And she didn't want to.

* * *

The next day they encountered something in the sand. "It's metal," said Gyneth, nudging sand away with one toe. "Let's see what it is."

They began uncovering it but before long, Haly recognized the gray metal hide. She pulled her hand away and stumbled backward, tripped, and landed on her backside on the down slope of the dune. "Gyneth!" she shouted. "Get away from it. It's a Devouring Silence!"

"Is it? Wow!"

"No," she said, "not wow. Not wow at all. Come on. Hurry!"

"But it's dead."

"We don't know that for certain," she said. "I saw one live once. You don't—just come on! Gyneth!"

He heard the panic in her voice and he came away, but when she took his hand and started to hasten down the slope he didn't budge. "Don't get upset, but I want to take a closer look at it."

"Are you out of your mind?"

"No. I'm not. But I'm just thinking about the way they work, what they do. I—"

"If you're thinking about those things then you shouldn't even consider going near it."

"Will you listen to me for one second?"

Haly let out her breath. "Fine."

"Okay. Here's the thing. If Thela has the pen and she starts using it, we need something to counteract what she can do. Now this is just a hunch, but you know how they suck up all the light and the sound when they're taking captives."

"Yes."

"What if that's a kind of erasing and we can use it to erase what Thela writes?"

"That's crazy. How do you know it works that way?"

"I don't know. I told you. It's a hunch. I'd like to—"

"No."

"You haven't even let me finish."

"We're not putting Eggs in Devouring Silences and setting them loose. How would we control them?"

"Maybe they're like the wing, and there's an interface."

She shuddered. "Let's hope it doesn't come to that."

"But if it does, wouldn't it be a good idea for someone to try now, before it's too late?"

She looked at him. "You're serious about this."

He straightened his shoulders. "I want to try."

"It's too dangerous."

"Look who's talking."

"You're going to do it no matter what I say, aren't you?"

Gyneth didn't answer her. Haly sighed. She might as well be around, to try and rescue him if he needed rescuing. In defeat, she gestured to him to proceed.

Gyneth walked up beside the half-buried machine creature and placed a hand on its flank. Just as with the wing, a hatchway opened. Gyneth looked at her.

Haly hurried back across the sand. "I'm not letting you go in alone," she said. Her heart in her mouth, she followed him inside.

Within, it was much as the wing was, only instead of gold, everything was that dull-gray metal color. But there was a statue, just like in the wing.

"What do they mean, these statues?" she wondered

aloud. "Why would beings like the Ancients use human forms?"

"Endymion wrote that her cohort, Dylan, gave all the machines faces."

"I wonder why he did that."

"Well, we don't even know if these Devouring Silences, and the wing, are machines of the Ancients or artifacts of the book our world is based on."

"The Book of the Night."

He nodded.

"Let's read it and find out. Right now. Come on."

He smiled and turned to the statue. "Blessed Belrea," he said, "open for your children." He kissed the statue on the mouth, belly, and feet, just as they'd seen Clauda do with the statue inside the wing. And the statue opened.

But what came pouring out was not light.

It was the opposite of light. Haly had seen this before. She reached for Gyneth to pull him to safety, but it was too late. Tendrils wrapped around him and pulled him into the statue and it slammed shut. No. *No.*

She spun to the hatchway, opened it, and jumped through. She began digging through the sand to get at the creature's underbelly. She'd seen Selene do this. She could do this. But before she could wrest her knife from her belt and sink it into the flexible underside of the Devouring Silence, it was on the move. Haly was nearly buried in sand as it turned, and tunneled downward, out of reach.

She sat on the ground staring about her in stunned horror. Gone. He was just gone.

"He'll be back," she said to herself, forcing herself to at

least pretend to believe it. Anything else was too terrible. She waited.

What seemed like hours later but might only have been a few minutes, she felt a tremor beneath her palm. She jumped up and saw the sand hump up and then slide away to reveal the silver face of the Devouring Silence. Gyneth got out. Relief poured through her body to see him. He had a stunned expression and a big goofy smile on his face. "Haly. You have to try that."

She wrapped her arms around him and held him as tight as she could.

W e can get home a lot faster in that," said Gyneth that night as they sat around the campfire.

"I'm not sure I want to get home faster," said Haly. "Especially if it means going inside that thing. Gyneth, they were used to take slaves."

Gyneth nodded. "Yeah, but I think they do more than that. The tongue. I wasn't in there very long—"

"Too long, if you ask me," said Haly.

"But I sensed something with the tongue. Words."

"Words?"

"Yeah. I tasted words. You really need to check it out for yourself. Come on. It's not like you to be afraid of things."

She stared at him. "Not like me? Gyneth, I'm afraid of everything." She sighed and ran a finger through the dust, tracing curves and spiral. "I always have been."

"Well, okay, but you never let it stop you before."

His words rankled her, but she said, "That's because I

had no choice." She looked up and wished she hadn't. Gyneth probably thought he was hiding it well, but she saw the disappointment in his eyes. And he didn't even know about the book. "Okay," she said. "I'll try the Silence."

She immediately regretted her words. Why hadn't she just shown him the book instead? Still, she let him lead her over to the Silence, and he opened the hatch and they climbed inside. It was cool and dry, dark but for the jar of palm-glow Gyneth had opened. There were no bones in the cabin of this Silence. It smelled faintly of peppercorns, but that was all. No indication of what this thing had been used for.

Gyneth opened the statue. What poured out was the opposite of the light Haly had seen the few times she'd seen Clauda enter the interface in the wing. It was the nonlight of the Devouring Silence's tongue. She turned around. Gyneth put his hands on her shoulders. "Okay?"

She stared at him, at a loss for words.

"You know I wouldn't suggest something that would hurt you," he said.

She did know that.

"Just try it for a short time. You can come out whenever you want, just by willing it. Okay?"

"Yeah, okay." She took a deep breath and let herself fall backward into it.

She floated in nothingness. Immediately her tension melted away as she felt herself supported by what felt like thousands of tiny hands, cradling her. This was nice. She soaked in the sensation. Thoughts of the book, the pen, Endymion, Thela, and the Thesians all fell away and she found herself completely at ease, and utterly empty. The novelty of the sensation was so acute that for quite some time she was aware of nothing else besides the inflow and outflow of her breath.

And as she focused more and more on that, she saw the first tendrils of unlight.

Clauda had described the lines of light which connected her with the wing. These were just the same—sinuous, elusive—but they were made of darkness instead.

Haly knew better than to reach for them with her mind or her body. She waited as they gathered close. The touch of the first one left her mind alert, though her body felt numb. Then another touched her and another, and Haly's awareness of her body dissolved like sandstone under a waterfall.

The earth was to her as the sky to a bird or the sea to a fish. Haly now felt herself to be a sleek creature of the earth. She rolled and dived, tunneling for the sheer joy of feeling the land flowing over her metal skin.

Experimentally, she opened her mouth and let her long, tentacled tongue roll out to taste the earth she moved through.

"The Plain of Ayor was a sparse and arid land."

The words were dry and dusty on her tongue. Haly-in-the-Silence snapped her tongue back in. Her human heart pounded against her ribs but the part of her that was the Devouring Silence simply rolled along through the earth as if nothing unusual had happened.

Haly-in-the-Silence opened her mouth again and let one thin tendril out to touch the soil again. "Belrea lived in a small village five days' walk from anyplace else."

She drew her tongue back in again and tunneled up to the surface. Once there she disengaged her mind from the songlines and the statue opened. She rushed out of the beast and stood on the plain, turning in a slow circle, blinking in the sun.

The plain looked just as it always had. There were no sinkholes to indicate that the land she'd "tasted" had disappeared. No discolored patches or swaths of dead silverleaf to show there had been any effect from the creature's tongue at all. "Okay, okay," she muttered under her breath.

"Haly!" Gyneth rushed out of the Silence and ran toward her. "Are you all right?"

She took a deep breath. She'd left her satchel on the floor in the Silence. Had he looked inside? Had he found the book? She searched his face but found nothing but concern for her.

"I'm fine. Fine. I just . . . wow!" She let her joy in the experience of melding with the Silence overcome her other concerns, for the moment. "That was amazing!"

"So . . ." Gyneth scuffed one toe in the sand. "Can we keep it?"

Haly couldn't help but smile. "It would be a lot easier than walking the rest of the way."

They moved all their stuff into the cabin of the Silence. Once Gyneth had interfaced and started them on their way home, Haly fumbled in her satchel for the paperback novel *The Book of the Night*. She opened it and scanned the pages until she came to the part that read "The plain of Ayor was a sparse and arid land" and then flipped through it again until she found "Belrea lived in a small village five days' walk from anyplace else."

The book fell from her fingers and she sat down fast enough to make her backside sting. But her mind was too occupied to take much notice. "The same words," she whispered. "The very same words."

And she'd tasted them. "Molecules." Despite the heat of the day, she shivered. An idea slowly coalesced in her mind. She remembered Hilloa talking about her "three sticks in a bag" model of the universe. *The sticks can be anything.*

13

Thela's Challenge

P o awoke to the sound of distant shouting. Beside him
Thela stirred. They both sat up as the voices got louder.

"Thela Tadamos! Come out and face your country."

A challenge.

Thela arose and wrapped her robe about her. She strode
to the door, as upright and proud as if she were leading
the procession on Mother Day. She made no effort to
smooth her hair. It fanned out around her in a wild and
regal tangle.

She threw open the door. Beyond it Po saw a woman
with salt-and-pepper hair, about a head shorter than Thela.
Behind her was a crowd of women.

"Plata. So you've finally got your courage up. Is this
supposed to be dramatic timing, or are you afraid if you
wait until morning you'll lose your nerve?"

"Day or night is irrelevant to me when our country languishes. And I knew I would find you here, dallying with your half-breed consort. You care more for him than you do for running Ilysies these days. It seems fitting to challenge you in his bower."

Thela's voice was low. "Will you fight me here, too, then?"

"In the ring. These are my witnesses. He can be yours."

"You're joking."

"You seem to have more regard for him than you do for your advisors, or even your heir."

"If you mean to challenge me, Plata, then do so. If you're just trying to make a point, these theatrics do not serve your purpose."

"Summon your heir, then."

Thela's nostrils flared. "Very well."

In twenty minutes' time, a group had assembled in the exercise yard. Plata and Thela had stripped and now faced each other, both holding the traditional curved knife.

On Plata's side of the ring stood the delegation of women who had accompanied her to Po's chamber. On Thela's side stood Jolaz, Mab, Uphine, Po, and Myr, who had also awakened, and begged to come along.

"She seeks advantage in doing this in the middle of the night," said Jolaz. "Thela would have more supporters if she'd issued her challenge in broad daylight."

"Don't be so sure," said Uphine, and Po was shocked to see Mab nod in agreement.

Thela and Plata circled each other. Unlike practice fights, where the opponents wore armor covering the vital areas, this was a serious duel. They faced each other naked. It could well be a fight to the death.

Thela had the reach on Plata, but Plata was more muscular. "Your lust for your male has clouded your thinking," said Plata.

"Are you trying to talk me to death?" said Thela.

Plata dug one heel into the sand and launched herself at Thela. She drove one shoulder into Thela's solar plexis. Thela fell on her back. Plata dropped on top of her, straddling Thela's hips and raising the knife.

Thela jabbed her fingers into Plata's eye. The woman screamed and covered her face with her hands. Thela took advantage of the moment and threw her off.

But she'd done no permanent injury to Plata's eye. Before Thela could follow up with a slice or a kick, Plata had leaped to her feet. The two circled each other once more. "You think you can do a better job leading Ilysies than I have?"

"I think your steppe-born husband can do a better job," said Plata. "Under your reign we've lost our army, our flying machine, and our dominance in the Plain of Ayor. What are we now?"

"A rich country with no enemies. You forget that the Singers were on the verge of invading us and they are a threat no longer. Thesia has its own business to attend to, and the Libyrinth is harmless."

"The fact that you're comfortable making that assumption should tell all here just how far you've fallen. The Thela I knew would never be so blind."

Thela rushed her. She brought her knife in low and might have disemboweled Plata if the woman had not turned and taken the slash across the hip instead. Blood streamed down her thigh, but she seemed unimpaired by it. She caught Thela's knife arm and forced it upward.

Thela twisted and broke free but Plata shoved her. Thela fell face-first in the sand. Before she could get up or roll over, Plata wrested the knife from Thela's hand and cast it out of the ring. Thela whipped around and kicked out at Plata, but she dodged out of the way.

"You're disarmed. You're defeated."

"I'm not dead yet," said Thela.

Plata charged her.

Thela leaped up, dodged Plata, and then sprang out of the ring. Po gasped. What was she doing? It was illegal to retrieve a weapon once it was cast out of the ring.

Thela didn't go after her knife. She ran from the exercise yard.

"What are you doing?" shouted Plata. "You can't! You coward!"

The spectators were in an uproar. Po turned to Myr. "I can't believe it," he said.

"This is disgrace for all of us," said Myr.

Then Po saw Mab smiling. His stomach turned into a stone. He ran after Thela, his heart battering against his ribs.

Ahead, he could hear Thela's footsteps slapping against the stone floors. She was headed to his bower, where the pen was. Could he overtake her? Could he prevent her from what she was about to do? He ran faster.

He rounded the corner and saw the door to his apartments closing up ahead. He reached it just before it latched and he threw it open and plunged inside.

"Good, don't let them in," said Thela. She stood near the bed, the pen in her hands.

Po slammed the door shut behind him and bolted it shut. *No.*

"Now why didn't I make use of this sooner?" Thela's gaze lingered on him a moment before she began to write. Po wanted nothing more than to run across the room and wrest the pen from her grasp, but he couldn't move. He was barring the door. Because that was what Thela wanted.

The end of the pen opened like a flower and little motes of light drifted from it like pollen. As she wrote, words, golden and glowing, hung in midair. "Plata, daughter of Hecat, from Quatra north of Videsis, is my most ardent political supporter."

Po could do nothing but watch as the words shimmered and faded, and reality shifted. Out in the hallway, voices lifted in confusion. "Why have you stopped?" someone demanded.

"Thela surely knows what she's about," said Plata. "There's no need for us to interfere."

"What are you talking about? You challenged her. She fled! She's a coward. Go in there and execute her and restore honor to the throne!"

"Execute her? Our most brilliant leader? Never!"

Thela's tongue poked out from the corner of her mouth as she thought. She nodded and lifted the pen again. "Plata, whom I just wrote about, never challenged me. She and the others with her in the hallway will return to their beds and go to sleep. When they awake, they will believe that the events that took place in the Ilysian palace on this night were a dream, and they will not speak of it for as long as they live."

In the hallway, the voices fell silent. Po heard footsteps retreating.

Po tried to force himself to cross the room and wrest the pen from Thela. Now that her former challenger had retreated, he could leave the door and come to her side. He could touch her. He could lean his head on her shoulder and caress her arm. But when he tried to reach for the pen, he found himself doing something else entirely.

"Not right now, dear," said Thela. "I'm thinking."

Po went and sat down on the couch.

"How could I have allowed myself to come so close to losing the throne when I had this at my disposal?" She hefted the pen in one hand. She glanced at him and then away.

She wrote, "Adept Ymin Ykobos is outside the door to this room, ready to examine me."

"Po, open the door," she said, once the words had faded.

He did, and there stood Ymin Ykobos, looking vaguely confused. "I'm here to examine her majesty," she told him.

"Ymin, accompany me to my quarters." Thela turned to face him. "We will leave you now, Po. Await me here. You will make me unhappy if you do anything else."

Po had memorized what she'd written about him with the pen, back in the Corvariate Citadel: "In all but one respect, Po is as he was before I last wielded the pen. The only difference is that now, he will only do what makes me happy."

Somehow, she knew he was the reason she hadn't been using the pen. And she wasn't taking any chances now. That was why she had summoned Ymin Ykobos. Soon his teacher would confirm what he had done.

14

The Book of the Night

Haly and Gyneth caused quite a stir when they returned home to the Libyrinth.

"I told you we should have surfaced farther away and walked in," said Haly, looking around at the ring of spectators their arrival had attracted. Many of them held pitchforks and other implements, and were just lowering them in a manner that suggested they'd been raised in preparation for attack moments ago. In the distance she could see other people running toward the Libyrinth.

"But that would have meant missing the look on Peliac's face," Gyneth murmured under his breath. Louder, he said, "Someone should go after them and let them know everything's all right."

Rossiter took off at a run.

"What is the meaning of this?" demanded Peliac.

"And welcome home," said Clauda, stepping out from the throng, Selene a pace behind her.

"Clauda! You're alive!" Haly threw herself in her friend's arms and hugged her tight. "Selene found you?"

"Yeah."

"I knew she would." Haly looked up, to see Selene smiling in a way she had never seen her smile before. Haly glanced again at Clauda. Her friend gave a little nod and raised an eyebrow. Ah, good. "Finally."

Selene blushed and Clauda laughed out loud.

"So . . . why have you come home in a Devouring Silence?" asked Clauda.

"There's a lot to explain, and I want to hear about your journey, too. But we're starving. Let's go in and get something to eat."

Over fried onions and pulse, fresh bread and preserved plums, Haly, Gyneth, Selene, and Clauda caught up on one another's adventures. Many others stopped by to say hello or update one of them on some other development.

"So we just got back yesterday," said Selene.

"And there's been no word about Jan, Hilloa, and Baris? Or Po?" asked Haly.

"Nothing," said Peliac, who had seated herself nearby and occasionally interjected a comment.

Haly looked around at all of them. It was time. She couldn't put it off any longer. "There's something else. Something I found when I was with Endymion." She turned to Gyneth. "I just couldn't talk about it before. You'll see."

They all waited in silence as Haly took the paperback novel *The Book of the Night* from her satchel. "This is . . . well, I just don't know what to make of this."

"What is it?" said Selene. She peered over Haly's shoulder. "Oh! Goddess!"

Soon others had gathered around. Gyneth's eyes went wide. Peliac gasped. "What? What does this mean?" she said.

Haly shook her head. She opened the book and read the first page. "Belrea and Yammon lived in a small village in the middle of a vast plain known as the Plain of Ayor. It was a dry, sparse land, offering little to sustain the people, apart from an abundance of silverleaf bushes that provided forage for the goats. With great effort, the villagers coaxed crops of barley and pulse and onions to grow in the meager dusty soil, but the goats were more reliable. It was Belrea's job to take them out of their paddock each morning and watch over them while they grazed. This is because she was the daughter of the village's head woman and man. Belrea was the village goat girl, an honor she took very seriously."

Haly struggled for words, and failed. She simply handed the book to Gyneth to read. She watched his eyes grow wider and wider as he read, and at last he looked up from the page. "The goat girl?"

"What?" said Peliac. "Let me see."

Wordlessly, still holding Haly's gaze with his own, Gyneth handed the book to Peliac. Selene and Clauda read over her shoulder.

"What does this mean?" asked Selene when they'd all read the first couple of pages and handed it on to others.

"I don't know," said Haly. "I do know that this—" She took the book back from Burke and examined it more closely. On the spine was a little image of a starburst with a rocket ship sailing across it. "Parker Millennium, Science Fiction" read the imprint. "—was published as fiction. It's a novel, not history. Not biography."

"Are you sure?" said Peliac. "How can you tell?"

"Maybe it was rebound at some point by someone who wished to confuse matters."

Selene shook her head. "That doesn't make any sense. Listen to this: 'Yammon and his best friend Iscarion also lived in the village, but they were from much poorer families. Every morning they went out to the fields and tilled the soil and watered the crops and weeded the rows.'"

"But Belrea was born in Ilysies! She was the first Ilysian queen. She's not an Ayorite. And Yammon and Iscarion grew up as slaves to the Ancients! None of this is true!" Spittle formed in white flecks at the corners of Peliac's mouth.

"This is fiction," said Haly, a funny feeling building in the pit of her stomach. "It doesn't have to be true."

"Then this story is a fabrication based on our historical figures?" opined Gyneth.

Haly flipped to the copyright page, as if the fact that it was an offset print book were not proof enough. "It predates our Yammon, Iscarion, and Belrea," she said, pointing at the copyright date: 2098 by Roger Theselaides.

On her way to breakfast the next morning, Haly encountered Selene, Clauda, and Arche at the console. "Have you read the rest of it?" Arche asked Selene.

"Yes."

"What happens?"

"Yammon, Belrea, and Iscarion become friends. There's a romance between Belrea and Yammon, and some hints at a love triangle, with Iscarion being in love with Yammon, though the author never really commits himself in that regard."

"Why not?"

"Probably afraid to. The people of Old Earth were weird about same-sex romantic and sexual relationships. It's impossible to say whether the author himself shied away from the topic, or if he gave in to pressure from his publisher."

"They couldn't just write what they wanted?"

"Oh, heavens no. Publishing was a business driven by profit. And while the majority of publishing was done with ink on paper, books and the shelf space for them in the places where they were purchased were very tightly controlled. Anyway, in this book they all became friends and then their village was destroyed by the night wind, a sort of dark tornado that is controlled by a group of powerful people known as the Ancients. All that the night wind sucks up is instantly transported to a stone citadel where the Ancients live, protected by slaves they've mind-controlled from the villages they've captured. And guess what the slaves are armed with?"

"What?"

"Mind lancets."

"Mind lancets?"

"Yep."

"Huh."

"I know. Anyway, the three of them have to defeat the Ancients and liberate all the villagers that have been captured. Which of course they do, in the end."

"How do they accomplish it?"

Haly moved on and their conversation fell out of earshot.

Within hours, word of the paperback novel *The Book of the Night* had spread throughout the community at the Libyrinth, and speculation was running wild. Overnight, the book copying activities of the Community of the Libyrinth switched from *The Book of the Night* by Iscarion to the paperback novel *The Book of the Night* by Roger Theselaides. Everyone wanted a copy.

"Belrea, Yammon, and Iscarion were named after the characters in the book, it's obvious. No other conclusion makes any sense," said Nieth in the line for breakfast.

"And the Plain of Ayor, as well?" challenged Arche.

"Yes! Clearly the Ancients adored this book, as is evidenced by it being beside the last Ancient."

Haly sighed, got her bowl of porridge, and sat in the far corner of the dining hall, but it was little help. Everywhere Haly went, people were reading it out loud to one another, and speculating on what it meant that a book written and printed millennia ago so closely resembled events from their own world's history.

"They called it the Corvariate Citadel because it lay enshrouded in darkness as black as a raven's wing," Ock read, surrounded by a little group in the Alcove of the Dog. "Clouds perpetually blotted out the sun and it was said that the darkness emanated from deep within the citadel, where the Ancients kept an orb that held all the powers of night and darkness, and it was these they used to enslave the Ayorites."

Of course, there were some differences between their world and the one presented in the novel, but those seemed to be just as captivating to people as the similarities were.

As she passed the kitchen she heard Hepsebah reading to Burke, Vinnais, and Rossiter. " 'It's bad luck to break a mirror,' said Yammon.

'Worse luck than remaining slaves of the Ancients all our lives?'

'I'll do it,' said Iscarion. 'I always have bad luck anyway. What difference does it make?'

'And I'll get into the temple.'

'It's too dangerous,' Yammon and Iscarion both said at the same time.

'No. I'll be fine. I'll present myself at the gate as a maid of the night. They'll be happy to have me. Once I'm inside, I'll use this.' She showed them the short mind lancet Iscarion had made. 'They won't be expecting it.'

"The three of them looked at one another. Yammon gave a heavy sigh at last, and nodded."

"So Belrea was there when the Ancients were overthrown," said Rossiter.

Haly stopped. She couldn't help herself. She wished she'd never told anybody about this book. Now everyone was acting as if it was the real *Book of the Night*. But it wasn't. It couldn't be. "We don't know what it means," she said. "This book was written long before our world even existed. It's not a history of the overthrow of the Ancients. For all we know, it's just a coincidence."

"A coincidence, Haly?" asked Burke.

"It could be." She knew she sounded defensive. "Consider how many books we're surrounded by, here. I mean, no one has ever come to the bottom of the Libyrinth. It keeps going down and down, and eventually, you have to turn around. For all we know, there are an infinite number of books. Therefore, every possible combination of

THE BOOK OF THE NIGHT

letters and words could be represented by a book some-where in the Libyrinth. This could just be . . . one permu-tation, with no real meaning at all."

"But you didn't find this book in the Libyrinth," said Hepsebah. "You found it beside the last Ancient."

"Maybe she liked it because it was similar to our world. It could be as simple as—"

"Haly! There you are." Gyneth stood in the doorway, breathing hard, his cheeks red. "I want to show you some-thing."

Haly was ashamed that her first thought was, what now? She forced a smile and permitted Gyneth to take her hand and lead her away from her argument with Burke and Hepsebah.

Gyneth took her down the spiral staircase in the cen-ter of the Great Hall, the one that led to the face at the bottom of the Libyrinth where Gyneth had installed the Egg on Redemption Day.

Selene and Peliac followed them.

He stood before the face that held the Egg and said, "Play."

The mouth opened.

Gyneth grinned.

"It—did you do that just now?"

"Yeah. The whole Libyrinth system is set up to be op-erated by voice commands. But you need to know what the right words are. I've been examining the circuitry and I figured out that it can do much more than just re-trieve books."

"Like what?" said Peliac, rather challengingly, Haly thought.

But Gyneth was only mildly daunted. "I'm not sure,

exactly, but for instance, I *think* the P-L-A-Y command recites the book."

"Really."

"Yes. Reads it aloud. But I'm not sure where the speakers are. I mean this, down here. This is operating system stuff. Upstairs at the console is the user interface. But I haven't found anything that might emit sound, unless it's just the audio output for the command console and they used it for everything."

Haly leaned over the parted lips of the face. She reached out and traced her fingertips over the smooth, curving metal. It felt warm. "For whom text is song," she murmured. She peered between the parted lips. "There's something in there."

"Teeth?" said Peliac.

It wasn't teeth. "It's a little metal shelf."

Gyneth peered inside. "It looks like it's designed to hold a book. One thing I've noticed about ancient technology is that they can be peculiarly literal. Maybe that's where you put the book you want recited."

"Better not try it until you're sure," said Peliac. "You don't really know what it does."

For once Haly agreed with her. Gyneth looked a bit disappointed, but said, "I'll keep investigating the circuitry until we know for sure."

The next day, Haly was at the main console when Clauda came up to her. "What do you think about Gyneth's discoveries about the operating system?"

"You've heard about that?" Of course she had. Everybody had. The news had fanned the flames of speculation and now the theories were becoming wilder by the minute. "I don't know what to think about it. We don't know enough yet."

"But the lips opened at the command 'play.' Surely that must mean something."

"Not necessarily," said Haly. "It probably just means that it will recite a book placed in there."

"But if you're so certain, why won't you let Gyneth test it?" asked Vinnais.

"It's not a question of me 'letting' Gyneth do anything. All of us present at the time agreed it was best not to take any chances until we know exactly what it does."

"But if all it does is recite the book, what's the harm?"

"We don't know that for sure."

"So you think it might do more?"

"I've been wondering about that myself," said Gyneth, coming up from the hatch in the center of the Great Hall. "I've just been examining the circuitry, and I don't think it recites the book in the mouth at all. There's a lot of connections leading from that book holder down, not out into areas where you'd expect to find speakers but down so far I had to give up and turn around.

"I don't think 'play' means 'read aloud,'" said Gyneth. She stared at him. "What do you mean?"

"Just that it means something else. Maybe . . . maybe 'play' means 'enact.' Maybe the reason Belrea, Yammon, and Iscarion are named in the paperback *Book of the Night* is that they *were* in the paperback *Book of the Night*. They were . . . characters."

"No!" she was furious with him for saying that. "What a horrible thing to even suggest!"

Gyneth seemed confused. "But . . . we have to examine

every possibility, and when it comes to the People Who Walk Sideways in Time, well, what *weren't* they capable of?"

"And just because it's possible doesn't mean it's true. Circuitry isn't everything. This book is an Old Earth novel that obviously influenced the people living here many generations ago. I think it's worth considering that sometimes the simplest explanation is the correct explanation. Iscarion, Yammon, and Belrea named themselves and the plain after the people and places in this book and Iscarion changed his name to Theselaides and titled his account of the overthrow of the Ancients after his favorite novel," said Haly. "Revolutionaries and activists throughout time have been influenced by great works of literature."

"But surely it's worth considering if—"

"No! Consider? Consider that we aren't real? That this whole world is just a . . . a construct? That we're just . . . some kind of . . . program? I won't. I don't see how any good can come of such an idea."

"It's just an idea, Haly. Since when are you afraid of those?"

She knew he was right, but her horror of what they might discover overwhelmed her reason. "I can't talk about this. I won't." She turned away, pretending not to see the hurt and confusion in his eyes. Or the unease and disappointment in the eyes of so many others.

15

To the Rescue

Po paced the sitting area of his chamber. His heart pounded out the seconds in slow motion. He didn't know how, but Thela knew he'd been controlling her with his kinesiology. He was certain of it. That was why she'd summoned Ymin Ykobos to examine her. Had the adept discovered his work yet? It was only a matter of time.

What would Thela do when the truth was confirmed? With every breath he expected to be transformed into a goat, or to lose his arms and legs and mouth, as he had before. Or to simply cease to exist altogether.

But nothing happened. Thela's revenge was inevitable. Doubtless, she wanted to be present to witness whatever it was she intended doing to him. Worst of all was the knowledge that he had failed. She would wield the pen with abandon now, and the whole world would become her plaything as surely as if she were an Ancient herself.

Through the archway to his exercise yard came a sound. Po went and looked out into the night garden. It was empty. But then it came again. A rustling, as of something moving through the undergrowth on the other side of the wall facing the ocean.

"Stay out of the weeds," someone whispered.

"If I get any farther from the wall I'm going to wind up at the bottom of this cliff," said someone else.

"Shh!"

As the voices registered, Po's heart seemed to stop. He ran to the wall and peered through the latticework. "Jan? Baris?" he whispered.

"Po." He knew that whisper, too. The moonlight gleamed in Hilloa's dark hair. "Oh, thank the Tales, you're still alive."

Terror filled him. Behind Hilloa, Baris and Jan smiled and clapped each other on the back. "See? I told you it would work," said Baris.

"You all have to get out of here, right now," said Po. "Run!"

"No way," said Hilloa. "Not without you."

"We came to rescue you, Po," said Jan, as if explaining something that should be obvious. He grabbed the crevices in the bricks and started to climb.

"No, I mean it. Leave. Now."

They didn't listen to him. In a heartbeat, all three of them had scaled the wall and stood in the garden. Hilloa embraced him. For one brief moment he let himself sink into her softness. He breathed deeply, drinking in her smell of honeysuckle, sea spray, and sweat. Other hands clapped him on the back and gripped his shoulders.

"Poacher," said Jan. "Are you okay?"

Po tore himself from Hilloa's arms. He stepped back from all of them and forced himself to look mad. It wasn't easy. It was pure joy to see them—joy, and terror. "Your timing couldn't be worse," he said. "I've been preventing Thela from using the pen—"

"See, I told you guys," said Hilloa.

"But now she knows. She's . . . she's going to . . ." He shook. He was on the verge of bursting into tears in front of them, again. Only this time it was for a good reason. "You have to get out of here, she can't find you here. She's coming. Go! *Please.*"

All three shook their heads. Hilloa said, "If she knows you've interfered—was it kinesiology? Did you use your kinesiology to—"

"You're in danger, too. More than we are," said Jan.

"You'll just make it worse for me if she finds you here. And she's using the pen now. She can do anything she wants."

"Then come with us." Hilloa grabbed his hand and tugged. "Come on, what are you waiting for? Let's go."

"I can't," he said. It was true. He could let Hilloa drag him to the wall, he could climb it and sit on top, but he could no more climb down the other side than sprout wings and fly over it.

"She's controlling you," said Hilloa.

He couldn't answer.

The sound of a door opening came to them from inside his chamber. Po couldn't move, couldn't speak.

"Well," said Thela, standing in the archway to the yard.

His three friends rushed her at once. Thela looked at him. Po tackled Baris. They fell to the ground. The impact blew Baris's breath in Po's face. Mother. What had he been eating?

Po pulled his fist back. Baris stared at him, mouth open. "What?"

"What are you doing?" yelled Jan. He grabbed Po's cocked elbow with one hand and wrapped an arm underneath Po's other arm. He'd grown in the past few months. He managed to lever Po up off of Baris a bit.

Po kneed Baris in the most accessible place. "Fuck!" screamed Baris. "What is wrong with you!"

"She's controlling him," said Jan.

"It's the pen!" cried Hilloa. Po couldn't see her, but her voice sounded strained. It came from the direction of the archway.

Po shook Jan off. He pivoted and swung his fist into Jan's jaw as hard as possible. Shit! Jan flew back and landed on his back in the grass.

Hilloa and Thela played tug-of-war with the pen. "Give it to me!" said Hilloa.

Thela pulled back and looked over Hilloa's head, straight at Po. "You know what will make me happy."

No. No.

The grass was cool and slick beneath his feet as he took the five strides needed to come up behind Hilloa and wrap an arm around her neck.

"No fucking way!" cried Jan. And then Baris hurtled into Po, pushing both of them into Thela.

Thela kicked Hilloa and wrested the pen from her. She backed into the room. "Make me happy, Po."

He tightened his arm around Hilloa's neck. She gasped. "What? Why? Oh!" And then she didn't have the air to speak anymore.

"Fucker!" screamed Baris, punching Po in the side of the head.

Pain exploded across Po's skull and the next thing he knew, Hilloa had twisted around to face him. "She's controlling you, Po."

"I know!"

Jan came in low, hitting Po behind the knees with his shoulder. Po flew forward. Hilloa reached out to catch him and Baris tried to block her. They all went down in a heap upon the threshold and for a moment everything was a tangle of arms and legs.

When Po managed to free his head from Hilloa's armpit and look up at Thela, the words she'd written already hovered in midair. "The three people tangled with Po on the floor of his chambers in the Ilysian Palace are gone."

Before he could draw breath, the words shimmered and disappeared, along with his friends. Gone. Po slumped to the floor without Baris's bulk propping him up. He sat up and reached out through the empty air where Hilloa had been a moment before. He turned to where Jan had been lying across his leg. Gone, all of them.

He was alone with his queen.

Thela held tight to the pen and watched him from the other side of the room. "Your accomplishments as an adept go beyond those of any of your colleagues." The look in her eyes was steely, remote. "You deceived me, Po."

Po shook his head.

"Don't bore me by trying to deny it. Adept Ykobos herself said she'd never seen an energy working like the one you did on me. All to keep me from using this." She lifted the pen. "Of course it's my fault. I was too subtle by far, writing that you would only do what makes me happy. I thought I was protected, but it turns out that what I want, and what may, in the end, make me happy, are not at all the same thing.

"Still, it was sweet of you to try to mend my broken heart, even if it did nearly lose me my kingdom. That's how I figured it out, you know.

"When I found myself eating sand in the ring, about to lose my throne and possibly my life, I realized something was wrong. I never would have allowed things to reach that point when I had the pen at my disposal. I would have written Plata out of existence weeks ago—unless something, or someone, had prevented me. And who has been there day and night, always eager to give me a treatment, to rub my feat and soothe me with his remarkable kinesthetic abilities? Oh, Po. What am I going to do with you?"

He didn't answer her.

"You are such a unique creature. A male adept of such power . . . To simply kill you seems wasteful. But I must prevent you from causing any more trouble, and you need to learn a lesson."

She paused, tapping the pen against her chin. "I know." She lifted the pen and wrote, "Po takes his right index finger in his left hand."

Dread filled him. Po tried not to, but just as he'd been unable to keep from choking Hilloa, just as trying to take the pen from Thela by force was unthinkable even now, he grasped his right index finger.

"Po bends his right index finger back against the joint until it breaks," she wrote; the words, glowing, hung in the air between them.

Po started bending his finger backward. "Stop," he said, not sure if he was saying that to himself, or to her. "Please! No!"

Still, he bent it back, despite the pain, despite everything. His mind exploded in the wet snap of his finger breaking. When his vision cleared, he was on the floor and his finger was a wet throb of heat and pain. He looked up at Thela, tears on his cheeks. She lifted the pen again. "Po takes his right middle finger in his left hand," she wrote.

16

Thela's World

Selene sat up and rubbed the grit of sleep from her eyes. She felt as if she'd awakened from much more than a single night's sleep. She'd awakened from a lifetime of wrong thinking. She never should have been jealous of the time her mother spent caring for Ilysies and training her heir, Jolaz. How childish of her. She should have been grateful for what time her mother could spare her. And she should have dedicated her own time to finding ways to make Queen Thela's job easier, instead of running away to the Libyrinth. "Oh," she said, under her breath, looking out the window at the lightening sky. "Oh."

Selene took a deep breath. The cool morning air cleansed her of the errors of the past. She pulled her hair back from her face and looked down at Clauda, who stirred in the bed.

Clauda blinked and yawned. She pushed herself up and

shook her head. "Suck a goat," she said. "I've got to give Queen Thela her wing back."

"Yes." Pleasure at the thought of Thela's reaction to that warmed Selene. "You must. I'll help you. We'll do it together."

They rode out with a team from the Libyrinth to the woods where Clauda had crashed. With all those people, plus block and tackle, it was the matter of an afternoon to unearth the wing and free it from the trees. They rested for the night and in the morning, Selene climbed into the chamber and Clauda entered the statue, and they headed home.

T he Libyrinth is gratefully under the rule of Ilysies."

"The Corvariate Citadel is an Ilysian city."

"The Plain of Ayor grows crops of barley as lush as those in the Ilysian Valley."

Line by line, day by day, Thela changed the world. It pleased her to keep Po near, and since he was groggy on Ease as often as not, that meant she conducted most of her business from his bower.

He awoke to find her stroking the side of his face. He tried to pull away but his body was leaden with Ease. His hands felt like two loaves of bread, hot from the oven and studded with glass.

Thela took in his reaction and gave him a sad smile. "You cannot lie to me anymore," she said. "I fixed all that."

He actually found that a comfort. If he was bound to tell the truth, he had to *know* the truth, and that meant that his mind, his feelings, were his own at last.

"So tell me, do you believe that I love you?"

His stomach turned. "Yes." *Mother*. So much for a sense of relief. He wondered at himself. After all she had done to him, how could he believe she loved him? *Well, maybe it's what she thinks love is.*

Was that why she hadn't killed him outright?

Po watched Thela as she read correspondence. She sighed and set a letter down beside her on the couch. She took up the pen. "The Shenashian ambassador of trade has lifted the tariff on barley exports," she wrote.

From where Po sat he could see through the archway into the yard. Lightning suddenly flickered across the sky outside. It was a clear, warm day. Yet for an instant the sky went black. A split second later, everything was normal again. Had he imagined it? He looked at Thela. She sat with her back to the doorway and seemed not to have noticed. She picked the letter up again and read it and smiled. "That's better." She turned to the next letter in her stack of correspondence.

L ater that day Thela left his bower and Ymin Ykobos came to tend him.

"You never should have done that to her," she said under her breath as she fed him. "I'm not sure *how* you did it. When I discovered it, I was so shocked I simply reacted. Of course, I would have been duty bound to tell her the truth anyway." Her gaze fell on bandaged hands. "You were a great adept," she said. "It's too bad."

"What, you mean they won't heal?"

"Well, they'll heal, eventually. But without intervention it's very unlikely they'll ever be as strong as they were, and as for channeling energy in kinesthetic trance . . ." She shook her head.

"Without intervention? But you're an adept. You can intervene! Please!"

Ymin gave him a stricken look. "I can't. She's forbidden it."

"She's taking kinesiology from me." The realization sent a jet of hot agony through his heart. Suddenly the desire to hurt Thela overwhelmed him. He wanted to kill her—for his friends and for his hands. But as long as she had the pen, there was little anyone could do against her. "You must try to take the pen away from her," Po told Ymin.

"The pen?"

"You don't know of it? She has a pen. It looks like a wand in the shape of a flower. It's very dangerous. Anything written with it becomes true," he said.

Ymin smiled at him and pushed the hair back from his forehead. "Ease can make one imagine all sorts of things," she said.

"No. It's true. It's real! You haven't seen it? Ask Mab. Mab knows." That was a risk, but it was important that Ymin believe him. She was the only person he had access to who might be willing and able to take it from Thela.

"Mab?"

"Thela's spy."

"That old rumor? Oh, Po. The Ease has the better of you. Everyone knows that's a myth. Thela has no spies."

Was she joking? Everyone knew Thela had spies. Po stared at Ymin and she looked back at him with absolute sincerity. Uh-oh. Thela had changed that, too. What else had she written while he was asleep?

"You'll have to be careful. You may need allies," he told her. "I'll do what I can but gather those you trust and those who are critical of Thela. The sooner the better, before she—"

"Critical of Thela?" said Ymin. "Who would be critical of Thela?"

When Ymin left, Po forced himself to get out of bed. He went outside and lay on his back in the grass. He stared up at the blue sky, at infinity. If he could take flight, like the wing, he'd be free. He closed his eyes and pretended to soar high above the plain, looking down on it in all its many shades of tan and gray. When had he begun to love the plain and its emptiness?

Of course it was empty no more, tan and gray no more. It was as green and lush as Ilysies now. Or so Thela had written. Were there ever unintended consequences to her decrees? He had no way of knowing.

Suddenly daylight flickered to night and then back to day again. That had happened a couple of times in the past few days. It worried him. He thought it might have to do with how much Thela was using the pen. It seemed impossible that something so powerful could not cause unintended consequences.

In *The Book of the Night* Endymion had told Iscarion he needed to "refresh" this world. And Hilloa had that theory of dimensions and pocket universes—the sticks in the bag. They could be anything, she'd said.

What if this world was not a terraformed asteroid, but a whole pocket dimension? And what if the "sticks" of this dimension, the forces that gave it space and time, were stories? Perhaps the world became barren because it needed more stories. And perhaps Thela using the pen to edit the "stories" that were already here was further weakening the fabric of existence.

At the moment the land was prosperous, but what would happen if these odd day-to-night shifts continued, or worsened? If the pen had caused them, then maybe there was a way to use the pen to fix them.

"Hey," someone said.

Po opened his eyes, squinting in the sun. Careful not to use his hands, he rolled onto his side and pushed himself up with one elbow.

A dark shape stood on the other side of the latticed brick wall—Myr.

"Hey," Po said in return.

There was a scraping sound and Myr's dark head appeared over the top of the wall. Po's heart raced. That was all he needed now, an attack by a jealous male. He struggled to his feet. It was awkward, not using his hands. Everything was awkward.

He managed to gain his feet and he started backing away. Until he noticed that Myr was not coming after him. He sat on top of the wall watching Po, a frown on his face. "What happened to you?" he asked Po. "I heard you screaming the other night."

Po took a deep breath, and decided to tell Myr everything. He couldn't handle being alone anymore. He needed a friend, even if it was another male. He opened his mouth. "Queen Thela—" he said, but that was as far as he got. The words, held inside for so long, all tried to rush out of him at once and he choked. Heat rushed to his face and he struggled for breath. His own sob sounded harsh and raw in his ears. His vision wavered as scalding tears overflowed them and ran down his face.

He couldn't see. He heard Myr land in the yard, and his footsteps. Po rubbed his face in the crook of his elbow to clear his vision.

Myr stood a few paces away, staring and looking uncertain.

Pain, rage, and grief made Po reckless. "If you want to kill me, here's your big chance." He lifted his bandaged hands. "I can't stop you."

Myr looked from his face to his hands and then back again. "What happened?" he repeated.

Po swallowed the knot in his throat and managed to say, "She made me break them."

"She? You mean Queen Thela?"

He nodded. He was past words now. The look of horror on Myr's face, the act of speaking of what had happened all brought the reality back to him more vividly, somehow, than the constant ache of his broken bones and the sight of his bandaged hands.

And his friends. His best friends, who'd come to rescue him, were gone. Gone where? Just gone. *Don't think about that.*

"Oh," said Myr. He stepped closer and rested a hand on Po's shoulder, lightly, like a bird that might fly away again at any moment. "I'm sorry."

Po swallowed more tears and forced speech from his raw throat. "Why should you care? You should be glad. This is a big opportunity for you."

"No," said Myr. "She's still obsessed with you. I haven't seen her in days. Not since you sent her to me."

"What are you talking about?"

"Don't deny it. I heard you tell her to visit me. And she did, to make you happy. She loves you."

Po could not support the naivety of Myr's words. He sank to the ground under their weight, and Myr sat with him. He rested his hand on Po's shoulder again and squeezed.

"I hate her," said Po.

"Well she loves you, though it may not benefit you." He nodded to Po's hands, which were lying in his lap, useless. "She really made you break them yourself?"

Po nodded. Tears rolled down his face. "Finger by finger."

Myr said nothing for a moment. He moved his hand to Po's other shoulder and pulled Po against him. "That's horrible. How did you manage to obey?"

"I had no choice. She has this pen." An idea came to him. "It's very dangerous. It's a device of the Ancients. Anything she writes with it comes true. She wrote me br-breaking m-my f-f-f—"

"Shh," said Myr. "You don't have to say it."

Po let himself sink against Myr. In some ways this was the most incredible thing that had happened to him so far. He was accepting comfort from another male.

But he didn't have to pretend anything with Myr. And since Po would love nothing better than for Thela to forget he even existed, he wasn't in competition with Myr anymore.

And Myr seemed to sense this. For the better part of an hour, they simply sat together. Clouds rolled in from the east and the yard cooled. Po shivered.

"Come on," said Myr, standing. He helped Po up by the elbows and guided him inside. He helped Po down onto the couch and fetched a cup of water, which he held to Po's mouth. Po drank gratefully.

It was so odd, being tended to by another male. It was completely outside Po's frame of reference. What was it like for Myr? "This is weird," he said, when he'd finished drinking and Myr had set the cup aside.

Myr smiled a little crookedly. "Yeah." He sat down in the chair beside the couch. "But I heard you. I was up all night that night. I don't care if you're my rival—nobody deserves that." His eyes grew wide.

"Do you realize what you just said?" asked Po.

Myr opened his mouth, paused, then closed it again. He stared out the archway into the yard. "Not until I said it, but . . . you did me a good turn when you didn't have to, and . . . I won't take it back. It's true."

"Do you believe me about the pen?"

Myr stared at him, fear and speculation in his eyes. "Is there anything else I can do for you? Are you hungry? Do you need . . . anything?"

"The pen is real."

Myr's larynx bobbed. "Strange things have been happening."

Po nodded.

"Mynae is gone."

Po didn't say anything. He just kept staring at Myr.

"She displeased Thela when she gave a private performance for Alys Memnon. Now no one knows where she is. It's like she's just vanished."

"With the pen she can do that and much more," said Po. "Have you noticed the weather lately?"

"The lighting?"

"I think it's a side effect somehow. She's using the pen a lot. It happens when she's written several things in a row with it."

"What else has she written?" asked Myr.

"There's been so much. Remember when the river flooded?"

"I heard about it in practice."

"That was one of the mistakes."

"And the rabbits?"

"That, too."

Myr took a deep breath and sat back. Po watched him. He stared at nothing, picking at a loose thread on the hem of his tunic.

"She's not just a threat to others," said Po. "It's only a matter of time before she comes to harm herself. But you can protect her."

Myr met Po's eyes. His gaze burned with thwarted intensity. Good. He'd hit a nerve. "For her sake, you must steal the pen."

A fine sheen of sweat stood out on Myr's brow. He looked like a rabbit caught in a trap. Had Po moved too soon?

"And do what with it?" he asked.

"Take a boat out past the breakers and drop it into the ocean."

Myr stared at Po in silence. Po held his gaze. "And when she discovers that it's gone?"

His heart pounded. "We'll make it look like it was me."

"She'll kill you."

He shrugged.

Myr's eyes grew bright. He turned from Po and rested his head in his hands. "I don't like this," he said, his voice thick. "I'm just her consort. I'm just supposed to keep up my appearance and please the queen in bed. This is . . . I shouldn't have to deal with this."

"I know," said Po.

Myr whirled on him. "Is this what you learned at the Libyrinth?"

Po opened his mouth but Myr cut him off. "If this is liberation, you can keep it!" He stood and strode toward the door. "I don't want to deal with this." He left.

17

Conspiracy

Po decided that if Ymin Ykobos wouldn't heal his hands, he'd try to do it himself.

It took him days of concentration just to get past the pain and enter kinesthetic trance. He'd never tried to do this on himself before. Would it even work?

He bit through one end of a bandage and slowly unwrapped it using his mouth to pull the gauze away. He tried not to move his fingers but that was almost impossible. With every shift, hot spikes of pain drilled through the general ache and brought tears to his eyes.

But that wasn't as bad as the sight of his mangled hand. The fingers were swollen, the joints bruised a deep purple. He closed his eyes and started unwrapping his other hand.

He had blessedly little recollection of breaking the

fingers of his left hand. It had been even worse, of course, because he'd had to do it with the broken fingers of his right. He kept passing out, but Thela revived him. Near the end, he was eager to finish, simply so he could stop.

Now Po placed the palms of his misshapen hands together, and breathed. It was not like the visions he had when attuning himself to others. It was . . . He experienced himself—his energy pathways, his breath and blood and the electrical impulses of his nervous system—from the inside. It was like being caught in the rushing current of a stream, swept away through the twists and turns and eddies of his body and mind's functioning.

It was all in constant motion, too swift for him to touch, observe, or manipulate. It wasn't going to work.

Po tried to withdraw to normal consciousness, but he couldn't do that, either. He was caught in the stream of his own being and he couldn't get his head above water. He was drowning.

Suddenly a tree branch dipped into the river just ahead. Po grabbed for it. The black tide of pain that flooded him forced the remaining air from his lungs but a second later he was out of the trance, lying on his back in his bed, gasping.

Ymin Ykobos looked down at him, her eyes wild. "What in the name of the Mother are you doing?" She held his hands apart by the wrists. Her look of horror only deepened as she took in the bandages scattered on the bed. "You did this yourself?"

He nodded.

"Mother." She placed his hands gently on his chest and rubbed her face. "Why?"

Wasn't it obvious? "If you're forbidden to heal my hands, I thought perhaps I could do it myself."

"But you know how dangerous that is."

"I've done a few things with kinesiology no one's supposed to be able to do. I thought maybe I could do this, too. I knew it was a risk, but if it would return to me the use of my hands, it would be worth it."

"The use of your hands?"

"As an adept."

"It means that much to you?"

"Of course."

Ymin sighed. "But you're a consort of the queen! The whole reason your mother apprenticed you to me in the first place was because she feared you would not be chosen by a good woman. But now you have secured for yourself the best consortship any male could hope for. What more could you want?"

"What more? How about a wife who doesn't force me to break my own hands?"

Ymin reddened. "Well, that was extreme. But you betrayed her! And did she execute you for your crime, or cast you aside? No. She kept you."

"I don't want to be kept. I'm an adept. I want to heal. Just because I'm a male doesn't mean I'm only good for fucking and siring. But none of that makes any difference now, because if Thela keeps on with what she's doing she'll destroy us all anyway."

Ymin sighed. "Shh. Try to calm down, Po. You're being hysterical. Here." She took a packet of powder from the pocket of her robe and stirred the contents into a cup of water. "Drink this. You need to relax. And I have to rewrap your hands, so it'll be just as well if you can sleep through that."

Po hesitated. He didn't want the Ease. He wanted to keep arguing with Ymin. But at the same time, he was so tired, and his hands hurt so much. . . . He nodded and let her put the cup to his lips. He drank and slept.

I heard what you said to Adept Ykobos," said Myr. It was later that day, or maybe the next, Po wasn't sure. "Do you really believe that?"

Po was still groggy from the Ease Ymin had given him. It had been a healthy dose. "Believe what?"

"That you can be an adept even though you're a male."

Po wanted to either laugh or cry. He decided to laugh. "Yeah, I do."

Myr frowned. "What's so funny?"

"Nothing. Not you. Don't get pissed. It's just . . . Oh, Goddess . . ." Tears won in the end anyway and for a little while, Po couldn't speak. "Being male doesn't make you stupid, Myr," he said, when he was able. "We're not really all that different from women."

"How can you say that?"

"Yes, we're different, obviously, but we're all human. We're more alike than we are different. That's what I mean."

"But we're so emotional, it overpowers our thinking. Everybody knows that."

"Maybe we're like that because everybody expects us to be like that. I've met men from other places and they're not like we are. If they can be different, so can we, if we want to be."

"I'm proud of who I am," said Myr. He sounded a little defensive.

That night a great wail went up all over the city, and perhaps beyond. It sounded as if all of Ilysies cried out in anguish. Nearer, within the palace, Po heard people running, shouting—more screams and cries. What had Thela done now?

It was late. Ymin Ykobos had fed and bathed Po and he lay in bed. Hours passed and an unearthly silence fell. Po was thirsty. A ewer with a straw sat on a table beside the bower.

Sitting up without using your hands was awkward. He lay there wondering if it was worth the effort. He heard footsteps. He strained his neck to raise his head, half hoping and half fearing it was Thela. It wasn't. In the dim light from the stars outside, Po saw a shadow enter the room. But not from the door; from the garden. It was Myr. Po lay his head back down. "Myr," he whispered. Relief that he still lived poured through him like fresh, cool water.

Myr padded to his bedside and sat down. "Do you need anything?"

"Water, please."

Myr helped him to sit up and drink. When he had his fill he sank back down on the bed. Po rolled to one side to face him. He could barely make out his face. His eyes glittered like starlight reflected on a still sea.

"People are dropping dead in droves," said Myr. "Anyone I've ever heard say anything critical of Thela is dead . . . except you."

"Do you see now?"

Myr's eyes glittered in the faint light. "Okay. I'll do it."

"Good. Just be careful."

Po stopped taking Ease. He discovered his room was no longer guarded. Perhaps Thela felt that with the pen there was no need. Or perhaps, following the purge, there simply weren't enough guards.

He was walking around the outer perimeter of the parade ground when he saw something glittering in the sky. It wasn't the sun, but something reflecting the sun. As he watched, it grew larger, taking on a crescent shape he knew well.

The bull dancers who had been practicing in the grass paused and looked up, shielding their eyes from the glare.

The wing came closer. In fact, it seemed to be coming right at them.

What on earth did Clauda mean by even flying over Ilysies, let alone buzzing the palace?

His spirits rose with the thought that she was coming for him, and sank again with the realization that if that were so he'd have to explain to her what had happened to Hilloa, Baris, and Jan.

And then his brain caught up with the rest of him, and his stomach clenched.

Sure enough, seconds later, just as the wing was truly visible in detail, Queen Thela stepped out of the gate and onto the receiving platform, accompanied by Jolaz and several other minor dignitaries. She spotted Po and sent Uphine over to collect him. He joined the others on the platform.

The wing crested the palace wall, raising a wind that ruffled Po's hair and fluttered in Thela's robes. It sank gently to the ground in the center of the yard—the bull dancers had long since scattered—and the hatchway opened.

Clauda came out. Po remembered that day he'd been fighting with Baris in the stables when Clauda came in from flying the wing. His heart felt hot and tight, as it always did when he remembered his vanished friends, which was why he tried not to think of them.

Po wanted to run to her, but he stayed where he was. Clauda crossed the yard and knelt at Thela's feet. "Your Majesty, the wing and its pilot are yours to command."

The sight made Po ill but her words made him break out in a cold sweat.

But then Selene emerged from the wing as well. All the moisture drained from Po's mouth and his heart pounded. Selene? What—why?

She, too, crossed the yard. She knelt before Thela, then prostrated herself, kissing her feet.

She looked up at her mother and tears glittered in her eyes. "I've been wrong about everything. Can you forgive me?"

"Of course." Thela grasped her daughter by the shoulders and lifted her to her feet. They embraced.

When the greetings were over and Steward Sopopholis was leading Clauda and Selene to their quarters, Po trailed behind. He knew Thela had changed them, but he couldn't convince his body that they were not his rescuers. He lingered in the doorway after the steward left.

"Po!" Clauda ran to embrace him. He held his hands out to his sides and let her arms encircle him. He rested his cheek on top of her head and closed his eyes, and for a moment he indulged the fantasy that he was safe at last.

"Oh, Po," said Selene, coming up beside him and resting a hand on his shoulder. "It's so good to see you again. We didn't know what had happened to you. We searched and searched, but . . ."

"Thela brought me here."

Selene squeezed his shoulder and Clauda released him and stepped back. "Oh, that's all right, then," said Selene.

He shook his head. "She has the pen. She's using it on you to make you say these things. She used it to kill Hilloa, Baris, and Jan. She's killed a lot of people with it." He lifted his hands. "She made me break my hands."

They stared at him in dismay. They looked at each other and back at him again. "Oh, Po," said Clauda. "What in the world did you do to deserve such a punishment?"

Panic dumped adrenaline into his bloodstream. This was like going mad. This wasn't Clauda, even though it looked like her. This wasn't Selene. They were gone just as surely as Hilloa and Baris and Jan. Only in a way, this was worse. Thela made them betray their true identities.

"Well, whatever it was, I'm sure you've learned your lesson now," said Selene. "Are you still Thela's consort?"

Was he? He was uncertain. She hadn't been taking her pleasure of him since the night she'd discovered his betrayal. "Yes," he said anyway, because what was the point of saying anything else?

"Oh well, you're lucky, then," said Selene.

"Do you remember what you said to me just before Mab took the pen?" he asked her when he found his voice again.

"Yes, and I'm sorry. I'm afraid we all misled you, Po. In fact, my expectations of you, and those of the rest of us at the Libyrinth, were entirely unfair. It was unreasonable for us to expect you to simply shed your role as a male overnight. And even if you could have, what would have been the result? A male running around acting like a woman? Who wants that? Certainly not you, and you were wise enough to realize that, even if only instinctively. Thank goodness you clung to tradition, Po. Good for you. You're a fine male and you have a vital role to play. You don't need to be anything else."

Po couldn't seem to breathe. His throat and chest were paralyzed. His mind raced, trying to think of something to say. There was nothing.

Clauda stood beside Selene, nodding in agreement.

"I have to go now," he said, and went in search of Myr.

He found him in his room. "Have you had any luck finding out where she keeps the pen?" he asked.

Myr looked up. "She keeps it on her person," he said. "She won't be parted from it."

"Even when you're alone together?"

"That's a laugh. She's not visiting me."

"Still?"

Myr shrugged.

"Well you have to sneak into her chamber at night while she's sleeping and take it. Only when you do, don't drop it in the ocean. Bring it to me instead."

"I can't take it," said Myr.

"Don't you believe me? You know she used it to kill all those people, and—"

"That doesn't matter," said Myr. "I mean it does. I'd do

something about it if I could, but I can't take the pen from her. She'll know it's gone almost immediately. She'll just take it back and kill me. It won't do any good."

Po left to find Jolaz standing in the hallway outside.

She tilted her head to the corridor leading to the left, toward her quarters. "Come on," she said.

Po followed her, astonishment giving every step a surreal quality, as if he were in a dream.

Her chamber was much like any Ilysian private quarters. Jolaz shut the door behind them and sank onto one of the couches surrounding the low table in the center of the room, gesturing for Po to join her. "My people have swept the spy holes, we can talk safely, for now."

Talk? About what?

"First of all I want to say that I'm sorry that happened to you." She nodded at his hands. She stared at him, searching his face. "Everybody is."

What could he say? He waited, instead.

"Does she—she has something that she used to make you do that to yourself, doesn't she? Something she's using to do all kinds of things."

Could he trust Jolaz? Did it really matter? She was in a better position than most to do something about the pen and she had plenty of motivation for preventing Thela from remaining all-powerful. What difference did it make if she betrayed him, used him? If she could stop Thela, it would be worth it.

He told her about the pen. "I suspected something of the sort," she said. "But it was today, when Selene showed up and made obeisance to her mother, that I knew for sure. Then, all kinds of other things started to fall into place."

She stood and paced the room. "This isn't good. I've always been loyal to Thela. On the whole she's been a good queen. One of our best, in my opinion. But this device, this pen." She broke off and sat down across from him. "What I'm about to say is strictly between us. If it gets out I'll know you talked and I have people who will make what happened to your hands seem like a back rub."

"Okay. I don't have any reason to tell on you. You've checked up on me, I'm sure you know that."

She gave a short, sharp nod. "Just making sure you know."

He waited.

"This pen encourages the very worst tendencies in Thela. If she has a fault, it's in being overly ambitious, overly ruthless. Her rule is her life. There's no balance with her. Frankly, it's been astounding the way she's taken to you. It's the most she's ever indulged in a personal life.

"If she were a bit more balanced, more grounded, she'd be an even greater queen than she already is, because she'd understand her subjects better.

"But that's never been her focus. Her focus has always been power, seemingly for its own sake.

"I'm not like that. For me, power must always be evaluated as a means to an end. And those who climb too high fall hard and fast. I believe in realistic expectations, worthy adversaries, and stability. Perfect things don't last. I want Ilysies to endure forever, not rule the world."

"Why are you telling me all this? I'm just a male."

Jolaz laughed. "Yes. You're just a male the way the Libyrinth is just a library. You're an adept. You've met the last Ancient. You *performed kinesiology* on the last Ancient. And you used kinesiology to control Thela herself."

Po started. "How do you know I—"

Jolaz grinned. It was odd; she usually looked so serious—like Selene. "I didn't, until now. But I guessed. The two of you returned suddenly and unannounced after a sojourn in the Corvariate Citadel. Thela now has a device of the Ancients. It's unlikely she got it here. It probably came from the citadel, yet she's only using it now, weeks after her return. Something—or someone—was preventing her from wielding it." Jolaz sank back on the couch with a sigh. "Too bad I didn't recruit you or you didn't approach me before she figured out what you were doing. I could have mounted a real challenge to her rule, not like that half-assed maneuver by Plata."

"Yes, but would you have?"

Jolaz considered the question, one finger tapping on her thigh. "Probably not. Anyway, it's too late now. Any whiff of disloyalty and I'll disappear, or worse. There's a rat in the kitchens that bears a striking resemblance to Plata.

"I can only imagine how she reacted when Ykobos blew your cover. Well, I don't have to imagine. But what astounds me is that she didn't kill you outright. The only explanation I can think of is that she, too, is aware of how powerful you are—and potentially useful."

"Do you think you can get the pen away from her?" he asked.

"Someone must. A thing like that is inherently corrupting. For someone like Thela—well, there's no hope for her unless . . . maybe there's no hope for her, period."

If Jolaz believed that, she'd be unable to act against Thela's immediate plans. She'd been bound in loyalty to Thela, like the rest of the Ilysians who were still alive.

She must believe that what she was doing was for Thela's ultimate benefit. "I wrote that Thela will be redeemed, but I forgot to write when," he said.

"Okay, okay," said Jolaz, pacing again. Under her breath, so faintly Po could barely hear it, she said, "I have to at least try, for her sake." She turned to him. "We have to get the pen away from her, first and foremost. After that, we can rewrite the things she's written and then . . . can we write the pen out of existence?"

"I don't know, but it's the first thing I'd try."

She nodded. "Where does she keep the pen?"

"Myr says she keeps it with her at all times," said Po.

"Myr? You've been talking to Myr?"

He shouldn't have said that. Po schooled his features to blank and tried to pretend he hadn't heard her.

"Don't worry, I won't get either of you in trouble. If he's working with you, that's an added asset. No one will suspect that two consorts are cooperating with each other. We can use that."

"If you get the pen from her, what will you do with it?"

"Can its effects be reversed?"

"Yes." He told her about the greening of the plain.

"Okay," said Jolaz. "Okay—there's hope, then. We just have to think of a way to get access to the pen.

"If she's got it with her at all times then the thing to do might be brutally simple. We just rush her and take it. Two of us hold her down while the third uses the pen to undo her work and destroy the pen. It would be best to do it at a time when she's alone and unguarded, of course."

"Do you realize what you're asking? That means at least one male has to lay hands on Thela in violence."

Jolaz paused. "Mmm. Yes. And not you, of course." She

nodded to his hands. "I'll have to do it on my own, then. Perhaps . . . chloroform. Yes. I'll get some chloroform from Adept Ykobos. You or Myr will lure Thela to someplace where I'm hiding and I'll get her from behind. Then I can take the pen and rescue her and all of us from its corruption. I like it. It's simple, and the simple plans are always the best."

And who will stop you from becoming the next Thela?

Po left Jolaz's quarters and returned to the consort's wing. Myr was in his yard, exercising again.

"You don't have to steal the pen," he told him.

"Good, because I can't. And I can't betray Thela. I can't even—"

"I just need you to signal me the next time Thela visits you. Sing her a song, and I'll hear you, and—"

"I'm sorry," said Myr.

"What?"

Footsteps rustled in the grass behind him, but before he could even turn, two soldiers stepped to either side and grabbed him by the upper arms, holding him immobile.

Thela came around into his view. "Did you think I wouldn't know you were talking to Jolaz? I suppose not. She seemed surprised, too. But no security measure can stand against this," she waved the pen. "Thela knows what others wish to conceal from Thela." She smiled. "And now . . ."

Po drew a deep breath and closed his eyes. He didn't want to see what she wrote. Whatever it was, it would be beyond his endurance. "Please," he said. "Just kill me."

She chuckled. "Yes, of course, my dear. But your death should serve the nation, don't you think?"

He shuddered, and if it weren't for the soldiers holding

him up he would have fallen. Terror blotted out thought as he awaited what would come.

Seconds passed. He breathed in and out. One of the soldiers adjusted her stance. Distantly, Po heard a seagull cry.

Something settled around the crown of his head. He flinched, but nothing else happened. The circlet resting on his brow didn't weigh much, but it was a bit scratchy. He knew what it was without seeing it, without touching it. It was his crown. He was the Barley King.

18

The Barley King

Haly awoke on the day of the Barley King's processional and smiled in anticipation of the festivities. She sat up and nudged Gyneth, who still slept by her side. "Get up, lazy."

He opened his eyes. For a moment, as they looked at each other, she had the oddest feeling. As if they had once been partners, not mistress and consort. Gyneth smiled and kissed her and Haly let the odd notion drift away. "Fetch me my best white gown and draw me a bath."

She looked out the window of her tower room, at the splendor that was the Ilysian Libyrinth. Thanks to Empress Thela and her bounty, they prospered. The fields were green for as far as the eye could see and every day more people came here to study. It was a good thing they had lengthy written instructions from the empress as to just which subjects should be pursued and which shunned, or Haly would not know how to guide so many enthusiastic minds.

Gyneth returned with her bathwater and her robe, as white as a cloud on a sunny day. She relaxed into the hot water and let him wash her. There was a knock on the door.

"Shall I send them away, Holy One?" asked Gyneth.

It seemed odd to Haly that he would ask that, and then, odd that it seemed odd. She shook her head. "No, let them enter."

It was Clauda. "I'm ready to fly you to the ceremony, Holy One," she said.

"That's good. We'll go directly after breakfast. Have you eaten?"

"Just a roll when I first woke."

"Keep me company, then. Once my bath is done, we'll eat together."

Later, sitting together at a little table crowded with dishes of fish, fresh bread, berries, eggs, and yogurt, Haly noticed that Clauda was barely picking at her meal. In fact, she was methodically shredding a roll into smaller and smaller pieces. "What's bothering you?"

Clauda appeared to be startled out of her thoughts. "Nothing, Holy One."

"Nonsense. There is something. You were in my service a long time before you became the empress's pilot. You can't hide from me. Something concerns you."

"I don't wish to trouble you with it."

"Not trouble. Satisfy my curiosity."

Clauda hesitated, then said, "When I fly the wing, I sometimes have strange thoughts."

"What kinds of strange thoughts?"

Clauda studied her plate. She looked about the room. She seemed to be searching for some way out of admitting whatever it was to Haly. This made Haly more determined than ever to wrest the truth from her.

"You're keeping me waiting."

"Forgive me, Holy One. Sometimes, when I fly the wing, I think that things were very different, not long ago. You and I . . . we were friends, not master and servant. And . . . Ilysies . . . Empress Thela . . . we did not look upon her as the wise benefactor that she is." Clauda laughed, but it sounded forced. "It must be the altitude, that makes such ridiculous notions seem real."

A little shiver crept up Haly's spine. She stood and closed the shutter on the window to block the draft. "Obviously. Don't trouble yourself over such things. Put them firmly from your mind and focus on doing your duty."

As they stepped out of Haly's chamber, they encountered a Nod huddling against the wall on the other side of the hallway. It was the first one Haly had seen in days, and it looked ill. Its skin, normally a robust red, was pink, with alarming patches of gray here and there. It trembled, as if from weakness or fever. "What does she say?" it croaked.

Concerned, Haly got to her knees and examined the creature more closely. Its eyes were rheumy, the whites yellow. "What's wrong, Nod?"

"The more it writes, the weaker we become."

"The more what writes, Nod?" Haly was confused. "I thought you wanted more people to write."

"Not with that pen."

Haly glanced up at Clauda, who shook her head. "I don't understand, Nod. What can we do to help?"

"Give Nod the pen."

"What pen?"

"The pen of the Makers."

Haly sat back on her heels.

"Do you know what he's talking about?" asked Clauda.

"No. Do you?"

"Makers means the Ancients, right?"

Haly nodded. "I think so."

"Have you ever heard of a pen the Ancients used? Maybe one with special properties?"

"No," said Haly. She picked the Nod up. "Why don't you come with us today, Nod. Maybe Empress Thela can help."

The creature shrieked. "She's the one doing this! She'll destroy us!" The Nod struggled feebly in Haly's grip.

"I'm sure you're mistaken, Nod," said Haly. "Empress Thela is wise and good. She would never hurt you."

"No! She takes Nod's job away!"

Haly sighed. "Come on. You'll see." She tucked the Nod in the crook of her arm and turned to Clauda. "Let's go."

Po peered through the curtain of the litter that bore him along the parade route. Directly ahead of him was the platform where Empress Thela sat in state, accepting the accolades of the crowds that surrounded them. They were still in the city of Ilysies but many people from the countryside had come into town in the past day or so to see the spectacle from its outset. They would follow along as the procession left the city, wound up through the mountains, and then continued out onto the plain.

Thela sat on a throne even grander than the Lit King's had been. Jolaz sat at Thela's right hand, soberly nodding, and on the whole, looking rather embarrassed by all the fuss. Po had only met her briefly. He had gotten the impression she was not at all pleased with recent events.

Selene sat at Thela's left side, and her gaze was for her mother alone. It gave Po a very funny feeling, the way the princess doted on her mother. It wasn't right. Though, of course, Thela was worthy of admiration from one and all, the blind love in Selene's face when she greeted her mother didn't fit with the former Libyrarian's personality. For that matter, it was unlike her to relinquish her post as a Libyrarian and agree to serve her mother's interests in the Corvariate Citadel.

Po searched the crowds, hoping against hope for some glimpse of Ayma, Haly, Clauda, or even, Mother help him, Siblea. But of course it was a pointless pursuit. The chances that he would spot them, even if they were still alive, were miniscule. He chided himself for even entertaining the idea that any of them still lived, except that he could not rule out the possibility that Thela might have lied in order to destroy his hope and make him more biddable.

Only it had not had the effect she might have hoped for. Despite everything, he found himself often imagining a life with Hilloa that was entirely unlike anything he'd ever known. That time that they'd spent together in the citadel, terrifying as it had been, had also been unique. Once they had gotten past their expectations of each other they had been as equals, neither asking of the other anything they themselves were not ready to give. He was glad he'd had a chance to experience that.

The first stop on the procession was traditionally the Barley King's hometown, and they did not deviate from that custom. After a long day traveling up into the foothills of the Lian Mountains, they reached his village at dusk.

The gentle rays of the setting sun cast the little town in golden tones of nostalgia. There was the big olive tree in the center square, with the spring beside it marked out with white stones. The small houses scattered about the hillside were made of the same stone, which glowed amber in the sunset.

It seemed like the whole town came out to meet them, led by Po's mother, his aunt Minerva, and Magistrate Malinas. It was strange to see them again. They looked so much older, and smaller.

The procession came to a halt beneath the spreading branches of the big olive tree and Empress Thela descended from her litter. Po's mother dipped a cup of water from the spring and offered it to Thela. "These waters feed the Ilysi River; may they nourish you as well, my queen."

"As one mother to another, I gratefully accept your gift, and am renewed by it, as the land will accept and be renewed by the gift of the fruit of your womb. Today you are a mother, tomorrow you will be the mother of all Ilysies."

Thela drank, and the whole town erupted in cheering.

Wine was brought forth and lanterns were hung in the trees. Drums began to play. Po was escorted down from his litter by his mother and his aunt. "I'm so proud of you!" said Minerva, beaming.

His mother grabbed him and hugged him hard. She pulled his head down to her shoulder. Po felt like he was a little boy again. All around them people were celebrating, but she held him so tight he could barely breathe. "I'm so sorry," she whispered in his ear. "I never would have sent you to the palace if I'd known this would happen." He heard her stifle a sob.

"The queen is waiting for us to drink with her, Philomena, and all the village women will want to dance with Po tonight," said Minerva. "Come."

Po's mother crushed him to her once more and then released him, standing back, forcing a smile through her tears. "Wait!" Po grabbed for her hand, but Minerva drew her away with a firm arm around her shoulders and a determined smile. Meanwhile, more women were gathering around Po.

"Will the Barley King honor me with the first dance?" asked Magistrate Malinas.

Po had never been the center of so much attention in his life. Women of all ages, shapes, and sizes waited for their chance to dance with him. They plied him with cups of wine and morsels of food. He quickly got drunk, which made it easier to forget that he was going to die the next day, and that made it easier to enjoy the party.

He didn't see his mother again that day.

Po awoke in his litter, his head pounding. The procession was already leaving town and the lurching of his platform made his stomach roil. He thrust open the curtain and leaned over the edge of the platform and was sick.

The morning sun was harsh in his eyes, sharpening his headache to a piercing agony. The sun that had been so gentle the evening before now cast the village in a harsh light. Blinking, Po took in the cast-off cups stained with wine, the scattered bones of roast fowl, and greasy papers that had held fried dough sticks.

Most of the village followed them. Po pulled his head back inside. He thought of looking out the back to see if he could spot his mother, but he wasn't sure he wanted to. There was nothing she could do for him. Seeing her would just make more pain for both of them.

In another hour or two, they would be at the place where the ceremony would occur. Soon he would walk to the chopping block and face the Destroyer. He did not want to. He thought of all the times he had offered up his life, in mortification, in guilt and fear and desperation. He'd had no idea what he was really talking about. He did not want to die. He missed his life already. His village, his mother and his aunt and his cousins. His life at the palace and at the Libyrinth. Adept Ykobos, Myr, Haly, Burke, Ock, Zam. He wanted all of it back. He did not want this honor. He wanted the chance to find out who he might become, if he could ever put to use the lesson of the Redemption.

As if in response to his thoughts, the sky turned black and the ground glowed white. People screamed. Po felt a tearing sensation, not so much inside as all around and through him. Did the others feel that as well? In the next breath, everything was back to normal again. He looked up ahead, and saw Thela writing in Endymion's journal with the pen. What was she doing now?

Po had the now-familiar sensation of something slipping from his consciousness. It was a fine, clear day, and had been since morning.

The Plain of Ayor was not flat like the Great Plains on Old Earth's North America. It undulated. The procession wound up and down low, gently sloping hills and valleys. It was a perfect day.

It was early afternoon by the time they reached the place where the ceremony would take place. It was a large, shallow depression similar to the one in which the Libyrinth was situated. It was almost perfectly round, and in its center was a flat slab of rock. Po could not seem to take his eyes off of that rock. He imagined his blood spilling over it.

He remembered what he'd written with the pen that night before Plata challenged Thela: "Queen Thela will know Redemption," and "The story Kip told Po in the vegetable garden at Minerva's house in the town of Nikos is true."

Kip's tale. An old goat's beard about how men's tears and blood make plants grow. Would there be a lush jungle here, this evening?

Wind fluttered the canopy of Po's litter and on the other side of the valley, the wing came to rest. Po's heart pounded harder as he saw Haly and Clauda disembark, along with Siblea and several others.

Empress Thela's procession came to a halt and attendants scurried about, setting up a long table and laying out a feast. Selene came to Po's litter and waited while he disembarked. She looked at him as if she were lost. He thought perhaps he looked the same way. Neither of them said a word as Thela summoned them to meet the delegation from the Libyrinth.

Haly smiled and embraced him. Po closed his eyes, breathing in her smell and remembering the day she had confided in him that she was not sure the community would make it. "Oh, Po, we're all so proud of you," she said.

At her words, Po's last hope died. She embraced the ritual. She had hated it before. He remembered how angry she'd been when he'd suggested it all those weeks ago, after Thela had tricked him and set fire to the Libyrinth's crop. But now, everything was different. Everyone was different.

Clauda, too, embraced him. She said little. Like Selene, she seemed to be perpetually slightly confused, as if she sensed something was wrong but could not put a name to it. Haly had with her a Nod, a poor, sickly one. As Thela approached them it screeched and launched itself at her. "She must give it back!"

Thela backed up and one of her guards stepped in front of her. The guard seized the Nod by the neck.

"Stop!" said Haly. "I apologize, Empress." She bowed low. "But please, restrain your woman from harming the Nod. It is sacred to us."

Thela's eyes narrowed as she stared at the creature struggling in the guard's grip. "Odd custom."

Po had a feeling a note would be made, and soon, regarding the Nods, or the lack thereof.

Thela nodded, and Clauda retrieved the Nod from the guard. "I will put it where it cannot disturb us," she said.

They all sat down, Po in the place of honor between Haly and Thela. Across from them sat his mother, his aunt, and Magistrate Malinas. After one lone, doleful stare, Po and his mother didn't look at each other again. He could not eat, could not concentrate on the conversation around him. Down in the valley, near the flat rock which would be the last thing he'd see, the musicians were setting up. Already he felt the pulse of the drums in his bloodstream, marking out the remaining beats of his heart. His mouth was dry. He wanted to get up and run. But he couldn't do that.

He looked up and down the table. Everyone was eating and talking and laughing. How could they do that? How could they carry on as if everything was fine when his life was about to end? He wanted to cry out, to beg for help. But he couldn't do that, either.

The sky went black. Everything that was light colored went dark. Everything that was dark colored went light. It was as if the whole world became its opposite. It didn't go away immediately this time. In the space between two wagons on the far side of the valley, Po saw four figures in robes.

"What is this?" said Haly, and she turned to Thela. "What have you done?"

Clauda stood and hastened in the direction of the wing. "She's doing it all, somehow. Making us think these things."

Haly was on her feet and confronting Queen Thela. "What have you done?"

The world snapped back to its regular appearance. For

a moment everyone stared about in silence. Clauda, already several paces away, stood very still. Haly looked at Thela and then at Po as if wondering how and why she was standing there, leaning toward the empress in this confrontational way. Then she straightened and took her seat. Clauda returned to the table. Everyone resumed eating again. Po looked back to where he'd seen the robed figures, but they were gone.

From nearby, Po heard thumping and muffled shrieks. A crate that had been used to store dishes was shaking. Clauda kept glancing that way, though everyone else ignored it. Po caught Clauda's eye. She mouthed one word: Nod.

The meal ended. As servants began clearing away the dishes, Po wished he had the pen so he could bring time to a stop.

Jolaz and Selene led him to a tent where he was dressed in the ceremonial tunic and anointed with verbena oil. The crown of barley was placed upon his head. Each of the women embraced him. He clung to Selene. "I don't want this," he whispered.

"Shh," she said. "My mother is wise. Your sacrifice will make the land fertile."

"It already is fertile."

"Po, it must be done."

"You didn't used to be like this. You hated this."

"Now, now. That's enough, Po. You're imagining things."

Jolaz took Po's hand, very gently, and drew it away from Selene. She could squeeze it if she wished. Po took a deep breath against the tears that threatened to spill from his eyes and he let himself be drawn away. Still he stared at Selene, willing her to remember.

Selene held open the tent flap and Po stepped through. People lined up on either side of the opening, creating a human corridor down which he must walk. The drums beat. He took the first step. The observers threw rose petals upon him and in his path. Po tasted bile at the back of his throat, a sharp contrast to the sweet smell of the blossoms.

He had wanted this, many times, and now he had it. There was no escape. The best he could hope for was that what he had written with the pen would come to pass. Po exhaled and took the next step.

It was both ages and an instant, that he walked the corridor of celebrants amid blossoms. It wound around the rim of the valley and spiraled down. The drums were an echo of the blood pounding in his ears. At every turn of the corridor, he expected to see her: the Destroyer, with her scythe.

The faces of the people glowed. They beamed at him, grateful for his gift. He was barefoot. The drums were like the heartbeat of the world; he felt it as a living thing beneath his feet, and as he walked to his death, he breathed with it.

Kinesthetic trance came over him as smoothly and effortlessly as a wave of water. One step, and he was Po, walking between rows of people, and when his next step landed, he was with the whole world.

This world was broken and had been broken many times before. His shattered hands ached with the pain of it. Each time the pen was used, another bone was broken. Human bones mended in time, and so did these, though neither would ever be the same shape again. But he was just a person. The world had to hold up all of them, and since the pen had been discovered, it had been wielded far too many times. The forces that gave their world structure were crumbling.

Po dropped to his knees. "I will crawl the rest of the way," he announced. He had heard of Barley Kings doing such things and it being remarked upon as a sign of special devotion. He strongly suspected it was just a delaying tactic. In his case, it was going to be painful. He breathed deeply and stayed with the pain of the world. When he went down on his elbows and wrists, it still hurt like hell. But now he could use his hands. He pressed them against the ground, heedless of the pain, the tears and sweat that rolled from him in beads. He closed his eyes, forced himself to keep crawling, keep breathing.

He expected that if a visualization came, it would be something organic, a tree or a flower or a forest. Those were the forms his mind usually used to represent the energies he experienced in kinesthetic trance. But this time, what came was a memory.

He was in the Great Hall at the Libyrinth, that day after lunch when he'd argued with Siblea for the first time. Hilloa was showing them all her sticks-and-bag model of the universe. "The sticks can be anything," she said, and her words floated in the air between them, letters made out of tiny sticks. Po crawled along the winding length of one of those sticks and it, too, was made of letters, winding and twining around one another.

Now he was back on the ground, on his way to the sacrificial altar. The people on either side of him were dense collections of words, each a story unto itself, as was every grain of soil beneath him.

Stories were made of words, and words were made of

sounds. Song and Story. Hilloa's sticks were still vibrations, no matter what you called them. It was all rhythm, movement, life. Strings of words, thoughts, intentions, and wishes all wound together to form sinuous vines which in turn formed everything. They were songlines, the Name of the Ocean, the Last Wind of the World. They were the fabric of existence.

Only something was wrong with them. They had gaps in them, and in other places they had thickened where more had been added that did not belong. Breaks, scar tissue. He focused on one of those breaks and very nearly fell through it, into another dimension entirely. He glimpsed it in the distance: a flat desert plain and a great metal sphere. He clung to the edge of a letter, one in a language he did not recognize, his hands screaming. He used the pain as a rope, to connect with the other half of the broken letter, making up the portion that had been erased. The effort left him exhausted, drained of more than just strength. But it wasn't enough. The rents were everywhere. If he tried to mend them all he would die.

Everything shook and he opened his eyes. He had been crawling, all this time. Back in his body, the pain of his hands was overwhelming. He gasped. Tears ran down his face and dripped onto the ground. Where they landed, green things sprouted. Kip's story was coming true. He had made it so with the pen. Was that better because it was a story that was already told in this world, or worse, or of no consequence either way?

Ahead of him he saw Haly and Clauda at the end of the line. He was almost there. He glanced behind him. Flowers and grasses grew in a trail behind him. He came at last to the end of the line. There was the rock that would be his sacrificial altar, and beside it stood Thela, dressed in the red robe of the Destroyer, with the scythe in her hand.

19

Sacrifice

He knelt before Thela and she lifted him up. She kissed him and held him close. "Your gift will bring prosperity to the whole land."

Over her shoulder, Po saw a trail of flowers and vines sprouting up where he had crawled. He didn't want to die, but at least this time her words were not just symbolic. He lay down upon the altar stone, his eyes meeting hers as she raised the scythe.

The world flickered to its negative image again. A thunderclap rang out and an arc of argent fire split the sky. At first it looked like a winding arc of lightning running from horizon to horizon, but then the fissure widened, pushing back the darkness on both sides. Thela looked up and her mouth opened in shock. "Stop!" shouted Haly.

Turning his head, Po could see her running toward them. Over her shoulder she called out to Clauda, "Get Nod."

The plants he had brought to life with his tears withered and died. Haly was acting like Haly again. And behind her, there was a disturbance and he heard Selene yelling something he could not make out. Everything that had been written with the pen was unraveling. Which meant he did not have to obey Thela, either.

The scythe whistled through the air and Po rolled to the side. The blade missed his neck but he felt a sharp pain as it nicked his cheek. "Lie still!" yelled Thela.

Po jumped to his feet. Over her shoulder he saw three robed figures striding down the slope of the valley toward him. Amid all the reversed hues, they alone looked normal. Their robes were brown, their faces tan—three faces he never thought he'd see again.

Thela set the scythe aside and pulled the pen from her robe.

Po plowed into her, knocking them both to the ground. As they fell he saw the pen fly from her hand.

She landed on his right hand and he blacked out from the pain. When he opened his eyes again, he was on his back, on the altar stone. She stood above him with the scythe, and beyond her, the sky was tearing itself apart. The scintillating line of lightning had widened to a river, ever growing, the argent light pushing back the darkness on both sides. Rain fell, but it was not rain. Flakes of paper drifted down, like ash or snow. One landed on his nose and he briefly saw the word "and" before it crumbled to dust.

Thela raised the scythe. "Don't worry, Po," she said.

"Your sacrifice will put all this chaos to an end. I've written that it will be so."

Po tried to roll away but she was standing on his arm. He closed his eyes. He heard a clatter and a scream, and felt a piercing pain in his shoulder. His shoulder?

"Yammon's tonsils, Jan, you almost killed him yourself."

"Sorry. My hand slipped."

He knew those voices. The pressure on his arm was gone. He sat up. Jan and Baris each had Queen Thela by one arm, and Hilloa knelt by his side. All three of them looked normal, unlike everything else. Thela struggled in their grip but they did not let go. Jan wrested the scythe from Thela's hands and threw it to the ground.

Po looked at Hilloa. She reached out and touched his face. Her hand was warm. "You're back," he said.

She smiled. "We thought we found you, and got caught by Thela, but now . . . here we are." She frowned. "Where are we, anyway?"

Po couldn't answer her. He pulled her to him and held her tight, burying his face in her hair. He breathed in the smell of her. She was alive.

"No! It's mine!" cried Thela. Hilloa pulled away and Po looked up to see Haly holding the pen and Thela struggling in Jan and Baris's grip. Thela broke away and threw herself at Haly. She wrapped her hands around Haly's neck, choking her. "Give it to me."

Po picked up the scythe, ignoring the agony that lanced up his arms as he used his fingers to grip the haft.

The women rolled over and over. His grip on the scythe was clumsy. He was just as likely to do Haly harm as Thela. He dropped the implement and wrapped his arms around Thela, crying out as the struggling bodies bumped and bashed his barely mended bones. He pulled Thela away and held her tight as she struggled. His arms were wrapped tightly around her rib cage. He was taller than her, and stronger. It worked. Haly got to her feet, breathing hard.

"No!" Thela fought and kicked and writhed as Haly stepped back, holding the pen. "You abomination!" Thela screamed at him. He had no answer for that.

The ground beneath them shook. Po stumbled. Thela landed a foot hard on his instep. He gasped and she broke free and lunged at Haly, who was a few paces away, examining the pen. "Look out!" shouted Po, and leaped after Thela.

Haly dodged to one side. Thela tried to swerve to grab the pen from her but Po collided with her before she could turn. Thela went tumbling toward the altar stone. The ground shook again and she fell. Po grabbed for her but his hands, which had endured a great deal already, simply could not grasp her in time. They clutched at empty air. There was a horrible, slicing, crunching sound and the blade of the scythe poked out the front of Thela's robe, blood dripping from its blade.

Thela stared at him, astonished. She reached for him and he went to her.

"Ithalia."

She blinked and gave the faintest of nods. "I can see now. If I could just have stayed Ithalia."

He nodded. Footsteps crunched behind him and he saw Selene standing there. "Mother."

Po moved aside and Selene took her mother's hand. "I'm sorry," said Thela. "I didn't understand, but now . . .

now I see . . ." Thela stared at Selene until the light went out of her eyes.

Selene dropped her hand and turned to Po.

"I'm sorry, Selene, I—"

She shook her head. "No. Not another word of apology from you." And then she grabbed him, held him tight, her tears damp against his shoulder. "Seven Tales, we almost killed you."

The ground beneath them heaved and they fell to their knees. "We're all going to die if this keeps up," he said.

"What is it? What's happening?"

He was about to try to encapsulate everything he knew about the pen, but that was when Clauda showed up with Nod.

The creature took one look at Po and pointed at him. "He must finish what he began."

Haly, Clauda, and Selene all looked at Po.

"I don't know what he means," he said.

"Mend the letters," said Nod, "and destroy the pen."

A shiver ran through Po. He stared at Nod. "I can't, there are too many. It hurts too much. I'll—"

"Nod will help."

Would Nod prevent him from dying? Po doubted it. Haly, Clauda, and Selene were looking between Po and Nod. "What are you talking about?" said Selene.

Po didn't want to explain it to them. He wasn't sure if that was because they'd ask it of him also, or try to talk him out of it. He reached out and put his hand on Nod's head. He tried to breathe with Nod. Nod did not breathe, but the kinesthetic trance came over him all the same and he knew that what they all saw as Nod, whether plural or singular, was really just the extrusion into this plane of existence of a much, much larger being. If this could be done, Nod would make it possible.

The ground shook again and another arc of lightning joined the first, quartering the sky now. "He must hurry!"

Po nodded. "Put him on my back," Po told Clauda, getting to his hands and knees.

"But your hands!" said Haly.

It didn't matter. The pain was now so constant, he hardly noticed the slicing sensation as his fingers touched the ground. No, he still did not want to die, but at least this was for something more than a queen's ego and a nation's pride. Po breathed with the world and gave her broken body his pain, his blood, his love, and his life.

Haly watched as Po, on his hands and knees, closed his eyes and began to crawl. Nod rode on his shoulders, carrying the pen. It was the oddest spectacle of all the many bizarre things she had witnessed that day.

At first, whatever they were doing seemed to have no effect. But gradually the tremors in the earth ceased and the sky began to close up again. And then the light returned to normal.

That was when they noticed that other things were returning as well. The lushness of the land, for instance, and something else much more troubling. Haly caught herself thinking how appropriate it was that Po gave himself to the land like a true Barley King. She started and grabbed Selene by the arm.

Selene returned an equally horrified look. "I just thought

that I should spend the rest of my days creating a perfect statue of my mother, in gold, and carry it about from village to village so all might revere her."

Clauda glanced between both of them. "The changes Queen Thela wrought with the pen are reasserting themselves now that the destabilization is being mended." Haly looked about at the assembled crowd. Many people were looking torn, confused.

A chill ran through Haly. "Where are Baris, Hilloa, and Jan?"

They looked about, but could not find them.

"Nod," she shouted, and ran in the direction of Po's hunched form.

If anything, the vegetation around Po, and wherever he had been, was the thickest of all. Vines and shoots wrapped around his arms and legs, continually being uprooted and sprouting again when he moved.

Nod glared at her as she approached. "She must not interfere!"

"But Nod, everything the pen wrought is coming back."

"Yes, well, if beasties do not like what they write then perhaps they should choose some less permanent place to experiment."

"But it wasn't us, Nod. It was Queen Thela. It was all Queen Thela."

"Huh. She does not know as much as she thinks she does."

"You're right. But please, can you just . . . undo what she wrote? Can you do that?"

"You'll make the land barren again," said Clauda.

"But we're losing who we are!"

"You want to retain your true nature?"

"Yes!"

"Very well, then." Using both hands, Nod wrote with the pen, "The things Thela Tadamos wrote with her pen will not change the basic nature of those they concern."

"That's . . . is that . . . ?"

"That's better," said Selene.

Nod lifted the pen again.

"Nod, what are you—"

"If beasties keep tinkering this boy will die for nothing. Is that what she wants?"

"No!"

Nod wrote, "The pen no longer exists."

And it was gone.

"Wait!" cried Haly. "Hilloa, Baris, and Jan! Where did they go?"

"They're gone," said Selene. "Gone."

"That's done now," said Nod. "No more back and forth. He is almost finished. Not so many gaps left now, but he needs Nod's help and Nod can only do this from the outside. No getting back in again, either. I must go while there is still space." He looked up at Haly. "Thank you for my story." And with that, he became smaller and smaller, until he disappeared.

This was the last of the repairs, and Po was at the end of all that he had to offer. He reached across the gap in existence with splintered fingers and pulled the ends of the broken strands together. As they joined, he felt the Song, once more in tune, thrumming through the whole of being. He let go, and let it take him.

20

Journey to the Bottom of the Libyrinth

Haly, Clauda, and Selene gathered around Po's prone body. He lay on his stomach, arms outstretched, barely visible amid the lush vegetation that sprang up all around him.

Haly turned to Selene. "Fetch Adept Ykobos, will you?"

Selene nodded. How pale she looked, how drawn. Haly supposed they must all look like that, haunted by the things they had done under Thela's rule.

Haly herself remembered acting the haughty queen, ordering around those nearby her—particularly the men. Oh, Tales, Gyneth—she looked about for him, but before she could find him, Selene had returned with Adept Ykobos.

The adept's robes were stained with blood. Haly guessed she'd been trying to revive her fallen queen. "Thela is dead," said Ykobos, confirming Haly's surmise.

Haly sighed, unable to prevent the rush of relief that coursed through her at those words.

"What of Po?" she asked. "Is he alive?"

Ykobos knelt beside his prone form. She placed one hand between his shoulder blades and closed her eyes. Seconds later her eyes sprang open again and she pulled her hand back as if burned. "Mother," she murmured, standing.

A tremor shook the earth and they all fought for balance. Ykobos stared at Po, alarm etched in the arch of her brows.

"What?" said Selene. "What is it?"

"Po," said Clauda. "Is he . . ." She broke away from Haly and knelt at his side. She reached out to touch him, to roll him over.

"Don't!" cried Ykobos.

"Why?" said Haly. "What's going on, Adept? What did you feel?"

Ykobos crossed her arms and tucked her hands in her armpits, as if she could block herself off from the world. "He's deep in trance. It's not like anything I've ever encountered before. He's . . . connected with . . . with everything. The whole world. . . ."

The sky flickered again and the ground trembled.

"He's holding it together," she finished.

"Holding it together?" said Selene. "What does that mean?"

"It means what it means," said Ykobos. "He's enmeshed with an energy structure the size of which I've never encountered before. I think it's the whole world."

"Thela's use of the pen weakened the fabric of existence," said Clauda.

"And Po's using his own energy to strengthen the fibers," said Selene.

"Or at least prevent them from unraveling entirely, yes," said Ykobos.

"But he's just one boy," said Haly. "How can he survive that?"

"Nod is helping, right?"

"But Nod was weakened, too."

"What if they both fail? How can he survive?"

Ykobos stared at her in stony silence for a moment. "He won't. And when he dies, the world will die with him."

Clauda shook her head. She stared at Haly, a crease between her brows. "He's not going to die. If the pen weakened the fabric of reality, and Po's now holding it together, then that means we have to find a way to strengthen those fundamental structures again."

"That's easier said than done," said Haly. "We don't even know what those structures are, let alone how to fortify them if we did."

But Clauda knew what they were.

"This world was made by the People Who Walk Sideways in Time," she said. "One of their own devices broke it. What can be broken can be mended. We'll fix it and then he can let go and come back to us."

They all stared at her. No one wanted to point out the truth. "We're not the People Who Walk Sideways in Time," said Haly. "Such things are beyond us."

If possible, Clauda's expression became even more fierce. "For shame! The Ancients were once ordinary people—Earth people. With the same body of knowledge at their disposal as we have, they figured out how to harness universes and create new worlds. Nothing is impossible unless we let it be," she said, and headed off toward the Libyrinth.

Selene sat on the western edge of the community, beyond the fields, where scattered rocks dotted the low hills. She stared off into the undulating, barren landscape. If it weren't for Clauda, Selene might just do herself and everyone else a favor and walk out into the western plain, never to return.

Her guilt over Po was a bottomless well, but what she hadn't expected was the searing sense of loss at her mother's death.

Regret dogged her every step. Time and again she imagined herself pushing Thela aside before the blade could pierce her heart, and then Thela, looking up at her in gratitude.

It wasn't so far-fetched. Before they had wound up on opposite sides of Thela's quest for power, she'd often shown affection for Selene.

And Selene had rebuffed her. Now, every unanswered letter, every cold, resentful retort came back to haunt her. And to think that once she'd thought Thela's absence would set her free.

"Hey, cut that out."

It was Clauda. Selene turned and raised an eyebrow, trying to look innocent.

"Don't pretend you don't know what I'm talking about," she said. "You're doing it again. Wallowing in regret. You have to stop."

Clauda was right. What she was doing was self-indulgent,

and it wasn't getting them any closer to stabilizing their world or helping Po. "I'm sorry."

Clauda sighed. "That's not what I mean. You're already sorry enough. You're too sorry. I'm not trying to give you something else to be sorry about."

Selene nodded. "Sor—" She stopped herself.

Clauda laughed and gave her a sideways hug. Selene savored the weight of Clauda's head against her shoulder. "C'mere," said Clauda.

She led Selene to the shelter of a rock outcrop. They sat down facing each other. "Selene, can you remember a time when you didn't worry?"

The question caught her off guard. "I've never thought about it."

Clauda nodded. "Well, think about it. Now. I'll wait."

Selene contemplated the question. At length, she said, "When I was small, I used to visit my sire, Van. This would have been . . . I guess I was about six. Mother set him aside after I was born—he was old—but she gave him a nice villa in town and he was surrounded by friends. He had this wonderful garden, and a library that let right onto it. I loved it there. We'd play hide-and-seek and then I'd browse through the library. He'd let me take any book I wanted and read it in the garden. There was this pear tree there with low branches and I'd climb up there and read for hours."

"I've never heard you mention your father before."

Selene nodded. "He was very intelligent, gentle, and kind. He had a keen sense of humor and he loved to laugh."

"Was. He's passed now?"

Selene nodded. If Clauda's aim was to cheer her up,

this wasn't working. She felt as if she could dissolve into tears at any moment.

"What happened?"

"The little lion inside devoured him."

Clauda's lips parted, but she seemed at a loss. "I'm so sorry. How old were you?"

"Twelve."

"That was when your mother chose her heir, too?"

"Yes." Selene had never really put the two events into context with each other. She'd been heartbroken over Van's death. And when her mother chose Jolaz as her heir, and by necessity started focusing her time and attention on her successor, she'd been terribly jealous of Jolaz, though even then, she had no desire for the throne.

"So you lost both of them," said Clauda, summing it up with characteristic bluntness.

"I didn't think of it that way, but I suppose it's true." Selene watched a beetle crawl across the ground and disappear beneath a rock. "She was willing to sacrifice me. Why should I care that she's gone?"

"She was the only mother you have. Just because she wasn't a good one, just because you really are better off without her, that doesn't mean you can't mourn her. As long as she was alive there was always the chance of mending your relationship."

Selene raised an eyebrow.

"Okay, a very slim chance, but now she's taken even that away."

Selene glared at Clauda, suddenly overwhelmed with anger. "What is your point?" Goddess, the little Ayorite could be annoying.

"That's right," said Clauda. "Be mad. At me, at Thela or Mab or the cancer that killed Van. At Time, the Seven Tales, or the Song, but not at yourself, Selene."

"And why shouldn't I take responsibility for my actions?" she said.

"If that's what you're doing, it'd be one thing, but it's not. What happened to Po is not your fault. And you're not responsible for anything else Thela did, either. You're beating yourself up for things you had no control over, and it's crippling you, and we need you."

Selene sank her face in her hands. "I'm trying, Clauda. Believe it or not, I'm trying as hard as I can."

"That's why I think you need a different approach. It's why I asked you about a time when you were carefree. Here." Something nudged Selene in the shoulder.

She looked up to see Clauda holding out a book and a pen. Frowning, Selene took the items. She opened the book. The pages were blank. "What's this?"

"You're always reading, Selene. And you're always trying to contain your feelings. I think you need to reverse that flow. I think you need to let yourself feel everything, and write it all down."

Haly combed the stacks, focusing her attention on one volume after another, searching for anything that might lead to an answer to their dilemma.

"All of the adults are talking about the flu pandemic. A lot of people are sick and can't get upgrades." It was a book voice.

Haly could hear other voices as well, the voices of people. Teams searched the stacks on foot now. The Liby-

rinth was an elaborate clockwork and the frequent tremors had bent the tracks upon which the shelves ran,
rendering them inoperable. Bit by bit, they were loosing
everything they'd gained since the Redemption.

"People can't get upgrades because nobody can say for
sure that the source code hasn't been corrupted. I can't
believe this. I was supposed to upgrade next week. This is
so unfair!"

The voice, despite its outrage, was faint, as if it came
from a great distance. If that was the case, then it must
be information she badly needed to hear.

"I told Lysander she wanted to be a meat puppet."

Haly walked in one direction, and then another, trying
to judge if the voice got any louder.

After some trial and error, she thought she'd pinpointed
the direction of the book, but in the maze of shelves, it was
impossible to travel in a straight line.

A long corridor of shelves forced her to go at right angles to her desired heading and when she came to the end
of it, and could at last turn in the direction she needed,
she realized that the voices of the other Libyrarians had
fallen silent, as had the book she'd been searching for.
And the books around her were ones she'd never known
before.

"Moving cautiously, she continued down the street.
No rubbish cluttered the gutters here; no cars were parked
at the curb."

"Declining the bridge, they took the Mickle Boulevard
exit and looped east into the city's bleak, rubbled heart."

"Already we have gone out of our depth."

Haly couldn't believe it. After a childhood spent wandering these stacks she had contrived to get lost in the

Libyrinth now, at this late date. "Hello! Anyone?" she shouted as she'd been doing intermittently for the past several hours, but the only voices that answered her were those of books.

Disbelief gave way to panic. Haly resisted the urge to run. The best thing to do was stay where she was. She knew that. She turned in a circle in the little alcove she'd halted in, stretching her awareness out, searching for books she knew.

If she could find just one of them, she could use it to guide her back to familiar territory.

" 'You've never been this far outside before, have you?' he said at last."

"In this freedom, they ride the waves of birth and death in perfect peace."

"We made so many deviations up and down lanes, and were such a long time delivering a bedstead at a public-house, and calling at other places, that I was quite tired, and very glad, when we saw Yarmouth."

But these books were all strange to her.

She went to the end of the aisle and looked up and down the next passage. At the end of that passage she found that it came to a dead end. A shelf of books had come off its track and pressed up against those on the other side.

She turned around and went back the way she came; only now she couldn't remember if *Understanding Our Mind* was where she'd turned to the right, or whether she'd come into this aisle farther up, where *David Copperfield* recited his tale.

This was ridiculous. She of all people couldn't get lost in the Libyrinth. All she had to do was remember the books she'd heard on her way here.

But she'd been so focused on the distant voice of that one particular book that she hadn't been paying attention.

Suddenly, the maze of the Libyrinth seemed vaster than it ever had before. Haly felt it stretching out around her in all directions. No one knew where it ended. Maybe it never did. She could wander in here forever, never finding her way to daylight.

The narrow-spaced shelves pressed in upon her. The books, always her companions in the past, now seemed forbidding, alien. She didn't know any of these books. She didn't belong here. This was their world, a world of words, not meant for mortal beings.

Haly had never felt so small or alone, even when she'd been a prisoner of the Singers.

Her breath came in rapid gasps. She fought down the panic, forcing herself to breathe deep. She'd be fine. She had plenty of food. All she had to do was find one book she knew, and follow its voice to known territory.

She stretched her awareness out, searching for the first title that came to mind—*The Curse of Chalion*—but she couldn't hear it. Too far away, no doubt.

"Haly? Haly!"

It was Gyneth. Haly's heart leaped. "Here!" she shouted. "I'm over here!"

Through the shelves she saw lights. She heard their footsteps. "Stay where you are. I'm coming!"

Relief flooded her with warmth, and then Gyneth turned the corner and she threw herself into his arms. "I was lost," she said. "Lost."

"Yes," he said, his voice shaking. "But I found you."

*　*　*

I think we turn here," said Gyneth.

"But we've been at this corner before," said Haly. "And that passage leads downward. We keep spiraling downward. We need to try and go up."

"Well, what do you think we should do? Do you know any of these books at all?"

She didn't. Humiliation momentarily overcame her frustration and guilt. They'd been wandering around for hours now, trying to find their way. In rescuing her, Gyneth had only gotten himself lost as well.

"Wait, what's that?" he said, holding out his jar of palm-glow and pointing beyond the corner in question. Something gleamed a different color than the shelves around them.

They hastened toward it and found a railing surrounding a narrow, spiral staircase similar to the one that led down from beneath the seal in the center of the Great Hall.

"Another staircase," said Gyneth.

"But it leads down," said Haly. "We need to go up."

Gyneth looked at her. In the shadowy green light of the palm-glow, she could see the gleam in his eyes. "But I wonder where it leads."

"Gyneth—"

"It's not like we're getting anywhere anyhow. And we have plenty of food and water. Besides, we might find something down there that will help us make it back up again."

"Like an elevator?"

"Who knows?"

Haly stared at him. "I don't want us to wind up like my parents, two skeletons huddled in the stacks."

"We won't. We'll be careful."

Haly sighed. "Well, maybe just a little ways."

They descended the lace-like iron spiral staircase. It seemed to be a continuation of the one that led down to the face, which meant they should be able to get back again, later, if they could find where the face was from the level where this staircase began.

Around them the songlines in the tunnel glowed. It was like moving through a column of air in the ocean, surrounded by undulating, sun-spangled water.

The Song was so strong here she felt it humming though her body. What would happen if she tried to focus on an individual book voice right now? She reached out for the one that flickered in and out of her awareness so unpredictably.

Haly stretched her awareness out in all directions, using the unity of the Song to sift through words like grains of sand.

"Grant is not getting updates on his link. It's like the whole world is down."

Haly focused her awareness on the voice. Just as before, it skittered away from her, but before it receded into silence once more, she got a flash of an image—a pink notebook laying on a floor somewhere, half obscured by something above it. Just as it faded she got a sense of a direction, far, far below them—deeper than she would have thought possible.

They followed the spiraling staircase down through more and more shelves of books. The shelves became even more closely spaced than they were above, and before long she couldn't make out any shelves at all, just a solid wall of books, pressed against one another and sitting directly atop each other.

She looked at Gyneth. He took in the sight with his mouth open.

Farther down, the bindings of the books began to blend, forming one enormous cylindrical book, countless titles running across its spine.

Haly and Gyneth tightened their grip on each other and continued down. The bindings gave way. Words, free of page, book, and binding swirled around them, spiraling up from a vortex far below.

They had reached the bottom of the staircase now and stood on a little platform. Nothing but a thin metal railing separated them from the maelstrom of words that swirled around them.

"See?" said Gyneth. "This is why I think this world, our world, is made of words and made to enact words. I think we live in a giant machine created by the People Who Walk Sideways in Time to bring their favorite books to life, and that we are the descendents of the characters in whatever book was left playing when they all lost interest and went away, or died off."

"Well, maybe our world is made of words. By Hilloa's theory, anything can make up the dimensions in a pocket universe, and words are sounds and sounds are part of the Song. But I won't accept the idea that we're not real. I don't see the evidence for it, here or in anything else you've shown me."

"Sometimes I think you wouldn't accept it even if you had incontrovertible proof."

"I think you're right."

"What? You admit it?" Gyneth gaped at her.

"Consider what that would mean. If we start believing we're just characters in a book, and we're not real, then it doesn't matter what we do. It's not so important, Gyneth, what the truth is, as how we live and treat one another."

"But . . . don't you want to know?"

She saw the hunger in his face. That thirst to learn, to discover the truth. It was so much stronger than her own. "I never realized how brave you are, and sometimes reckless. But I should have. When I showed you words for the first time—"

"I was horrified."

"Only at first. Soon you were asking me to teach you to write—something that hadn't even occurred to me."

"I remember. I felt so betrayed, at first by you but then by my teachers. I was taught that words would blind me and make me deaf to the Song. When I found out I'd been lied to, I never wanted the truth kept from me again. That's why I want to know what our world really is. That's why I think it's important. The truth may be good and it may be bad, but it belongs to everyone. Lies live in service to those who make them."

She caught her breath. "Oh." She felt as if he'd pulled her back from the edge of an abyss. How close had she come to becoming like Censor Orrin, or the Lit King, or Queen Thela? Had it started like this for them, as well? With all the best intentions and a little human weakness? "I see. Gyneth, thank you. You're right." She took a deep breath, and felt lighter.

He took her hand and squeezed it. "You're not responsible for whatever we discover. You can't control it. Don't demand so much of yourself."

"Okay. But let's go back up now, okay?" she said.

"Yeah, just a minute." He turned to the railing and leaned over it.

"What are you doing? Be careful."

"I just want to see if I can see the bottom. Is there another layer below the words? What's that made of?"

He leaned even farther out over the railing. Haly started toward him, to grab him and pull him back.

The top of his head bumped into some of the words streaming past. They began to tumble and turn, and the world trembled.

"Oops," he said, and started to back away.

Haly sighed with relief and dropped her arm that she'd flung out to reach for him.

Neither of them spotted the errant *J* until it had snagged in the hood of his robe.

Gyneth gasped as the letter yanked him backward over the railing. Haly lunged for him as he teetered, the metal rail across his back. He cartwheeled his arms.

But the *J* kept pulling. Haly's hands closed over empty air as Gyneth tilted back and fell.

She leaned out over the rail, reaching for him. He grabbed for her hand. As their fingers brushed, the *J* tilted under his full weight and at last let go of him.

"No!" The metal rail bit into Haly's midsection as she tried to reach him but he was already far below her, tumbling through words and space.

"Grab the letters!" she shouted, even as she saw he was trying to do just that. But the letters rolled each time he grasped them. As he fell faster and faster, he could not even catch at them. Haly caught one last glimpse of his face, looking up, eyes wide, lips moving though she couldn't make out what he said. And then he was gone.

21

Endymion's Journal

The book, when she found it, was an odd thing. It was bound in a pink material that was like leather but far more durable, and embossed with yellow flowers and a creature that resembled an Old Earth horse except that it had a single horn in the middle of its forehead.

The cover was fastened shut with a lock, but Haly didn't need to open it to know what it contained.

"This journal is the property of Endymion Harthwaite—Bowes, 9.5."

Haly sat down on the floor of the Libyrinth aisle where she'd found the book. She wasn't sure how long she'd been down here. She still had food, not that she ate much of it. Water was starting to run low, though.

She sighed, staring at the little locked book. She didn't want to listen to it. She wanted to read it. She tore off the little tab holding the book closed, and opened to the first page.

At the top were some numbers: 5.1.3037.

Maybe it was the date. They'd have their own calendar system. Or would they need one if they were outside of time? She set aside the question and began to read.

It will be my upgrade day tomorrow and in celebration, my parents are taking me and my friends to BookWorld. There's already been a great deal of discussion between Lysander and myself over what book we want to play in. They have everything there, and it's constantly updated so you don't have to wait, even if you want a story that someone just published on some obscure little meta site. It's kind of fun to browse. Everything is in Old Earth book form. It's so romantic. Mom gave me this paper diary, so I could make my own notes in a book just like the ones they have. Just like Old Earth.

They even have nonfiction titles, but who would want to play one of those I have no idea. Probably Dylan, he's such a geek.

All of the adults are talking about the flu pandemic. A lot of people are sick and can't get upgrades. Nancy's mom was afraid to let her go and she almost talked all of the parents into canceling the trip, but Lysander's dad said they were all a bunch of scaredy cats and he convinced even Nancy's mom to let her go. So it's all set.

5.2.3037
OMG, Lysander and I spent all day with Yammon today. This is so cool. We found him after he was cap-

tured by the Heteropisceans and tortured, so we got to take care of him. Tomorrow we're going to go with him to Tarsus and help him look for the wing. But we can't tell him where it is. Whenever we try to do something that would interfere with the story as it's written, our words just don't come out. No one can hear them. The idea is that people want to experience the story as it's written. Lysander and I think that's stupid. We want to be in the story, changing it, creating it anew; we want to be characters ourselves, not just spectators.

5.4.3037

So, Grant brought an uplink with him. The idea behind coming to BookWorld is to get away from real life for a while, but Grant can't do without his ChitChat. So anyway, tonight he was checking his messages and he caught a news clip about the pandemic. It's getting much worse. People can't get upgrades because nobody can say for sure that the source code hasn't been corrupted. I can't believe this. I was supposed to upgrade next week. This is so unfair!

5.5.3037

Lysander found me pouting about not being able to upgrade and she gave me what-for. "Don't you realize people are dying?" she said.

Dying? We don't die. That's ridiculous. That's what makes us better than meat puppets like the ones created for BookWorld. They die, we don't. We upgrade. We just keep getting smarter and more powerful and better. How can we die?

I told Lysander she wanted to be a meat puppet. I told
her she was so in love with Yammon that she'd lost all
perspective. She's forgotten that he's just a character in
a book. Not real like us.

5.10.3037
Dylan has a pen. I saw him with it yesterday after we
got back from the climactic battle. He was writing in
the air, something about all the machines having faces.
He must have stolen the pen from his mother, the engineer. I'm going to tell Lysander about it. She hasn't
been speaking to me because I said she wanted to be a
meat puppet but she'll forgive me now. If we can get
the pen from Dylan, we can make Yammon fall in love
with us.

5.12.3037
Our parents were supposed to come and get us today.
They didn't show up. Grant is not getting updates on
his link. It's like the whole world is down. We're sitting here at the BookStation, where they told us to
wait for them. *The Book of the Night* is still playing so
there's nothing to see for miles around but rocky desert and little scrubby bushes. I'd give my cookies just
to check my messages. I'm sure there's a reason they're
late, and if we had access to our mail, our in-boxes
would probably be overflowing with messages from
them explaining everything. But the fucking link is
down. How can that be? The link hasn't been down
since before our parents aggregated. That's old-school,
meat puppet shit, systems going down.

5.25.3037

It's been a week since I wrote in this. Our parents still haven't showed. Most of my friends think they're not coming. They think the pandemic killed everyone. They think we're alive only because we've been unlinked since we've been here, and they think Grant might spread the disease to us through his link. I can hear him screaming even now, though I think he's getting weaker. I just want to go home.

The next entry was dated 7.1.3972. If the first two numbers were months and days, and the last one was the year, then it had been hundreds of years since Endymion's last entry. It read:

The Book of the Night is playing again, and none of us can stop it because Pierce has written that we can't. It's hard to believe now that this was once my favorite book, that I chose over all the others, to be enacted for my birthday. I swear to the Seven Transcendent, if I ever get hold of the pen again, I'm going to set the characters free from their narrative and let the meat puppets take over this whole stupid world.

8.20.4011

The Devouring Silences were slave takers in *The Book of the Night*, but now Lysander and I have reconfigured them to be much more. Pierce must not be permitted to rewrite reality with the pen. He must be opposed. Lysander and Rebecca and I took a Devouring Silence apart and have reconfigured it to seek out rewritten parts of the book and erase them. If it works, we'll capture as many more as we can and reconfigure those as well. For the first time, I feel like there's hope for opposing Pierce and his regime.

3.9.4012

Lysander and I have the pen again! Pierce was so stupid. He got drunk on the Song and left it sitting in plain sight when he passed out.

Well, we don't have to worry about *him* anymore. And now, with the changes we made to the Devouring Silences, we'll never be powerless again!

3.9.4052

I can't believe it. Lysander has betrayed me. She refuses to liberate the meat puppets. And she won't play any new books, either. All she wants to do is work on her pet project, Ilysies, which isn't even part of the book to begin with. But if we play a new book—I want *Bone Dance*—it'll kill all the meat puppets and re-terraform the whole world, so of course she doesn't want that, because Ilysies would be destroyed, too.

I'm going out of my mind. If I have to watch this stupid book play out one more time—even with the variations we made—I'm going to kill them all myself.

The worst part is the end. They're so happy. They're celebrating, and the next instant, they're all just gone. And when they come back again, they're slaves again and they have to do it all over.

4.26.4052

Lysander's been reading this. To punish me for speaking against her, she's using the pen to create "stage plays" in the old theater. It's horrible. She makes the rest of us watch. I thought Pierce was bad but she's much worse. I have to figure out a way to stop her. Either get the pen away from her somehow, or . . . I don't know, something else.

1.12.4389

Rebecca and I are working on a project in secret. I have a way of hiding this journal from everyone now. Even Lysander. She must not know what we're up to.

The first thing is, we must determine if the characters are capable of making the transition from meat puppets to independent beings. I've taken Iscarion as a boy and I'm experimenting on him to find out. He hates it. Hates me, but I have to know. If we do this thing it has to be for something. It's too terrible otherwise.

3.19.4393

I let Iscarion go back to his narrative today. They are overthrowing a powerful regime so there's no need to free them from their narrative just yet. I've told Rebecca to go ahead with the device. If we start on it now it should be ready in time. The best time to employ it will be just as the characters are storming the Corvariate Citadel.

6.30.4393
All is in readiness. Rebecca and I have drawn straws to determine which of us will operate the device. It will be me. I'm not sure if I've won or lost.

7.3.4393
Lysander has commanded all of us to come to the citadel for a special performance. The timing is good. The characters will be at the height of their revolutionary fervor. Belrea, of course, is in what will become Ilysies again. But it doesn't matter. Wherever they are I will reach them all.

I will take the wing up and beam the key frequency across the whole planet.

The great discovery of our parents, the frequency that transcends dimensions, will liberate the meat puppets into real people who are capable of independent action.

And transcend us to the next level, whatever that might be. Perhaps it's death.

Except for me. I must remain to do the thing, to fly the wing and send the energy out.

7.3.4393
I will make them whole individuals with free will. It will kill us.

7.4.4393
It's done. And it worked!

I sank the wing off the coast of what used to be Tarsus and let myself be captured by Yammon and his followers.

Already they are deviating from the novel. Surely that's a good sign.

Now if only I could die, like my friends.

That was the last entry. Gyneth had been right. On some level, she'd known he was right but she wouldn't accept it.

Endymion and her friends were as advanced in comparison to humans as a human was to a fly. They might as well have been gods. And they were children.

Haly put the journal in her satchel next to the orb that held what remained of Endymion's consciousness. She got up and started walking.

I t took her another day, maybe longer, but she at last located Scaramouch and from there made her way back to the little doorway in the Alcove of the Fly that had once been the community's main access to the books.

"Haly!" cried Selene as she made her way to the console. "Seven Tales! We thought you were lost for good! Do you know how long you've been down there?"

Others gathered—Siblea, Peliac, Burke. She didn't want to talk to any of them.

"Haly!" It was Clauda, pushing past everyone else. Haly would have avoided her if she could but she was too tired. "Look at you! You're covered in dust. Oh, it's so good to see you!" Clauda hugged her. The warmth of her embrace could not penetrate the cold inside Haly, just as the Song could not penetrate it.

Clauda released her and stood back. "Where's Gyneth?

Oh . . ." She cast a stricken look at Selene, who reached
out for Haly as well. "Oh."

"He fell into a vortex of words at the bottom of the
Libyrinth," said Haly. "He's gone."

"Gone?" said Clauda. She grasped Haly by the arm.
"You mean *gone* gone?"

Haly nodded. "Yes. Dead gone. He—" She couldn't talk
about it.

"Haly, I'm so sorry. What happened?" Selene reached
out to her.

Haly couldn't bear it. Their concern, their kindness,
could not bring Gyneth back. All it did was make her feel
his loss even more. "Here." She shoved Endymion's journal at Selene's outstretched hand. "You'll find this interesting. Excuse me." She left the Great Hall and walked
out of the Libyrinth, through Tent Town, and out to the
low hill where she and Gyneth had left the Devouring
Silence.

22

Anything

Haly got back into the Devouring Silence and interfaced with it. She dove into the ground again and tunneled. This time she let her tongue slide out and taste the words of her world.

"Belrea set the last mirror in place and the dawn light struck it, turning the silvery surface to golden fire. The next mirror caught it and the next and the next, until from where she stood she could see all the windows of the Temple of Night ablaze with daylight. Shouts and cries poured forth from the windows as well. Belrea retreated to the cover of a doorway to one of the slave quarters—now deserted—just in time as guards and Ancients came running out of the temple.

"But their flight availed them not, for now they were

caught in the broad light of day, which they could not abide.

"As they writhed in the sunlight, smoke rising from their burning skin, Yammon and Iscarion's army attacked, swiftly putting them out of their misery.

"It was all over in moments.

"Yammon wiped the ichor from his sword and came to her, Iscarion at his side.

" 'They're gone,' he said. 'The Ancients can enslave us no more.'

"She put her arms around him and held him close, lifting her face up, into the wide blue sky of a new day.

"And now, the descendents of Yammon and Belrea populate the Plain of Ayor."

She paused. Those last words were not part of the paperback *Book of the Night*. Their texture was different, too—rougher, coarser. And they tasted sweet, like apricots and cream, and toasty, like roasted hazelnuts. Haly's favorite dish was fresh apricots with milk and hazelnuts. And she was hungry.

But what would happen if she ate those words? She pulled away and tunneled away as fast as she could before she devoured those words.

What would have happened if she had eaten them? If their world was made of words and the numbing effects of the Silence's tongue were activated by the act of eating, was that like erasing those words and with them the reality they described?

There'd been no effect from tasting the words that were part of the paperback novel *The Book of the Night*, but she hadn't been tempted to eat those. She surfaced and found herself on the outskirts of a village. In the distance she saw people farming. All was peaceful, for now. They hadn't noticed her and they hadn't fallen unconscious or disappeared as the result of her "tasting" those words. The drive to eat had been clearly separate from simply touching and tasting with her tongue. Did that mean that the Silence had to decide to use its tongue to numb people and carry them away? That it was a separate act from simply sensing things?

As she continued to explore, she was able to detect three different kinds of world-writing: original material left over from when *The Book of the Night* was playing; things written with the pen; and things which, because they had transpired since the book player had ceased functioning, were part of the world but had not been consciously written by anyone.

It was only the second kind that she concerned herself with.

"Everyone living in the Plain of Ayor is loyal to Thela Tadamos." Haly devoured it.

"Po can only do what makes me happy." Haly-in-the-Silence ate that one as well.

"The three people tangled with Po on the floor of his chambers in the Ilysian Palace are gone." She ate that, too.

Line by line she erased all that Thela had written, but she couldn't bring Gyneth back no matter what she did.

For a time Po seemed to be gaining ground on the breaks in the world, but suddenly great chasms opened up around him. Whole paragraphs disappeared right out from under him. He'd been joining "The sky during the day is blue, except when there are clouds" with "The sky at night is black and filled with stars, except when there are clouds," using an "and" he'd salvaged from a disintegrating fragment. Suddenly the whole part about the clouds and the day and the night and the blue broke away. He tried to cling to them but the force was too great. He knew that if he let go it would cast the world into eternal darkness. He hung on, but the words still drifted away from one another into incoherence. He dissolved with them, bits of him floating off in all directions, clinging futilely to isolated words, meaningless.

The earth shook and great chasms opened up. The sky flickered from blue to black to magenta to a checkerboard pattern, and every silverleaf bush in sight became an Old Earth fire hydrant.

Selene held Clauda tight at her side and lifted her arm to ward off the sheets of burning paper that rained down from the sky.

"What's happening?" cried Clauda.

"I think what Haly's doing with her Devouring Silence is making the destabilization worse."

"You think?"

They ran toward the shelter of an overturned cart. "I'm going to take the wing up," said Clauda. "Maybe there's something I can do."

"No!" Selene had to shout because suddenly the twelfth movement of the *Losian Concerto* blasted at high volume with every gust of wind. "It's too dangerous. Anything can happen to you up there now."

Clauda took Selene's face in both her hands and drew

her down for a kiss. The earth trembled again and they both fell. "Darling, anything can happen to us anywhere now. In fact, I think this"—she gestured at the surrounding chaos—"is the definition of anything."

Selene wanted to stop her but there was no stopping her, and it wouldn't have been right, even if there was. And she knew that. "I'll come with you."

"No."

"Clauda!"

"You can't do anything from inside the wing, Selene. You left me behind once and told me you needed me to come up with the other half of the plan. Remember?"

She remembered. Clauda had been so ill she couldn't even walk and Selene had left her behind in Thela's clutches, certain that Clauda would think of something, certain that she could be more effective on her own than she'd be following Selene.

Clauda nodded. "Now it's your turn. Think of something."

Before Selene could say another word, or even hug or kiss her goodbye, Clauda was up and away. Selene watched her run across a field of tablespoons and climb into the wing.

She was relieved when the wing became airborne but whether Clauda was really safer up there—an enormous bird flew through a crack in the sky and suddenly burst into hundreds of smaller birds—was anybody's guess.

Selene spotted a group of people running toward the Libyrinth. Among them was Siblea. He had a book in his hand.

Selene knew she didn't have intuition. She understood the phenomena whereby several pieces of information

come together to impart to a person knowledge of which
they are barely even aware, that they cannot name or con-
ceptualize. That was what was happening to her.

She didn't know why, but she knew she had to stop him.

She ran after him, part of a rising tide of people running
toward the relative shelter of the Libyrinth.

But not even the Libyrinth was the Libyrinth anymore.
The walls, the dome, the floor, it was all books now, books
flowing clockwise in a slow vortex.

Where the central console had been was a large circular hole, with steps made of books spiraling down into the
depths of the stacks.

Most people were huddling along the walls but Siblea
and his party—Selene saw Peliac and Ayma with him—
headed straight for the steps. Selene ran after them.

She followed Siblea and the others down the spiraling
stair of books, and down, and down. Lines of text, un-
moored from their tomes, floated up around them, undulating in long sinuous threads of words, like smoke, like
songlines.

They went down and down, into the bowels of the
Libyrinth to the face where the Egg had been installed by
Gyneth, to where the book player was.

She ran as fast as she could but Siblea was even longer
of leg than she was. She was just barely able to keep him
within sight around the curve of the stairs.

At last they reached the bottom. The face where the
Egg rested was one of the few things that had not changed.
Or at least, not changed much. The mouth was open now.
Siblea bent over it, the paperback novel *The Book of the
Night* in his hand.

"Stop! Siblea, no!"

He turned to face her, regret written in every gaunt line of his face. "It must be done, Selene." He gestured around him to the streaming chaos of books and words shifting and fragmenting all around them. "Can't you see that?"

She hastened to his side. Between the parted lips of the face was a space just the perfect size for a book to slide in. "But if you play that book, you'll cause the whole world to reset to the world of *The Book of the Night*. We're not in that book, Siblea. No one alive today in the Plain of Ayor is in that book!"

Siblea compressed his lips to a hard, flat line. "Do you think I don't know that?"

"You'll kill us all!" She reached for the book. If she could just get it away from him . . .

Siblea backed away from her. "And what's the alternative? The basic integrity of this world has been completely compromised by the pen and the Silence. We're all going to die anyway. At least this way the world will continue. It can start over. People will live here again."

He was right. "But Clauda, Haly . . ."

"Yes. And you, and me, and Ayma. Everyone." Tears streamed down his face. "I don't want to do it. I don't want to . . ." His voice faltered. He closed his eyes, and when he spoke again his voice had steadied. "But someone must and I'm the only one capable of it. I have to—" He broke off and rushed to the face.

Selene intercepted him, slamming hard into his chest and knocking him sideways. "No. There's got to be another way."

"What, then?" Spittle flew from Siblea's mouth. "You tell me. What?"

Selene reached into the pocket of her robe and took out

the book she'd been writing tirelessly ever since Po's sacrifice. "What about this?"

Siblea gave a little shake of his head. "What is it?"

"It's my account of all that has transpired since I first
discovered the location of Theselaides' *Book of the Night*
in the secret vault."

Siblea's gaze darted back and forth between her face
and the book in her hand. "An account of recent events?"

"As accurate as I could make it."

Siblea bit his lip. "Will it work?"

"I don't know. It's not finished."

"That's probably just as well."

"Open-ended."

"Yes." Siblea paced, waving one finger as he thought.
"Do you have a pen?"

"Of course."

"Write something like, 'There are many more people
alive in this book than are mentioned in it.'"

"Oh! Yes, I see." Selene took her pen, thought on it a
moment, and wrote, "There are many more people alive in
this world that this book is about than are mentioned in
these pages. They are the descendents of the people who
lived in the world of the paperback novel *The Book of the
Night* by Roger Theselaides and they lived through a time
when no book played in BookWorld. Those who are alive
now, as Selene Tadamos, daughter of Thela Tadamos, is
about to put this book in the book player, continue to live
whether they are mentioned in this book or not."

"Good. That's good," said Siblea. A sinkhole suddenly
appeared in the floor not ten paces from where the player
stood. Books poured down its steep slopes. "Hurry!"

Selene stood before the open mouth, her book in her

hands. Could she really do this? Her words would become this world's reality. She'd been as honest as she knew how to be, but—

"Hurry! For Yammon's sake!"

"Wait!" Selene opened the book again. The ground shook. She braced herself against the side of the face and wrote, above the first line, "This story begins where the words end."

Siblea put his hands on her shoulders. "You must. Now."

Selene closed her eyes. Praying to the Mother, the Ocean, Time, and the Seven Tales that this was right, she slid the book through the lips of the face at the bottom of the Libyrinth.

The lips closed and the eyes opened. A hum like the opening bars of the Song filled the air.

The books stopped sliding into the vortex. And then the flow reversed. Bit by bit the world knitted itself back together. The books slid back into their proper places and the shelves reformed. Stray wisps of text that had floated off drifted back and rejoined their books.

Clauda was relieved to find the wing relatively un-changed. She climbed inside, stepping over a foot-tall house populated by anthropomorphic mice in shorts and jackets. Once inside the wing she sealed the hatch, approached the statue, and said the proper words.

She sank into the interface and merged with the wing. And that was when all normality ceased. In the synesthetic perceptions of the wing, the chaos of their disintegrating world was magnified. The tremors and chasms raked her golden skin like claws. She fought for the sky to get away from the terrible upheaval on the ground, but that wasn't much better. Lightning sent shock waves of electricity skittering through her senses. The fiery paper scorched her skin when it touched her but did little damage. More frightening were the glimpses of deep maroon unspace she caught in the gaps in the sky through which they fell.

Clauda forced herself to focus on gaining altitude and getting an overall view of what was happening. If she could detect some pattern to what was going on, maybe . . .

But there was no pattern. No emerging order to the chaos. All she'd really done was get herself a better view for the end of the world.

And she'd left Selene down there alone.

But there was one speck of order amid the constantly shifting reality. A young man lay facedown in a field. His hands . . . his hands were fractured, and somehow, in their fragmentation they knitted in with the broken words of the world. He'd held it together so far but now his strength was failing.

Coherence. That was what the world needed. The people who had made this world, the People Who Walk Sideways in Time, transcended three-dimensional, temporal existence by comprehending and manipulating the underlying coherence implicate in the quantum structures of their world.

The Song was their key. It was a transcendent experience for those who listened to it because it was itself the sound of transcendence. With the right energy and the right instruments, any Ayorite could do the same so long as she knew the Song.

Clauda had long speculated that the light that emanated from the wing was the optical equivalent of the Song. She unleashed it now in a broad canopy, to encompass the whole world.

It seemed to help. The earth stopped shaking and the sky closed up. The rain of burning pages ceased.

But just as Clauda-in-the-Wing was congratulating herself on her success, new holes and fractures appeared, as bad if not worse than those before.

Someone was working against her, undoing all that she did. She searched for the source.

And what she found was Haly-in-the-Silence, grief-stricken, single-handedly trying to unwrite everything Queen Thela had written and devouring her world in the process.

Clauda used the wing's light beam to support Po, to bolster his coherence and help him to survive. Then she turned her attention to Haly.

Darkness met light, Silence met Song. "Haly-in-the-Silence," said Clauda-in-the-Wing, "it's time to stop. This was useful in the beginning but if you continue, you'll destroy us all."

"Destroy what? We're not real. We're just a construct, a program. We're not real."

"No. You've got it the wrong way around. The People Who Walk Sideways in Time were the programs, the constructs. We're meat puppets. For them, creating biological life was as simple as baking a loaf of bread. We're no collection of numbers and operations. We're real."

"But I don't know how to stop. I don't know how to get out. It's dark and I'm *hungry*."

"Follow me. Let me guide you." Clauda directed the wing's energy beam to Haly-in-the-Silence, surrounding her with light and warmth. "You are still our Redeemer."

The Silence followed the beam's path and surfaced. Clauda landed. They were in a canyon that may or may not have been there before. The world appeared to have stabilized, though she wasn't sure why.

Clauda disembarked from the wing just as Haly was climbing out of the Silence. The two old friends went to each other.

"Gyneth!" said Haly, her face wet.

"I know." Clauda hugged her. "I'm sorry."

23

Everything

Haly pulled the orb from her pocket. "This is what is left of Endymion. She told me she wanted to join her friends."

"She set us free. After what she did for us, we should do that for her," said Clauda.

Haly set the orb down on the ground and climbed the rocky side of the canyon. She took refuge behind an outcrop and watched as Clauda took the wing up into the air. She hovered over the canyon. A beam of golden light issued from the bottom of the wing and struck the ground. Dust and smoke flew up, but also something else: a figure made of light. A woman with straight shoulder-length hair and a rapt expression on her upturned face. She was made of light, or perhaps light caught in dust. She rose up, her outspread arms smearing in her passage, until they resembled wings.

And then the wind caught her and she was gone.

Clauda landed and got out and Haly climbed back down to the valley floor and they looked around on the ground where the orb had been. There was nothing there.

"Seven Tales, this stuff is thick."

"I know, did you ever see the like?"

"No, not even when Thela made the plain green."

"Hey, over here, I think I found him."

"Is he alive?"

"I don't know. Help me cut these vines away."

"Yammon's tonsils, he's a mess."

"Shut up and help me. Easy now. Watch it!"

From a great distance, Po felt something move. Something that was not the Song. There was pain there, too, but it was far away, and he was nestled in the embrace of the world. He paid it no mind.

Light and sound. Colors. At first he could make no sense of any of it. Shouldn't he be dead by now? And because that was a thought, he realized he must not be. He became aware that he breathed. Someone was squeezing his hand and saying, "Wake up for me, Po. Come on, now. We need you." It was Burke.

Po opened his eyes and blinked at the bright light. Burke's face slowly came into focus, and then, behind her, the infirmary tent at the community. He was home. He looked to where she held his hand. "Shouldn't that hurt?" he asked, his voice thick.

Burke smiled, and it erased the dread that had been there a moment ago. "Thela used the pen to do that to you, didn't she?"

He nodded. "Sort of."

She shrugged. "Well, Haly may have nearly killed us all in the process, but she did succeed in undoing all of Thela's work with the pen."

"That means that if she used the pen to kill—"

"Yes! They're alive. Look!" She lifted up the side of the tent so he could see out of it. There, in a field already sprouting with green things, stood Baris. He walked behind Hilloa, who drove the plow, drawn by Zam. Baris was doing something odd with his hands. Waving them. Jan was picking up rocks and throwing them in a wheelbarrow.

Zam spotted him first, and trumpeted. "Po!" shouted Hilloa, leaping from the plow. She, Jan, Baris, and Zam all ran across the field, Zam trumpeting but slowing her gait like a good elephant and not trampling the town.

"This is your fault, isn't it?" said Baris, blood dripping from his fingertips. Where it pattered on the ground, seedlings sprouted. "That stupid story of yours. Too bad I can't cry at the drop of a hat like you."

"Po! We thought you were dead," said Jan. He got down on his knees and hugged Po tight.

"I thought you were all dead," said Po.

"We were," said Hilloa. "Well, sort of. Maybe not really. We were just . . . not, I guess. Strange."

Jan released him and Hilloa hugged him.

"But now you're back. And . . . and the pen?"

"Gone. No more pen," said Hilloa, sitting down on the side of his cot. She took his hand. "This is what we're stuck with now. No changing things at the drop of a hat."

Po tightened his grip on her hand. His fingers were stiff, but there was no pain. "Good."

There were no bones to inter, but they waited the customary year anyway, and chose Gyneth's notebook and pencil as worthy substitutes. Alone in the stacks, Haly placed the box that held them behind Endymion's journal. She stood a moment and ran a finger slowly down its spine. "You'll be happy to know you were right about almost everything, Gyneth. And . . . I miss you."

But she didn't linger long. She'd mourned him every day since his fall, and now her grief was an accustomed thing, like an old garment, soft with repeated washing.

Despite the formation of the council, and the elections, her life was just as full as ever. She was an elected representative now under the leadership of Chair Burke, and she fought many battles with Councilmember Peliac, and spent many nights strategizing with Councilmember Rossiter. In all her decisions she did her best to bear in mind what Gyneth had said about truth.

The Song was with her still, and they all still shared in the daily tasks of life at the Libyrinth. In the last month or so she'd begun to think she might fall in love again someday, if she met the right person, but for now it was enough that she had time to read. She pulled a book from the shelf and walked up the stairs and out of the Great Hall.

She walked out into the thriving town that now surrounded the Libyrinth. They lived in peace with Ilysies and Thesia now, but they were their own country.

Everywhere there was activity. The sides of the infirmary tent were rolled up to let the cool breeze in. Inside she could see Po tending his patients. With Burke acting as chair of the council now, he was in charge. Hilloa ran in with a book in her hand and they embraced.

The wind picked up, ruffling Haly's hair and the roof of the tent. Haly looked up to see the wing soaring overhead. Clauda and Selene were off on another expedition exploring the lands beyond the sea.

Haly turned from the settlement and walked out to the outcrop that overlooked their lush fields. She lifted her face up to the sky. It was a cloudless day. The sky was a bright blue shading deeper at the zenith. That blue was infinity. She couldn't see it all from here, of course, but she knew she looked out, not just at her universe, but at all the universes in all the numberless tales of time. But this sky, this tale, this world was already so big. It was big enough for everything.

WHERE TO FIND WHAT THE BOOKS SAID

PROLOGUE

" 'We are all going on an Expedition,' said Christopher Robin, as he got up and brushed himself. 'Thank you, Pooh.' " A.A. Milne, *The World of Pooh*. New York: E.P. Dutton, 2010.

"Tucker Mouse took himself very seriously now that he was the manager of a famous concert artist." George Selden, *The Cricket in Times Square*. New York: Yearling, 1970.

"Once the fire lizards settled to the business of eating, Piemur glanced at Menolly, wondering if she'd heard the drum message." Anne McCaffrey, *Dragondrums*. New York: Del Rey, 1979.

" 'When he broke that commitment to art, to making beauty, to recording, to bearing witness, to saying yessiree to the life spirit, whose only request sometimes is just that you acknowledge you truly see it, he broke something in Hal. . . .' " Alice Walker, *The Temple of My Familiar*. New York: Harcourt, Brace & Jovanovich, 1989.

"After that I was lost for a long time, doing dreamtime without end while my body paid the price." Joan Vinge, *Psion*. New York: Tor Books, 1982.

Chapter 4

"The study of the origins of words may be regarded as a sort of archeology of our thought process," David Bohm, *Wholeness and the Implicate Order*. London: Routledge, 1980.

"Exhausted from old age, Moses' last act was to write down on a scroll all the important events that had happened to the Hebrew people." Leonard Shlain, *The Alphabet Versus the Goddess*. New York: Viking, 1998.

"Behind the child blared the noise of the TV set; the sound worked but not the picture." Philip K. Dick, *Clans of the Alphane Moon*. New York: Dell Publishing Co., 1964.

"When finally he found the bottom of his sadness he looked up and wiped his eyes on his forearm." Christopher Moore, *Coyote Blue*. New York: HarperCollins, 1994.

"It's true that you could ask the same question a hundred different times and get a hundred seemingly different answers. But the S'kang concept of "truth" was indirect, malleable, subtle." Joe Haldeman, *All My Sins Remembered*. New York: St. Martin's Press, 1977.

"But you don't think about tomorrow when people are feeding surplus grain to pigs and dogs. So when people are starving to death in the streets, you don't think about emptying storehouses to feed them. People die and you say *It's not my fault, it's the harvest.* How is this any different from stabbing someone to death and saying *It's not me, it's the sword?* Stop blaming harvests, and people everywhere under Heaven will come flocking to you." Mencius, *Mencius*, translated by David Hinton. Washington, D.C.: Counterpoint, 1998.

"On the contrary, I've found that there is always some beauty left—in nature, sunshine, freedom, in yourself; these can all help you. Look at these things, then you find yourself again, and God, and then you regain your balance." Anne Frank, *Anne Frank: The Diary of a Young Girl*. New York: Bantam Books, 1952.

CHAPTER 6

"Come with me, my love, come away. For the long wet months are past, the rains have fed the earth and left it bright with blossoms. Birds wing in the low sky, dove and songbird singing in the open air above. Each nourishing tree and vine, green fig and tender grape, green and tender fragrance. Come with me, my love, come away." *The Song of Songs*, translated by Marica Falk. San Francisco: HarperSanFrancisco, 1973.

CHAPTER 7

"Was this the best thing that had ever happened to him, or the worst?" Nina Kiriki Hoffman, *Catalyst*. San Francisco: Tachyon Publications, 2006.

"The cloak-and-dagger protocols, the risk of capture, and the soaring view from the windows of Joe's home could not have been better designed to appeal to the mind of an eleven-year-old boy who spent large parts of every day pretending to pose as the secret identity of a super-powered humanoid insect." Michael Chabon, *The Amazing Adventures of Kavalier & Clay*. New York: Picador U.S.A., 2000.

"Eventually, something would have to be done about his hands." Mary Doria Russell, *The Sparrow*. New York: Fawcett Columbine, 1996.

CHAPTER 20

"Moving cautiously, she continued down the street. No rubbish cluttered the gutters here; no cars were parked at the curb." Pat Murphy, *The City, Not Long After*. New York: Bantam Books, 1989.

"Declining the bridge, they took the Mickle Boulevard exit and looped east into the city's bleak, rubbled heart." James Morrow, *Only Begotten Daughter*. New York: Ace Books, 1990.

"Already we have gone out of our depth." Judith Gleason, *Oya, In Praise of the Goddess*. Boston: Shambala, 1987.

" 'You've never been this far outside before, have you?' he said at last." Elizabeth Hand, *Winterlong*. New York: Bantam Books, 1990.

"In this freedom, they ride the waves of birth and death in perfect peace." Thich Nhat Hanh, *Understanding Our Mind*. Berkeley: Parallax Press, 2006.

"We made so many deviations up and down lanes, and were such a long time delivering a bedstead at a public-house, and calling at other places, that I was quite tired, and very glad, when we saw Yarmouth." Charles Dickens, *David Copperfield*. New York: Bantam, 1850.

ABOUT THE AUTHOR

The Book of the Night is Pearl North's third young-adult novel. She is the author of *Libyrinth* and *The Boy from Ilysies,* the first two books in her Libyrinth trilogy. She has also written science fiction and fantasy for adults under another name. She lives near Detroit, Michigan.